# FOR THOSE WHO KNOW THE ENDING

## MALCOLM MACKAY

MANTLE

First published 2016 by Mantle
an imprint of Pan Macmillan
20 New Wharf Road, London N1 9RR
Associated companies throughout the world
www.panmacmillan.com

ISBN 978-1-4472-9159-6

1 3 5 7 9 8 6 4 2

A CIP catalogue record for this book is available from the British Library.

Typeset by Ellipsis Digital Limited, Glasgow
Printed and bound by CPI Group (UK) Ltd, Croydon, CR0 4YY

Visit www.panmacmillan.com to read more about all our books
and to buy them. You will also find features, author interviews and
news of any author events, and you can sign up for e-newsletters
so that you're always first to hear about our new releases.

# FOR THOSE WHO KNOW THE ENDING

# CHARACTERS

**Charlie Allen** – Charlie and his cousin Ian keep their street-dealing business mostly outside of Glasgow. Tried to work the city before and got their fingers burned, and they'll only go in again for the right deal.

**Ian Allen** – A chubby little fellow who runs a successful street-dealing business with Charlie. Everyone thinks they're brothers, and it's too much work to correct them all.

**Chris Argyle** – There aren't many who have a better importing business than Argyle. What he needs are dealers to distribute, and then he can seal a deal with a major organization.

**Brian 'BB' Bradley** – Bright young muscle, throwing his weight around for a living. If he makes no mistakes he might survive long enough to get as disillusioned as the veterans who give him his orders.

**Nate Colgan** – You wouldn't tell him he wasn't the toughest man in Glasgow to his face. Security consultant for the Jamieson organization, and it's a job with increasing complications.

**Rebecca Colgan** – If there's anyone in Glasgow who truly believes in the goodness of Nate Colgan it's his daughter Rebecca. If there's one person he truly loves back, it's her.

**Aiden Comrie** – He's worked the street for years, hoping his big break will come. Setting up a drug deal between Argyle and the Allens would be huge. This is his moment.

**Liam Duffy** – He might be young, but don't underestimate his ability. He wouldn't be a senior man for Chris Argyle if he didn't know exactly what he was doing.

**Dale Duggan** – To look at him you would think he was nothing, and that's the point. If you don't look at him twice you'll never see the guns he delivers to buyers.

**Lisa Fitzgerald** – She knew what Gully did for a living when she married him, but all these years later she thought he was out of that world. She hoped he was, anyway.

**Sally Fitzgerald** – Lisa and Gully had wanted a child for so long, and they only had Sally for eight years. It broke them both, and they're still trying to put the pieces back together.

**Stephen 'Gully' Fitzgerald** – Back in the day, if you worked in Glasgow's underworld, Gully was the man you feared punishment from most. He's older now, but being scary is like riding a bike to him.

**Alison Glenn** – Usman's great, and she does like spending time with him, but she worries about her job, about her long-term prospects. She's feeling the pressure.

**Peter Jamieson** – He built one of the biggest criminal organizations in the city, and just because he's in prison doesn't mean that he isn't still in charge.

**Marty Jones** – Started out as the sort of pimp and moneylender that everyone despised. Has grown into the sort of pimp and moneylender that people in the business have no choice but to respect.

**Akram Kassar** – It's not serious criminality, moving counterfeit goods around and trying to make a bit of slightly dishonest cash. He tries to put some work his little brother Usman's way when he can.

**Usman Kassar** – Don't be fooled by the youthfully goofy appearance, he's a smart kid. The kind who can plan big things, and keep those plans to himself until it's time to do the job.

**James Kealing** – An industry veteran, running a bunch of

warehouses he and his terrifying father started and keeping his profile low and profits high.

**Przemek Krawczyk** – The criminals he works for in Glasgow take their orders from Eastern Europe, so when they told him to look after Martin Sivok, he did. But he can only babysit so long.

**Alex MacArthur** – The oldest of the old organization bosses, a man clinging on to power while the young wolves eye up control of what he built.

**Ronnie Malone** – Nate had never had a protégé before, a young man he could teach the ways of the business. He took Ronnie under his wing, and it turned out to be a mistake.

**Joanne Mathie** – She wasn't looking for a relationship, but Martin makes her happy and she wants to make the best of that, even if the circumstances are . . . complicated.

**Skye Mathie** – Her mother has a boyfriend and that's pretty disgusting to begin with. Her mother seemingly preferring that boyfriend over her, well that just isn't fair.

**Sarah McFall** – She's the senior woman that the Allens use for all their important negotiations. Smart, but that's never enough, you have to be tough as hell too, and she is.

**Kelly Newbury** – She seems to want to become the woman in Nate Colgan's life, and she's quickly becoming a key employee for the Jamieson organization.

**Don Park** – Of all the people lining up to replace Alex MacArthur, none has a better chance than Park. If he could set up his own drug network with Argyle and the Allens, he'd be halfway to power.

**Martin Sivok** – He came to Scotland from the Czech Republic through necessity, not choice. Now that he's here he wants to build a life, and working in the criminal industry is the only way he knows how.

**John Young** – He was Peter Jamieson's right-hand man, and the same police investigations that swept Jamieson to prison caught Young too.

# 12.46 a.m.

It's been almost two hours. His legs are cramping. The plastic strips have dug into his wrists where he's pulled at them. Martin's become accustomed to the dark now. He can see the small door they came in. He can see the loading-bay shutters beside it they should have left by. There's little in the warehouse itself, metal shelves pushed back against three walls and a large empty floor space. Not quite empty. There's a man dressed in black, tied to a chair by thin plastic strips. Martin.

The cut on the top of his shaved head seems like it's stopped bleeding. Either that or it's become numb. The balaclava he was wearing is gone. He didn't take it off, and he can't see it anywhere. The blood had run down the side of his neck, trickling down inside his clothes. He had wriggled to try and scratch the itch, but that was no use. Now the blood has dried and his clothes are sticking to it. When he shakes his head slightly, he doesn't feel any more liquid movement up there, just the dizziness of effort. That's a positive. Cling on to that.

He's leaning forward, now that it seems his head will let him. Tried this a few minutes ago and the pain that shot behind his eyes demanded he lean back again. Spent the next few minutes fearing that crack to the head had done him permanent damage. Bloody hell, that hit was harder than it needed to be. He's looking down at the straps round his ankles. These aren't as noticeably tight as the ones round his wrists. Tight enough. A second strap looped through the first and into a small metal hoop in the floor. All to guarantee that he's not going anywhere.

Not that he could anyway. His hands tied behind him, his shoulders starting to burn. He doesn't have the strength for struggle. Two hours. Shouldn't take half this long, not if they knew what they were doing. The waiting is making it worse. Forcing him to sit still, knowing they're out there. Knowing they're on their way to kill him.

Martin Sivok has been in the country for a little over a year. Born in Czechoslovakia, raised in the Czech Republic. Worked minor jobs in Brno based around dealing. Then the minor jobs got major. Working for a gang that had connections all across Europe. It paid well, and he was willing to take the risks that well-paid work requires. But risks run fast. They catch up with you; so he left in a hurry. Had some help getting out from his former employers. That same gang had connections in Western Europe, told him they had some work for him in Scotland. Sure, Scotland, why not? Glasgow seemed all right, mostly because there was nobody here trying to arrest or kill him. Wasn't where he had been planning to spend a few years, but so what? Hadn't been planning anything at all. Life was a wide open field and he was young enough to wander into any corner of it.

He's moving again. Trying to wriggle in the seat to take some pressure off his shoulders, see if he can dim the pain. Trying to loosen the straps a little, but that's only making things worse. The plastic is digging into the flesh and he can feel it cut his wrist. Now a dribble of blood, running down into the palm of his hand. Feels the blood on his numbing fingers. He's sighing, for all the good it'll do.

Weird how dry his mouth is. He's licking his lips but his tongue isn't moist enough to help. He hasn't shouted, and he won't. No point when there's nobody to hear him. There's something, a slow drip it sounds like, coming from behind him. Must be raining again, the water running through a hole in the roof of the warehouse. Big bloody surprise that it's raining in this city. It's a cold night, but he still has his jacket on. Another small mercy. So that's his coat keeping him warm and he's not bleeding from the head any more. Two positives to focus on.

Plenty of negatives to ignore. Being tied to a chair in a warehouse in Clydebank in the middle of the night isn't a cheerful way to pass the time. Knowing that someone's about to turn up with the intention of killing you and the ability to make it happen. All of it a set-up, carefully constructed by others. And Joanne, sitting back at home, waiting for him to return, aware that this might be the night when he doesn't.

Martin's closing his eyes. He's been trying to stop himself from doing that for the last hour. Close your eyes and you don't know when you'll open them again. Maybe you never will. And if you do, your mind might be too addled to react properly to what's happening. Stay awake and stay alert. He can't, he's too sore and too tired and too drained. Too aware of what's to come this night to want to think about it.

# 1

They weren't as big and impressive as they had claimed. Not in Scotland, anyway. He knew how well connected they were in Eastern Europe because he'd seen it first hand. Worked those long-established and deep-running networks and made good money from them. But here he was, Martin Sivok, thirty-one, short, stocky and standing in a foreign country. He needed their connections to help him now if he was going to survive the upheaval working for them had brought about. They got him some work. Some. Like, a little. Crappy jobs for crappy money.

Back in Brno they had been the biggest gang in town and had enough strength to make sure they stayed that way. A healthy percentage of the high-value drugs coming into the city and the region passed through them. Money flowed in with it, and Martin got his cut because Martin did some very dirty jobs for them. They liked him, they valued him. That's why they helped him get west and get safe when he was running from the police.

They tried to find him work, but it wasn't the same when they stepped outside of their own territory. There were other people in Glasgow, people who had been here a long time.

Outsiders were growing rapidly in influence, but there was an old guard fighting to protect what had always been theirs. The gang that brought him across, they weren't looking for trouble with the old guard. Working with them in supply, rather than against them in distribution. Making less money but avoiding any real conflict, for now at least. It was a different tactic from the norm, and one that meant Martin and his skills had nowhere to play in Glasgow.

So he was bounced back to the bottom of the heap. Nobody wants to be down there in the gutter of the criminal industry, not for long. Even kids starting out, their motivation is to get upwardly mobile. Get into the clouds where the money and influence are hidden. Well Martin had been up there already; he had just lost altitude. Meant learning the ropes in the new place; going back to school.

Learn who's who, that's important. Work out who you can do jobs for and who you can't. Who you can trust and who'll throw you overboard as soon as they've used you. Who has a long-term future in the city and who's one step away from their ending. Work out who's fighting wars against who so that you can try and benefit from the inevitable work conflict provides. Oh, and work out what the fuck these people are saying. His English was pretty good before he got here, been speaking it in bits since high school. Watched a lot of American TV and listened to a lot of music sung in what he thought was the right language. First day off the plane in Glasgow and he realized he'd learned the wrong English.

Took a while to get used to everything, but he did. He completed the often menial jobs they provided for him and made very little money along the way. He was practically living off his savings the first time he met Usman Kassar. He had mentioned his situation, a couple of times, to an absurdly hairy Polish guy with good English that seemed to be running things for the old gang hereabouts.

'There must be other things you could get me. I have done much more than this, back home. I can do it again.' Hinting at the high-value work he had made a living from.

'I know what you did,' the hairy man said, shrugging. His name was full of Z's and Y's, but Martin could never remember in what order. 'There's nothing here. People here, they have their own men like you. Men they trust. Men they've known for years. They don't trust you.'

'I could do that work for you.'

'We aren't doing that here, and we won't be. I'm not teasing you here, kid. We have a good thing going that we won't screw up. London, sure, other cities maybe. But we have a deal in Glasgow. A good one. There are others though. As long as you aren't working against us, you don't have to only work for us.'

That was disheartening. He'd been working for one gang for more than ten years, worked their toughest jobs back home. Now he was out of sight and out of mind. Hey, you want to go work for someone else you go knock yourself out. He felt dismissed. They'd brought him here as a courtesy, a thank-you for all the profitable work he'd done for them in the past, but they probably assumed he'd find work with someone else right away. He had clung on to them for too long.

Joanne Mathie knew what she'd be coming home to. She'd spent the previous evening stocktaking at the bookshop and spent the night at her sister's. Had warned her daughter Skye she'd be back at ten o'clock the following morning, and any piles of partygoers better be cleared by then. Joanne would have been surprised if Skye had kept her word, so there was no shock when she opened the front door and found a sickly teenage girl blocking the corridor. Skye had thrown a party, and thrown the house around with it.

Joanne stepped over the girl in the corridor and went looking for her daughter. There were people in the living room and the kitchen, half of them asleep and the other half wishing they still were, nursing all kinds of headaches. Strangers asleep in various rooms and various positions. There was beer on the carpet and what looked like a bloodstain on the kitchen table that she didn't want to think about. Couldn't find Skye. Went upstairs looking for her. Found her in her bedroom, still under the quilt with a gormless-looking soul lying next to her.

'You get up,' Joanne shouted at her, before turning to the boy, 'and you get out.'

The boy did as he was told, not so much as a goodbye as he pulled on some clothes and sprinted for freedom. Joanne stood over the bed while Skye made no effort at all to move.

'What?' Skye shouted.

'I tell you you can have a party but I'll be back by ten so get the place cleaned up. That was all I asked of you. Have you taken a wee peek at a clock?'

'Just get out of my room,' Skye said petulantly, pulling the quilt over her head.

'This is the last time,' Joanne shouted, slamming the door behind her as she walked out of the room.

Went into her own bedroom and paused. A stocky, shaven-headed young man lying on the floor at the bottom of the bed, all on his own. Looked like he'd managed to have a happy enough time, aided only by a bottle and three cans lying beside him. Joanne kicked him good and hard on the ankle. A man lying on the floor of her bedroom uninvited, a kick was the least he deserved. He sat bolt upright, growling something in a language that may have been foreign or may have been drunken Glaswegian.

'Out,' Joanne said harshly, pointing at the door.

He got up and made to leave, pausing when he saw her begin to tidy up the mess he'd made. Walked back across and insisted on picking up everything he'd left on the floor, apologizing in broken English. Went downstairs with her, picking up more rubbish as he went. Refused to leave until he had helped her move furniture back into place, including tipping two sleeping people off the sofa and barking at them to leave when they dared complain. He had the place cleaned and cleared in a little over forty minutes. She felt obliged to offer him a cup of coffee.

Said his name was Martin, from the Czech Republic, and emphasized the fact he was single. Joanne was thirty-nine, tidy dark hair, a pretty face, and short, which suited Martin. Truth was he had no idea where he was and had no money for a taxi so leaving wasn't a tempting option. They chatted for almost an hour, Joanne enjoying this straightforward little man. He was smart and self-effacing, but there was an unmistakable edge to the quiet confidence that radiated from him. An ordinary face with eyes that routinely hinted at far more than was spoken.

He visited the house the following day, and things moved fast. Joanne was old enough to know her mind and not debate it. She liked Martin and Martin liked her so they spent a lot of time together. Three months after meeting and he had practically moved in.

Usman Kassar. Jesus, the first time Martin met him he was convinced the boy was a halfwit. Had a big puffy jacket, oversized red headphones draped round his neck and some goofy cap or hat on. He was dressed for attention. They were exchanging a large sum of money for a significant quantity of pills and his outfit could scarcely have been less suitable. Doing a drug deal in an outfit you'd have to be high to wear. Could have carried round a neon sign and he wouldn't have been any more conspicuous.

It was in the back office of a hairdressers in Hillhead that the deal was done. A group of Pakistanis with Scottish accents and Eastern Europeans with Eastern European accents. Everything had long since been agreed, this was just the twitchy handover. You do the negotiation first, separately. Don't negotiate with the gear on the table, that has a habit of clouding stupid people's judgement, which is typically not clear to begin with. Martin didn't know who any of them were, not even the guys he was there with. One was Polish, the other might have been Ukrainian, maybe Russian, didn't speak enough to clarify either way. Didn't matter, Martin was just there to make up the numbers.

There were polite handshakes to begin with. The gear was handed over, the cash moved the other way. The possible Ukrainian pocketed the packet of money, the man Usman was with took the bags of pills. That fellow seemed jolly, he and Usman happy with the deal. The sellers though seemed to be trying to play up to some inscrutable Eastern European stereotype, all scowls and shrugs that would disappear when there were no strangers around, so Martin played along. Give the people what they expect.

The possible Ukrainian and the other guy on Martin's side

left together. Left him, nothing more than hired muscle they didn't need any more, to make his own way home. He was starting to stroll down the street, hoping to bump into a bus stop, get himself closer to Joanne's house in Mount Florida, which was neither a mountain nor in Florida. They were good with names round here though, he would give them that. He heard footsteps scuffing along the pavement behind him.

Usman Kassar made up an excuse with his brother, told Akram he was going to meet a mate so couldn't take the pills back with him. Story accepted, and Usman went scuffing off down the street to catch up with the foreigner. A lazy person running, not getting their feet off the ground properly and not caring about the noise they made. Struggling to catch up with that little guy.

Wouldn't make a good first impression and he knew it, the little skinhead frowning over his shoulder at the approaching Usman. You're unarmed and alone and some guy you've just done a drug deal with is running towards you. Usman was on his own too, sure, but that didn't mean anything. He would be on his own if he was looking to attack. Akram would then drive up alongside so that he could jump straight into the car for a getaway. Sort of thing the foreigner had probably done before, back in the day, before he graduated to more complicated things.

Usman assumed he looked as impressive as he felt, young

and tough and bristling with masculine energy. He was busy hanging on to his oversized headphones, and his attempt at running had neither the pace nor the urgency of a man in a real hurry. Also, he sure as shit wasn't afraid of being seen.

'Here, mate, wait up,' he said, wheezing out the last couple of words. He had run fifty feet, at most. 'Slow down, slow down, man.'

Martin wasn't walking quickly. He stopped and looked at this young man. Martin was thirty-one, but he looked older; Usman was twenty-five, but he looked younger. Thin as a rail, smooth cheeked and full of grins. He stopped beside Martin with one of those trademark grins all over his face, leaning forward with his hands nearly at his knees, panting.

'You are not fit,' Martin said quietly. Going for the deadpan approach, because that was what they had played in the hair-dressers.

'Aye, no, I'm not. Smoking too much good stuff. I know it, man, I know it. Listen, pal, you're Martin, right, Martin Sivok?'

Martin frowned at that. First time anyone here had known his name before he'd told them and that made him suspicious. Someone had mentioned him to this kid and this kid had some way of profiting from it. Something else Martin had seen before. You hear a name and hear a few things that that name has done. You put pressure on that person, try and work an angle that puts money in your pocket. Blackmail, mainly. You give me money or I tell local police about you. Simple stuff if you can persuade the other person you have the balls to follow it through.

'Why do you want to know?' Martin said. Low tone, taking a single step forward to make the distance between him and this guy uncomfortably close. Let him see how quickly this could turn very nasty.

'Here, Jesus, calm yourself, man. It's nothing bad. Fuck's sake. Man, he said you'd be cool.'

'Who said?'

'Przemek. That how you say it? Przemek Krawczyk?' Neither pronunciation anywhere close to correct. 'I don't know how to pronounce his name. We just call him PK. Everyone round here does, or we'd be falling over our fucking tongues. The Polish guy. Big hair, big beard. You know him, right?'

Martin nodded. The name, a mangled spit of vowels, sounded at least in the ball park of the hairy Pole's. He knew him, just didn't know why he'd be talking to this guy about him.

'So?'

Usman looked at him and puffed out his cheeks. 'Man, you're hard work. He said you'd be cool about this. I don't know, maybe he was wrong. Look, he told me you were a serious guy, you know, a guy who did big jobs. Said you were bored of the shitty stuff they have you doing for them. Said you might be looking for something a wee bit better.'

Martin said nothing for a few seconds. They were out on the bloody street and this wasn't a conversation that sat comfortably in public, Usman knew. Two people had walked past them already and there were others coming into range. You don't approach a serious guy in the middle of the fucking street where people can see you. But, maybe Martin wasn't that serious any more. The Pole had said it was a while since he had pulled a big job, and reputations got swallowed fast.

'I'm interested in good work,' Martin said eventually. 'If it's serious. If it's properly organized. If it's with people I know and I trust. I don't know you,' he said, and turned away.

That reaction wasn't a surprise, the tough guy thinking he was swinging on the top branches of the tree. Always took men like him a while to realize that their celebrity only burned bright in their own neck of the woods, and now that they had left their home city some younger spark would be filling that vacuum.

Martin started to walk away, made it a few steps and found Usman bolting in front of him. He stood blocking the path, a big grin still on his face.

'Look, wee man, I know you're reluctant. Sure you are. You don't know me from Adam. Probably don't know the city very well either, am I right? You come over here and you don't get the sort of respect you got back home. People don't treat you the way they should. Am I right? Yeah I am, I'm right. I seen it before. We got guys come over and they think they can be the same thing here they were back home. Doesn't work that way, does it? You left behind whatever reputation you had back in the old country. So you need to find some right good jobs for yourself. Can't lean on your old chums, you need to find good jobs for yourself, and I got a couple of belters.'

'These belters,' Martin said, only half sure of what the word meant. 'You take them to your friend back there. Or another friend. I don't know you well enough to trust you.'

He made a step to walk past Usman. Shove past him, if that was what it took. You wouldn't know it to look at him but Usman was a determined man, happy to push his luck if it needed a nudge. He blocked Martin's path again and held up a placating hand.

'Right, here's the thing. I need a serious guy, right. I know you're a serious guy. You done the sort of thing I need help with, so this'll be easy for you. I got a bunch of jobs planned out, I been scouting for ages, got all the detail, right. But I get that you don't trust me because you don't know me, that's fine, so here's what we do. I'm going to give you my number, because I know you won't want to give me yours. You call me when you're ready and I'll tell you about one job. Just one to start, that's fair enough. You and me, we talk it out. I tell you all about it, and how you can make a good fifteen grand off it. A week's work, tops. Right?'

Martin stood and looked at him, considering it. Usman smiling, trying to look reasonable and persuasive. Couldn't do any harm to take the phone number even if he had no intention of ever phoning the guy. Everyone promised big money for little work. It was the detail that would separate Usman from the criminal herd, but Martin had little intention of phoning to hear it, he just wanted this conversation to be over.

'Fine, I will take your number,' Martin said, taking his phone out of his pocket.

Usman told him the number, told him how to spell his name as well. As Martin turned to walk away Usman put a hand on his shoulder and stopped him.

'I bet you're thinking that I'm some kind of bullshitter, eh? Big mouth kid and all that. Well I ain't. This job, it's a good one. I got all the plans and info to make it work clean. Just needs a driver and gunman, two-man job, me and you. But you wouldn't have to pull the trigger, no way. Minimum thirty grand return. Minimum. You think about it. Call me and we'll discuss it, I'll give you the details. Don't have to say yes, but at least talk to me about it. How are you ever going to get to know people in the business if you won't work with them?'

Usman nodded, convinced he'd nailed the speech with that last gem at the end. Throw in a catch-22 that only he can solve for the new guy in town. He turned and walked back down the street, his tall and thin frame rocking side to side as he walked. An affectation, an attempt to look like the coolest man in Glasgow. Hard to say who he thought he was impressing, but he seemed committed to it. Going for a gangster swagger.

Martin took a walk to the nearest bus stop, still unsure of where everything was here. Best way to learn your way about was to travel in ignorance, watching the city going past and waiting for it to get familiar. He would make a little money just for turning up at the drug handover they'd done today, but only a little. Working security, a job he was no good at. Not in Glasgow, anyway. Here he was just a short man with a mean look and a funny accent whose threats were mostly misheard. God, funny accents summed up half the city from where he was standing, but he was the odd one out. So he wasn't even intimidating here. No reputation. Nothing. He was starting from scratch, and how do you start from scratch without taking a chance on new people?

# 2

It was the bill for the car insurance that changed things. Joanne had decided, partly because Martin had unofficially moved in and Skye had unofficially moved out, that it was time to get another car. She'd had one until Skye was nearly old enough to drive, then quickly sold it. She didn't want to teach that girl how to drive; she was quite dangerous enough on foot.

Joanne had enough money to buy the car by herself, but Martin insisted on chipping in. It was pride, more than anything. Go halves on everything this early in the relationship to make Joanne see how useful he was. So he had to take two thousand, two hundred out of his savings. He told her he had the money and Joanne had little choice but to believe him.

'I have money of my own,' she told him. 'You don't have to match me penny for penny.'

'I have money too,' he said.

She knew what it was. This macho little guy who had earned his own money and paid his own way his whole life, unwilling to have his girlfriend provide anything for him now. She had no idea how much money he had, but he hadn't done much work since they'd got together.

Joanne was going to pay for vehicle tax, so Martin insisted on paying for the insurance. And that was it. She saw a change in him now. Martin seemed like he was worried about something, and that something could really only be money. It became obvious that he was looking for work, phoning people who could help him out. They had separate accounts, didn't talk much about money. Didn't talk about what he would do to earn some either.

They didn't talk about his work because it wasn't a subject either of them was sure their relationship was strong enough to handle yet. Joanne worked with her older sister in a book store that their parents had owned before them. The parents were dead now, Joanne's house had been theirs before they passed away. So Joanne had a nice house that she didn't have to pay for and just enough money coming in from her job. She didn't know what Martin was bringing to the table.

She didn't put pressure on him; he put all the necessary pressure on himself. She didn't ask about money, didn't ask about his work, didn't ask about his history. She was too smart for questions.

'I had to leave in a hurry,' he had told her early in the relationship. 'I was working for some people. Not good people.'

'I never thought you were a social worker, Martin.'

He wasn't 100 per cent on what social workers did over here, but he was 95 per cent sure it was a long way from what he had done. Beating people, torturing a few and killing some. He did what was required to make the money he wanted. Over here? Standing in the back of a hairdressers while other people did deals, silent and simple. Only there so that his side would have one more person at the handover than the other side. He was a fucking statue.

Those savings had been hard earned. Took him years of brutal work to put it all together, but he had expenses back home as well. A nice flat, a nice car, a lifestyle that burned through disposable income quickly. When you work those jobs to make that money, you become determined to enjoy it. And when you flee the country in the night, get yourself across Europe and find yourself hardly employable for a few months, the savings dwindle. If it had been him alone he wouldn't have called Usman. He would have lived poorly; worked with people he vaguely knew and worked his way up very gradually through the crowds of industry men in this city. He had to be careful, a man in his position. Make a wrong move and he'd be running from another country, this time without help. Don't let people know who you are or what you did. Pick the people you work with carefully. Problem was that he didn't need to earn just for himself, he was part of a couple now. When he woke up in the morning with Joanne wrapped around him, he knew he had to make the call.

Martin was alone in the house, sitting at the big kitchen table. The kitchen felt old, solid, classic. Everything looked expensive, almost antique, leftovers from Joanne's parents' time. He had his phone in front of him, Usman's name and number on the screen. Thinking about that goofy smile and that silly walk. No. No way. He couldn't work with a guy like that, too much risk. He would never have given him the time of day back home. Guy like that, he would have laughed in his face. Thirty grand minimum take with an even split, he had said though. A week's work, at the most. Top up his savings and he wouldn't have to work again for a few months. Wouldn't even have to pull the trigger.

It was funny, but he hardly thought about the police, not back home and not here. He'd never been caught. Came close, obviously, or he wouldn't have been bundled off to Glasgow in the first place, but he'd always got away. Wasn't scared of getting caught now, even if he was in unfamiliar surroundings. He believed he had the talent to do most jobs clean. It was the thought of the other half of the two-man job botching it, getting him a bad reputation, that put some fear in him. The thought that Usman was a clown and everyone knew it but Martin.

He phoned the hairy Pole instead.

'Przemek,' he said, getting the pronunciation right this time. The good start he needed. 'It's Martin Sivok. I want to ask you about this Usman Kassar.'

There was a pause of a few seconds, a memory being searched. 'What about him?'

'Why did you give him my name?'

'I knew he was looking for someone like you. I knew you were looking for someone like him.'

'You make it sound like you're sending us on a fucking date.' His English improving to the point that he now knew where to drop the customary swear into a Glaswegian sentence.

'Hey, what you two get up to is your business. He got in touch with you?'

'He says he has a job. He seems stupid to me. Very stupid. If I work with him, I feel like other people will not want to work with me, they'll think I'm stupid like him.'

'Usman? He's young, that's all. He dresses stupid, but all young people dress stupid, always did. Talk funny too. But he has reputation. His brother, maybe more, but he has too. People know that he's good at what he does. He's done things that are outside of dealing, that's the thing. His brother is just a dealer, we have worked with him, a reliable man. Usman, he does some things that his brother doesn't, so when he needs someone to help he can't go to Akram. Needs someone to do some of the things you used to do. I thought you and him would make money.'

'Huh.' It sounded reassuring. Almost reassuring enough. 'These jobs, what are they?'

'You would have to ask him, I suppose, he doesn't share his secrets with me. I think he targets single jobs, high value, some risk. Good money though. You have robbed places, I know this, you can do it again. It would be that sort of thing, I think. Look, talk to him. He is from round here so he knows the targets. I don't know them, not my area.'

That was all he could get out of the Pole and he had nobody else to ask. Nobody who would know Usman and his record in the city. He needed to make better connections among the local organizations. Something he mistakenly hadn't tried to do. Now he knew he was staying, it looked like Usman would be his first.

If he could just trust the boy more. If Usman had made a better first impression. The impression of youth. The impression of brashness. The impression of difference. These weren't attractive to Martin. Deal with them individually. Youth. Well, he was definitely younger than Martin, but maybe not by much. Acting young in the street wasn't a definite indicator of how he would perform on a job. A smart kid was a better colleague than a dumb adult. Brashness. Lot of brash people in the criminal industry, that was universally true. It was a defence mechanism sometimes, a second skin for those who had grown up in the business. Many were drawn to the industry because it matched their own bold and aggressive attitudes. And it wasn't like he had to love the boy, just work with him. Difference. Well, he was different. A Pakistani, although he was Scottish and spoke like it. But there were two other issues relating to difference. The first was that everyone here was different to Martin. The second was that every difference was forgiven when you were profitable. That was universal too, applied to the business in Brno as much as in Glasgow. Colour, nationality, religion, those were all clothes you wore. As long as the person underneath made money, nobody paid a whole lot of attention. You stop being profitable, people look for reasons to hate you and your differences become an issue.

Usman had put together a list of alternatives, none of them any more appealing than the foreigner. He needed a second pair of hands and they had to be willing to hold a gun. There was a couple of names on the very short shortlist, but he didn't trust either one of them. Freelancers, men that Usman had learned about through various stories of doubtful truth, and he was unhappy with them both. He knew nothing about the foreigner, and that ignorance put the little guy a step ahead.

The phone rang, Usman looking at the screen and seeing an unknown number. He had almost given up on hearing from the foreigner at that point.

'Hello.'

'Hello, Usman?'

'Yeah.' A slight pause, working out the accent. 'Is that Martin?'

'Yes it is.'

'Yeah, I thought it was. All right, cool, brilliant, you want to talk about the job, huh?'

'I do want to talk about the job. I am not saying I will do the job, but I want to talk about it. Not over the phone.'

'Nah, nah, not over the phone, obviously. We'll meet. You want to pick the venue?'

A little, gentle piece of reassurance. Usman smart enough to offer Martin control of the meeting. And it was instinct too, he asked it quickly and naturally, which should impress Martin.

'You tell me somewhere, I don't know,' Martin said. Keeping it deadpan, all the way, accepting that he didn't know the city well enough to pick a location.

'Right, sure, no bother. There's a flat above a Chinese takeaway in Mosspark, that's not too far from you. There's, like, a doorway sort of thing with steps, like a passage. Go in there and I'll have the door up to the flats open for you. I'll go in the back so we won't both be seen going in the same way. We can pretend we never met if we don't like the smell of each other, right?'

'That's fine,' Martin said.

Usman could hear him writing the address as he recited it. They said their goodbyes, Usman grinning in triumph as he did. The gunman was halfway into the job.

\*

It was only after he had hung up that Martin thought about what Usman had said. Not far from you. So Usman knew where he was staying. Knew where Joanne lived. Martin's first instinct was to be angry. When someone in the business lets you know the extent of their knowledge it's usually some sort of threat. Work for me or else. But not this time. He calmed quickly, realizing what it was. The kid was showing his professionalism. Showing Martin that he could find things out, set things up. Trying to make himself seem like the sort of person Martin would want to work with.

They had arranged to meet within the hour, better to get this done quickly. Better for both of them. If Usman couldn't win Martin round then it put an end to it quickly, let both of them look for alternatives. Usman could find someone else to help him; Martin could try and find another way of earning a living. If Usman was persuasive then it let them get started on the job straight away. Preparation time was always key; whatever the job was, you needed to plan it well and that meant taking your time.

He found the Chinese takeaway, found the passageway with the few steps leading up it that Usman had described. Martin looked up and down the street before he went in. A first meeting, always nervous, always paranoid. This could still be some sort of a set-up, although it wasn't entirely obvious what anyone could gain from setting him up round here.

He walked slowly along the passageway, feet scuffing a

little to make some deliberate noise, kill the silence and alert Usman that he was close. There was a door on his right, ajar. He reached for it, and as he did, it pulled back. Usman was standing there, grinning when Martin stepped quickly back, ready to go on the offensive.

'Don't look so nervous, wee man. Come away on in.' He held the door open, dressed marginally less stupidly this time. He had a T-shirt on over a long-sleeved top which looked daft to Martin, like the boy didn't know what order to put his clothes on, but otherwise just a normal pair of jeans and trainers. No headphones or jewellery or anything else that made him visible from space.

They went upstairs, into a dingy little flat that didn't match the flashy style Usman had been trying to present to the world outside. As they entered the living room, Martin made a show of looking around.

'This is yours?'

'Nah mate, this dump isn't really anyone's. Guy downstairs owns it. Loads of people use it for, you know, meetings, stuff like that. Nice wee place nobody pays attention to, you know what I mean. Sit down, sit down.'

Martin sat on one of the chairs and regarded the remarkably cheap furniture around him. A place for a meeting, but not a place you'd stay any longer than that. He looked at Usman and shrugged a little. It was up to him to start the talking.

'Right, yeah, the job. Here's the detail. I've known about this one for, shit, how long, couple of years at least. Had my eye on it that long, so there's nothing I don't know about it. What I haven't had before now is anyone that would do the job with me. See, I mostly don't work with people like you. Gunmen, I mean; not, like, foreign people. So I don't really know any gunmen properly, or anyone who could do a good impression of one. The few I know of, I wouldn't trust to do this. Got to pick the right person for a big thing like this, got to be done the right way. So I've been sitting on it, waiting for someone like you to come along.'

He had that gangster trait of being able to talk about a job without ever telling you anything about it. Spend enough time building fences around the details of the bad things you did, it becomes hard for anyone to get in the gate.

'You found me,' Martin said impatiently.

'Aye, yeah, so I did. So, right, the job itself. It's a bookies. You know what a bookies is?'

'Yes, I know.'

'Good. It's in Coatbridge. You know where that is?'

Martin frowned a little, tried to conjure a facial expression that made it clear he could learn quickly. It would take another few months for him to learn where the places whose names he heard were in relation to each other.

'Never mind, doesn't matter, I'll show you it anyway before we do the job and you'll probably only go there again by accident. So there's this bookies, and it makes enough money, they all do. Never see a poor bookie, do you? Anyway, yeah, this place makes okay money from its proper business, but that ain't what we're interested in. It's been used to store and clean money for a criminal organization for a few years now. You heard of the Jamieson organization? Big bastards, their boss is in the jail?'

Martin nodded, this one he'd heard of and remembered. 'I know of them.'

'Cool, right, well it's them that are storing cash there. See, they make all this dirty money and sometimes they need to store the actual hard cash. Just for a wee while though, you understand, they don't sit on dirty cash long. They have a good operation for cleaning their dirty cash as well, but a big organization like that, it's going to get money it didn't expect. There's going to be money that comes in before their people have worked out how to clean it. You keeping up?'

'Yes, I understand this.'

He did understand it, seen it before. Any good criminal gang has more than one way to clean dirty money, but even the best ways have limits. You clean only the amount you can without drawing attention to how much money is flowing through the legit company doing the cleaning. And you keep the amount you clean through each legitimate business consistent over a period of months so that there are no dramatic spikes or falls in numbers. Common sense.

It could come from any number of places. A business agreement that comes quickly, a sudden payment of a debt you thought would be paid gradually. Maybe someone owes them fifty grand and sells their house to pay it in one lump, leaving them with fifty grand to clean at once instead of fifty payments of a thousand pounds over the course of a year. So when you make a good amount of money you haven't planned for, you have to stash it somewhere for a while, filter it into the system gradually. In the meantime, the actual cash has to go somewhere. Not into a bank account, because that leaves a paper trail. You find somewhere safe to store it. A bookies would be a decent enough place, a legitimate business with a safe of its own.

'Good, right. So this place, it's run by a guy called Donny Gregor. Been in with the Jamieson organization for a good while, right proper bastard he is. Has a guy called Gavin Gauld that does a lot of work for him as well. They're the only two there that know the place is part owned by the organization and Gauld might not even know that Gregor keeps money for them. I wouldn't tell that arsehole anything of the sort. I have a list of all the other staff that work there but none of them are involved. We'll keep them well out of it. If we time this right, when we hit the place Gregor will be the only one there.'

Martin was already shaking his head angrily. This was full of holes that he could see, and probably a few more that he couldn't.

'No. You said you knew how much money would be there. You cannot know. You said there would be a lot. You don't know that.'

'Whoa, whoa, calm yourself down. I ain't finished yet. Hear me out, right. I don't know how much money exactly is in there right now, sure. And I won't know exactly how much money will go in there when they make a delivery. But I know how big the Jamieson organization is, right. And I know that when they get unexpected scores, that's where they put almost all of them in the first twenty-four hours. I think they move some of it afterwards so that it ain't all in the same place, yeah, but they can't do that for a while. Thing is, I know who moves the money, right. I know who delivers it there. All we got to do is wait for him to show up with the cash and that night we hit the place, clean it out.'

He was looking at Martin with a smile on his face, trying to encourage a response. Martin just nodded. There was still uncertainty about how much money there would be, but he was probably right to assume it would be a lot, even if the amount fluctuated week to week. Certainly would be a lot if they waltzed off with the bookies' clean money as well. And if Usman really knew who delivered the unexpected cash then they could be sure there would be something worth stealing when they went in. Watch the money arrive and move quickly.

'I get you there,' Usman said. 'You go in the back, I cover the front. You get Gregor to hand over the cash. I can supply you a weapon, don't you worry about that. We keep ourselves covered up at all times, obviously. Maybe write a note or something, because I don't want you having to talk with your funny wee accent tying up your tongue in there, that'll give the game away. But yeah, we can clean them out. Split fast, divvy up the dough and start to plan our next big score. Huh? Come on, it's great, right? Foolproof.'

Martin was silent for twenty very long seconds.

'He can't complain,' Usman said, cutting in. 'He can't go to the cops. We leave his clean money the fuck alone, only take the Jamieson cash, then he can't even mention it to his own employees, see?'

'I see,' Martin said slowly. Then said, 'No.'

'No? What d'you mean no? No?'

'No.'

'Aye, I got that. But why not?'

'You know this city well, yes?'

'Course I bloody do, this is my town, this is. Don't let the exotic good looks fool you, wee man, I was born and raised here. Don't doubt my knowledge of this place.'

Martin nodded. 'I don't doubt it. So you know this organization you will steal from is dangerous. This man, this Gregor, doesn't complain to the police. Of course he doesn't, because he doesn't need to. He complains to Jamieson, or whoever runs Jamieson's business now that this man is in jail. I know these things. Trust me. These big organizations, the safety of their money is the most important thing in the world to them. They will do very bad things to make it safe,' he said solemnly, speaking from experience. 'Money is more important to them than people. They will kill you for stealing from them. Trust me. I know. I have done the killing.'

Usman looked at him, frowning. That easy grin was finding it hard to surface now. 'I know that. Listen to me, Martin, right. I know about this job. You know about this job. Nobody else knows about this job. Even my own fucking brother I haven't told. My own brother, you understand that. I tell him everything. Haven't told him about this one, because I get it. You and me are the only ones who can know if we're going to get this done right. You go in through the back and you clean it out. You don't talk a word. Maybe, I don't know, you wear wedges or something to make you look taller. No offence, but you're wee enough to get noticed for it. Don't open your bloody gob either. You get the cash, I drive you away. That's it, wee man. That's it all. They think you worked alone. They don't know who you are and they got no way of finding out, if we both keep our traps shut. You hide the money properly; only start spending any of it a few months from now. We play this careful and right and we'll walk with good money. You know it.'

Martin didn't say anything. Usman was already working out how much the little Czech liked to use silence. It wasn't a lack of language skills. Well, not entirely. Martin knew that silence was unnerving, kept the other half of the conversation on their toes. You talk about killing people, you talk about robbing a place, and most people get chatty. Nerves make people talk. Silence is scary in this setting. Use it. Usman got that.

'I still think no,' Martin said quietly. 'I am new here. The risk . . .'

'You won't do a job in this city that doesn't have risk,' Usman told him. Not pressing him, not being aggressive. He was good at keeping his tone conversational, even when the first chance at nailing a lucrative job he'd been eyeing for so long was wriggling out of his grasp. 'I don't know what it was like back in . . . wherever-the-fuck-avakia, but round here there ain't one safe person to work for. You work for Jamieson and you piss off a bunch of other people that don't like Peter Jamieson. You work for Alex MacArthur and you piss off a big bunch of people who don't like him. You work for James Kealing and you piss off a whole other bunch of bastards you don't want to piss off. You work for the people you've already been working for and you'll have pissed off someone along the way. In fact, I'll tell you exactly who you pissed off. You heard of Chris Argyle?'

Martin shrugged and nodded. He had heard the name being mentioned. He knew that Argyle was the man from whom the hairy Pole and his people feared reprisal. They were treading on Argyle's toes, and Argyle was very protective of those tootsies.

'You worked against him. If he knows it, then you already

got yourself an enemy you don't want in this city. Him and all the wee tough nuts he's got working for him. All that work you do, man, anything for organizations, that's a real good way to make enemies. Good way to make yourself a target for people with a good aim. You pull a job like this and nobody knows it was you, nobody can pin anything on you, right. So you make no enemy. Means you don't boost your reputation round here, but you don't need reputation for a gig like this. Man, there's less risk doing this than doing the shitty wee jobs you been doing since you got here.' Usman finished with the sort of satisfied shrug that suggested he had created an argument that couldn't be countered.

Martin fell back into silence. Not to try and unnerve Usman, this time, just because he couldn't think of anything to say. The arrogant bastard was right, there was nothing left to argue with.

# 3

That wasn't the only attempt at recruitment going on in the city around that time. The criminal industry was always changing, people coming and going. New blood needed after old blood was spilled. Occasionally some very old blood was lured back to the life, and that's what the second meeting was about that day.

Nate Colgan had been careful with the phone call. He wanted to talk to Gully; he didn't want to talk to anyone else. Least of all did he want to talk to Gully's wife, Lisa. She was one of the few people in this world that Nate was in any way afraid of. Afraid of her sadness, afraid of her decency. She was to be avoided at all costs. If he called and she answered, it would upset her. The last thing she wanted was Gully working with people like Nate again, so the last thing Nate wanted was her finding out.

Stephen 'Gully' Fitzgerald was, to put it simply, the best. Just the goddamned best. There was no one, for a good few years, that could touch him when it came to being muscle in the criminal industry. He was tough beyond measure, ruthless and smart. He was also trustworthy and likeable, which was why Nate was calling. Must have been more than ten years since he was at the top of his game, sure, and people's memories are short. Now Nate Colgan was just about the best in the city, adorned with a skill-set Gully would have found familiar. There were people like Mikey Summers, Conn Griffiths and Jamie Stamford, too. Reputation belonged to them now because reputation was fickle, but for a while, Gully Fitzgerald was the undisputed king.

The reason he was the best was because he understood the business properly. He knew how to hurt people, how to terrify people, obviously, but he also knew where to draw the line. Gully never went too far, but he always went just far enough. Gully never had any little accidents. If he did you serious harm it's because that's what the job was. You took all that experience, the intelligence and the charm, and inevitably people learned from him. It was no coincidence that some of the best muscle in Glasgow in the last ten years had worked under Gully's wing when they were learning the business. Alan Bavidge had, and he'd been damn good at the job. Hadn't kept him out of his grave, but you needed to be more than good to avoid that. Nate had worked with him as well, modelled some of his work on Gully. Nate was a darker personality though, which was why his reputation was maybe even more fearsome and why nobody ended up learning from him.

There was a boy Nate had taken under his wing. A good kid, smart and tough, should have been perfect for the job. Nate had seen himself as the mentor, had seen Ronnie Malone as his not so enthusiastic apprentice. It didn't last. Ronnie was killed. Murdered by someone who was supposed to be working with them. It was dirty and pushed Nate out to the edge of his personality, further into himself and away from the rest of the world. He didn't want to work with anyone else, but what he wanted and what the organization needed could be at odds. Only one winner in that battle.

Nate, big, tough imposing Nate, was the security consultant, or some such bullshit title, for the Jamieson organization. It had been a one-man job, back when Peter Jamieson and his right-hand man John Young were on the outside and handled the day-to-day. Now, with them in prison, it was bigger than that, although he had tried to conquer it by himself after Ronnie. Didn't want anyone else he liked suffering for the job, but he couldn't do it alone. Too much work, too much risk. It was his responsibility to protect the organization from outside attacks, hold down anyone who might become a threat. One man can't guard the multiple faces of such a big organization.

Took some time to work out how to play it next. He needed a second pair of hands, but he wasn't going to take on another kid. No more master and apprentice shite, no more teaching on the job. Someone experienced, someone who already had the T-shirt. He thought about poaching Mikey or Conn away from their employer, Billy Patterson, given that he too worked for Jamieson. Didn't seem fair, they were needed where they were. There was also a trust issue there, lies had been told to

Nate around the time of Ronnie's death and Conn was one of the liars. You have to work with liars in the business, you either accept them or find another job, but Nate was still angry. Hadn't yet reconciled himself to what had happened, and couldn't trust himself to act properly around the liars. In the end, he kept coming back to the same tough, trustworthy old hand. Gully.

'You're looking well,' Nate said to him when Gully arrived at the office above the gadget shop. A little place in Govan that Marty Jones owned. Marty was one of the senior men running the organization in Jamieson's temporary absence.

'You old charmer,' Gully smiled. 'Lying bastard, but a charmer.' He walked across to the desk where Nate was sitting and sat in the chair opposite, leaning casually back.

He was a little shorter than Nate, at around six foot. Almost as broad, although softer in the muscles and a little wider in the gut. His sandy hair was as ruffled as it always was, but he was clean shaven and neatly dressed, which he hadn't always been. There was a time . . . Man, there was a time when Gully Fitzgerald was a wreck of a man. Back when Sally died, hit by a car. Eight years old. After everything Gully and Lisa had gone through to have a child, and they lost her like that. Total accident, she ran out onto the street, between two parked cars. Driver didn't see her, didn't have a chance. Driver was devastated, but it wasn't his fault. There was nobody to blame, nobody to lash out at, which probably made it worse. He'd been working for old Danny Knight at the time, acting as muscle, bodyguard and general fixer. Gully stopped working, hit the bottle. Nearly lost his wife because of that. But Gully had been off the drink for a while, and still out of the business at Lisa's insistence.

'You're looking about the same as you ever did,' Gully said now, a sort of compliment that was undoubtedly true.

Nate, at thirty-eight, was ten years the junior of the two. Where Gully had gone from youthful, bright blonde with twinkling dark eyes to sandy, lined and sad, Nate had just stayed the same. His dark hair had gone a little grey at the sides, but that made little difference. Made him more distinguished, if it did anything at all. Maybe some of the lines that seemed to have always been there had deepened, but he had aged very little in the last decade.

'As bad as ever,' Nate said with a smile. 'You, uh, earning these days?' He always spoke in a deep rumble, something he couldn't control. Even when he tried to sound a little softer, his words growled their way out of his mouth.

Gully shrugged. 'I'm not sucking pennies out of charity boxes yet.'

'But you're not working?'

Gully smiled a little. Every smile just seemed sad from him these days. Too much misery in the eyes. Too experienced and world-weary to be surprised by any joke or outburst. The smile was designed to tell Nate all of that, and nudge him gently along.

'All right, I'll get to the point,' Nate said. 'You know I'm running security for Jamieson these days. Making sure we put up the barricades in the right places.'

'I heard, yeah. You'll be busy then.'

'I am. And I could use a second pair of hands. Someone who knows the business. Someone who can do some of the dirty work when I'm not able or when I need a trustworthy second.'

There was a few seconds where Gully just looked down at the floor like he hadn't quite heard Nate. He wasn't trying to be dramatic; he had never been one for artificially creating silence. Gully had always been a good talker, comfortable with the sound of his own voice, but he was thinking about something.

'You know, I've only been to one funeral since Sally's. Couldn't face them. I just knew that I would see her in the coffin every time I went to one of the bloody things, and seeing her once was enough. Anyway, when the person that matters most dies, what do the rest of them matter, eh? No offence, Nate, but the world is now populated entirely by less important people. Anyway, one funeral. You met Alan Bavidge? You must have.'

'I think so,' Nate said. 'Knew of him anyway.' He of course knew of Bavidge, had seen him around and heard the stories

42

even if he hadn't worked with him. Heard the story of his brutal, messy death.

'Aye. He was a good wee lad, was Alan. Not built naturally for it like you, but he had the talent to make up for it. Had the guts. Had the brain for it as well. That was the downfall, you see. The brains. Smart enough to understand how bad the things he was doing were. That's where the darkness comes from. You've got it in you, the darkness, I've always seen it. It's because you have to go home and look at your wee girl and know that the things you do would sicken her. I had it. Still do, I suppose. Alan had it in spades. I taught him to be as good at the job as possible, but it was never enough, not in this filthy business.'

He'd never spoken this way to Nate before, or anyone else in the industry. Never. He had been sad and reflective, but this was way beyond mere sadness. This was angry and righteous and tragic all rolled into one destructive package. This was hard to say, mostly because every word of it was true. When Gully mentioned Nate's daughter, Rebecca, and what she would think of his work, it was an artful stab to the heart. Knowledge gained from bitter experience.

'So when Alan died I figured I should go along to the funeral. I should see him dead as well, because I had helped put him there. If he had been worse at the job then he wouldn't have lasted long enough in the industry to be killed by it. He'd have been knocked around and sent off to work somewhere decent instead. He was only important enough to be a target because he was good at it. He was my victim. I didn't stab him, but whatever bastard did, only did it because of the things I taught Alan.'

'Gully . . .'

'Hear me out, Nate,' he said, raising a hand. He hadn't looked Nate in the eye once throughout this speech. 'This business, it's going to kill us. You know that, don't you? Good men, they go off and play golf and get hit by lightning. Or they start travelling in their old age and have a heart attack in Thailand dodging ping-pong balls. That's how the good and the nearly good go out. Us, the bad, we get involved in this business. We line ourselves up behind people like Peter Jamieson and wait for the consequences to come and rip us apart. You know it'll kill you, don't you?'

Nate nodded; a smart enough man to have worked this out already. The long, sleepless nights after Ronnie was murdered when all he did was think about the way this industry killed off its own. 'Yeah, I figure it just might. Even if it doesn't, it'll ruin things just enough so that it might as well have.'

Gully nodded. That was as much as he needed to hear. He had to know that Nate understood, that he wasn't kidding himself about the work they would do and the life they would have. It had been a while since they worked together, back when Nate had seemed to believe that he could survive this. The young ones always believe they're strong enough to get through the industry unscathed. Gully would never work with a person like that again. No more naivety. No more kidding yourself. The only people capable of doing a good job in this shitty business are the ones who know a perfect job doesn't exist.

'I'll work with you, Nate,' Gully said, with a bit of a shrug that looked dismissive. 'I could do with the money. But I won't work much; just help you out when I can. No seven-day weeks. No all-nighters. Nothing I can't explain away to Lisa.'

Nate looked up at that. He knew Lisa hated the business, knew she would hate Gully getting involved. She'd never liked what he did, but after Sally's death it became something more ferocious. Nate hadn't thought Gully would even tell her that he was working.

'I'm going to tell her something,' Gully said. 'No more lying to her. Well, no more big lies, anyway. I'll downplay what I'm doing, stop her getting afraid, but I'm telling her something.'

Nate nodded. 'We'll make it – I don't know – part-time, I suppose. You can work when it suits, with the occasional call-out when I need proper backup.'

Gully nodded. That was what he was looking for, part-time work and part-time money. Been a long time since he dreamed of getting rich, or thought getting rich would make him happy. 'The boy, the one who was killed. You want to tell me what happened there?'

Nate sighed heavily, looked around the empty office for

words that would help a usually expressionless man explain how he felt about it. 'He was already working for Kevin Currie, working out of the St John. Daft stuff, setting people up with rooms off the books, that sort of rubbish. He was smart and tough so I took him on. Pushed him into it. He was good, reluctant at first but becoming enthusiastic. We got crossed on a big job. Russell Conrad. You ever meet him?'

Gully shook his head uncertainly. 'He's a gunman?'

'Was. Anyway, he killed Ronnie, the boy. That's why I've been working alone, why I need someone to come in and help.'

Gully smiled a little. 'Someone expendable. Someone else who can be a magnet for the bullets they're firing at you. Aye, I get it, I get it.'

Nate smiled. 'Aye, poor wee you. You're so weak and vulnerable. So easily exploited.'


Everything seemed hollow now. Every day was an empty space from morning to night, the gaps in her life where Sally had been. Lisa tried, pushed hard to make it feel like a life worth living, but the gap would not be filled. So it became an act, the sad woman who was coping as well as could be expected. An act that convinced most people, but not her husband.

It was a battle to rationalize what had happened to their daughter. Years of trying, then years of joy after they'd had her. Now the rest of their lives to suffer the loss. There had to be a reason, an explanation. Lisa wouldn't come right out and say it, but she considered the industry to be responsible for every bad thing that had happened to them. Like losing Sally was some punishment from God for what Gully had done with his life. Gully didn't believe it. If anyone was going to be punished for what he had done it would be himself. He believed Sally had died because the world was a naturally cruel and unpleasant place. That's what he told Lisa, and what she struggled to accept.

They didn't talk as much as they had. Existed in the same house, two people tied together by their shared horror. When Gully made the effort to talk, it usually led to an argument. He came in that day and sat down across the table from her. Looked at her with a slightly sheepish expression that usually meant he'd done something stupid. She'd seen that look a few times during the drunken years.

'I met Nate Colgan today,' he said to her. 'You remember Nate? Big lad, used to do some jobs with me when I was working for Danny.'

'I remember the name.'

'Aye, well, Nate's flown up to new heights in the world these days, senior man for Peter Jamieson. He's looking for reliable help for low-level work, part-time. I said I would think about it, talk to you about it.'

Lisa sat stiffly, trying not to show her sense of disgust. 'What's there to talk about? Do you want to do it?'

Gully shrugged. It was obvious that he didn't know how to speak to her any more, scared that anything he said would upset her. He seemed like a man terrified that he was one poorly chosen sentence away from pushing her over the edge.

'We could do with the money,' he said. 'It would only be easy work, a few hours a week.'

'You want to do it. You may as well.' She could see that he was going to do the work anyway. He might not have any enthusiasm for it, but it was a choice between work and spending more time at home. She didn't blame him for choosing work.

It was something else to put between them. Another screen that she could hide any hope of a return to normality behind. Normality would have been an insult to what they had lost. Him working in that industry again was another thing to hate. Another step towards the end.

Nate had what he wanted, but when was that ever enough? He had a man he respected and trusted to work alongside in Gully, but they would be working a job Nate didn't much like. Working for people he struggled to trust, the lingering hatred from Ronnie's death refusing to clear. It was never going to be any different. The industry was run by people only a fool would trust. Nate was no fool. Hate them, never trust them. Do their dirty work and take their money but never get attached. Always there, nagging at the back of his mind, the memory of

Ronnie Malone. A good kid, killed because of the job Nate forced him into. Now he was working with a friend, another person he cared about. Putting that friend in danger. So no, he wasn't happy.

There was an empty house waiting for him, something even Gully could better. Nate had a daughter, Rebecca, but she lived with her mother's parents, an arrangement that generally kept her away from the violence of Nate's life. He had her most weekends, and that brought him some joy and plenty of extra worry. There was a woman he was in danger of getting close to, despite himself. Her name was Kelly Newbury, and no matter how hard he tried to keep his distance from her, he couldn't quite get her out of his mind. He wanted someone else around, despite the risks.

He wanted something physical, but he needed something more, too. A beautiful younger woman, smart and aware of his work, Kelly worked in the business too. She knew what Nate did, knew the life he lived because of that work. She was, in many ways, the perfect woman for him. He wouldn't have to hide his true self. Still couldn't bring himself to call her. He felt too old and too dangerous. He was a man in a bubble; the only person he allowed close enough to share it was Rebecca. Doing work he didn't like for people he didn't trust. Keeping the woman he liked at arm's length because of it. He cursed his stupidity.

# 4

He didn't tell Joanne anything. She didn't ask, to be fair, so it's not like he lied to her. A lie of omission, if you insist on calling it a lie at all. If she had asked what he was working on, Martin would have told her, would have explained it to her in as much detail as she wanted. Part of him wanted her to ask, he wanted it to be that sort of relationship. Perhaps if they'd already established it as that sort of relationship, she would have asked, but it felt too early for total honesty. Lying about work was also an instinct he had never learned to crush.

See, for many years, back home, he worked just as hard keeping the job a secret as he did doing the work itself. He tried to hide it from family, but that became too hard so he lost touch with family. He tried to keep it from friends, but when that got too complicated he changed his friends. Only hung around with other people in the business, the kind of people who wouldn't care and wouldn't talk. They weren't always the kind of people he wanted as friends. Flashy and aggressive, industry people who defined themselves by the damage they did. And girlfriends. There were a few. Started out being girls he liked from outside the business, ended up being girls he didn't from inside. The business sent you on a downward spiral, even in your private life.

Now he had Joanne. A smart woman, outside the industry, and he wasn't going to lie to her. If she put her size-four down and said no way Josef, he would have backed out. Would have walked away from the life at her instruction. He had told himself again and again, he would back out, all she had to do was tell him. But she didn't.

She could see the expectation on his face. He had told her he was going to be working that day, and hadn't added anything else.

'Oh, right,' was all Joanne had said.

She knew it disappointed him, her not asking for more. He wanted to have to explain. Wanted her to want to know. Joanne understood the nature of Martin's work and she didn't feel like she had to know more than that. She was happy in ignorance, and she hadn't been happy for a long time. She had earned the right to decide how honest they were.

They went through their early morning routine. Sleepy sex and a long shower followed by a rushed breakfast. Joanne was going to be second to the bookshop, her sister there before her. Hated when that happened. Always felt that she had to be seen to work harder than Sophie to prove that her status as an unmarried single mother didn't make her some sort of failure.

She turned up for work on time and she put the hours in. Some mornings Martin slowed her down.

'I'm off. Will you be home when I get back?'

'Should be,' he said to her with a nod. Waited for her to ask a little more.

She nodded and kissed him, left without another word. Didn't give any outward sign that she cared about what he was doing. Left the house and drove into work. Thought about him constantly through the day. Wondered what he was doing and hoped that he was safe. She didn't want to know, because that felt right for the relationship. She didn't want to have to explain this to him, because explaining was almost as big a commitment as finding out. So she worked and pretended it was no big deal. Her, always trying to be respectable and law-abiding, fallen for a career criminal. Knowing he was pursuing that career even as she thought about him.

Her lack of interest, if we're being honest, hurt him. Just a little bit, but enough. The thought that maybe she didn't care, that maybe she only ever saw this as a short-term thing, a bit of fun. As soon as he disappointed her, got himself arrested, she would ditch him. But her lack of interest was limited only to his work; it wasn't representative of their relationship. He was worrying about nothing. He kept telling himself that as he left the house.

Joanne had taken the car, so he was back on the bus. The

city still didn't seem familiar to him, but it wasn't the concrete mystery he had first encountered. There were bits of it that he recognized when he looked out the window, others that he was sure he had seen but couldn't convince himself were in the same place as before. Others still seemed entirely new to him. He had moved around a lot since he arrived in Glasgow, tried to learn the place. You can get the basics, major landmarks, shopping areas, those sorts of things, but not the detail. You don't gain the knowledge a man in the business needs by looking out a bus window. Takes longer and it takes more effort. You have to be working in the city, day in, day out. You have to scout the place with all the professionalism you can muster. Even then, you won't learn every street; you won't learn every little hole that any city offers to hide in. He couldn't, after thirty years, tell you every part of Brno, just the bits that mattered. That was the problem with Glasgow; it was only just starting to matter to him.

He went north of the Clyde, then got another bus that took him east. He was going to Alexandra Park for the first time. Found it and then followed the directions he'd been given to find the fountain where he was supposed to wait. There were way more people there than he had expected and he grimaced to see them. He thought it would be some small fountain hidden among the trees where the deal could take place without anyone else seeing. Instead there must have been a dozen people sitting round the black edge of the grand fountain, chatting and killing a sunny lunch hour.

Straight away, Martin understood. The person he was meeting didn't trust him, wasn't sure that this Eastern European newcomer was reliable. Wasn't willing to accept that any new customer had honest intentions for their first meeting, that's why he wanted plenty of witnesses around. Made sense. Annoying, but it made sense. So Martin walked halfway round the fountain until he saw the man he thought he was looking for.

Dale Duggan was middle-aged and it didn't look like it had been an easy fifty years. He was overweight but still dressed in a thin, tight jumper. Maybe it had fitted at one time and maybe he just hadn't noticed how much weight he had put on. He couldn't have thought it was a good look, if he'd taken the time to notice what he was pouring himself into. The fact that his thick dark hair didn't look like it had battled a brush for some time suggested he didn't concern himself much with appearance. He was sitting on the curved edge of the fountain by himself, a blue plastic bag at his feet. Martin went over and sat near him. Not right beside him, not so close that a passer-by would realize they were there to meet. A few feet apart, a safe zone in between. Martin reached into his pocket and pulled out a brown envelope. He placed it on the safe zone, resting his hand on top of it for a few seconds, making sure that Dale had seen what was happening here. He took his hand away, glancing off in the opposite direction. Took two seconds for Dale to reach across and put his fat little hand on the envelope. Had to be quick, if it fell back into the water, that would be his wad of cash soaked. Once he had the envelope Duggan got up, slipped it into his trouser pocket and walked away.

Martin watched him go; made sure he was safely out of view before he moved. Duggan didn't trust Martin, but Martin wasn't dumb enough to trust Duggan either. Some guy he'd heard being mentioned by others in the business, that was hardly a glowing recommendation. Certainly no guarantee of professionalism and no guarantee that this was what it seemed to be. Duggan could have been setting him up.

He took a look around him and shuffled a few feet sideways until he was sitting in the spot Dale had vacated. Still warm. Martin sat and stared at the world around him for nearly ten minutes, taking in the park and the mostly happy workers on their lunch break. He took longer than he needed to, but careful was a valuable currency. There was nothing alarming, nothing to make him nervous. No police, nobody standing watching him. When he was as sure as he could be that it was safe, he picked up the plastic bag and strode out of the park.

Sitting on the bus with the bag on his knee, a shoebox inside the bag. Stupid thing to do. The kind of stupid you only do because you don't have a better option. He should be in a car; they shouldn't have met in public. Martin was clutching the bag, trying not to look like he was desperate for everyone to ignore him, which he absolutely was. There were two young men on the bus behind him, talking fast to each other. Their accents and the noise of the engine were killing the meaning of their words in Martin's ears, but it sounded like they were engaging in a game of one-upmanship. Women's names were being used as a means of scoring points, and each was questioning the other's honesty. Not far in front of him there was an old woman talking loudly. She was all on her own, and each sentence seemed to have very little connection to its predecessor. None of them were paying attention to the skinhead with the plastic bag.

It was a relief to get back into the house. Relief was soon swamped by guilt as he walked upstairs and into their bedroom. He took the shoebox out of the bag and looked inside. A small handgun, although not as small as he would have liked. Ammo, but not much because he shouldn't need any. Usman had said he would provide the gun but Martin had refused, insisted on getting one of his own. A gunman always should. Could never trust a weapon provided by someone else. Martin needed to make a connection with a seller in the city if he was going to be working here, and now seemed like the time to start. It meant storing it in the house before use though. Bringing a gun into Joanne's home.

If she didn't know it was there then she was innocent, that was what he kept telling himself. He pulled open the wardrobe and pushed the box in against the back beside the two other shoeboxes that belonged to him, both of which did at least contain shoes. It didn't look out of place and there was no reason why she would check inside it. And he hoped, prayed, that it wouldn't be there long.

It was weird being in the house without Joanne there. It still felt like he didn't belong. It was her house, and everything in it was hers, bought either by her or her parents. But slowly, very slowly, that was changing. He was starting to create his own little spaces inside it. Chairs that he always sat on, the cup that he always used, routines that belonged to him, and made tiny little fragments of their home his. Things that Joanne silently encouraged, making him a growing fixture in her life. She would only do that if she wanted him to stick around. That thought made him smile a little.

# 5

Donny Gregor's days were filled with the same, soul-crushing routine. Out of bed early, into the bookmakers he ran, watch people throw good money after bad, go home in the evening. Maybe it wouldn't have been so bad if he owned the place, but he didn't even have that dubious honour. He ran it for others, so others picked up almost all the rewards. Now and again something interesting would happen, but interesting usually meant criminal and the criminal activity that floated round his business just made him more nervous. It was a little thrill, sometimes, and it might have been worth it if he was profiting, but usually it just meant Gregor was getting a taste of the risk with none of the reward.

His bookies in Coatbridge was part-owned by Peter Jamieson, although Gregor was only partly sure of that. He had dealt directly with John Young, Jamieson's right-hand man, which was why he figured Jamieson owned some or all of the place, but Jamieson's name wasn't on the books. A few different people had their names on the books and it was likely some of them worked for Jamieson. Maybe some of them didn't even exist, but that didn't matter. Whoever they were, they never showed up or got in contact, and Jamieson had control.

That was where the little bit of excitement came stumbling into Gregor's life. Sometimes they would use the safe in the shop to store things. Money, he assumed, although he never saw inside the envelopes and didn't want to think about what else they might be putting in there. Didn't want to, but couldn't stop himself thinking about drugs or guns or worse. As long as he didn't see it, he could plead ignorance. They were very careful when it came to keeping their secrets, much more so now that Jamieson was in jail. People were paranoid and even the trustworthy were looked upon with suspicion. The new guy who delivered the cash, a scary big fellow, had asked a few questions the first time he showed up. Asked about people approaching Gregor, trying to use the place for their own ends, or trying to lean on him. There had been no one, thank God.

'And if anyone does come round here looking for anything, you'll be the first person I call, Mr . . .'

'Colgan.'

'Colgan, right. I'll remember that.'

Colgan was coming in through the front door of the bookies now, a sports bag over his shoulder. He looked routinely intimidating, the sort of guy that couldn't turn it off no matter the situation. He ignored the customers, mostly men, watching the racing on the TVs and walked across to the counter. Gregor had seen him come in and had noticeably positioned himself at the counter so that Nate wouldn't have to talk to any other member of staff.

'Mr Colgan,' he said with a smile, 'would you like to come through to the back?' Asked quietly. A little too obvious, perhaps.

'Yes please.'

Donny Gregor, Nate knew straight away, was one of those people who revelled in being around criminals. You could see the nerves in him, but you could also see the desperate effort to make himself useful. Try and strike up a friendship, then tell his equally pathetic wee friends about it afterwards. Tell people that he had met Nate Colgan, spoken to the man on equal terms. Hint that he's important to Peter Jamieson, try and make himself seem like he's some sort of big gangster. There were always plenty of people like that around; the kind who wanted to seem dangerous by association. Nate, and others like him, did a good job of avoiding the kind of people who were thrilled by their proximity to criminals, but Gregor was one of the few useful idiots.

The bookie led Nate through the side door to the offices at the back of the building. A couple of people might have turned to glance at the new arrival who was going straight through with the manager, but nobody let their look linger. You didn't need to know the business to know that Nate Colgan wasn't the sort of guy you got caught leaving your eye on. Gregor and

Nate disappeared through the back of the shop, along a short corridor, and through to the little office Gregor used.

There was nobody else there. The routine was, or should have been, Donny Gregor waiting out in the corridor to make sure they weren't interrupted while Nate put a particularly well-sealed package into the safe. This time Gregor had broken the routine. He had closed the door behind them, standing inside the room, self-consciously clearing his throat to make sure Nate knew he had something to say. Nate, with the bag still slung over his shoulder, stopped and looked down at the shorter man with a firm look. Inquisitive, yes, to start with, but more than that. Just a tiny little bit threatening. The sort of look that told Gregor he better have a damn good reason for breaching the reassuring set-up they always used.

'Listen, Nate, I was thinking of phoning you anyway, even if you hadn't turned up. I don't know, maybe calling you isn't the right way to do these things.'

'Why?' Nate asked. Gregor had the whiff of a man who was set to ramble.

'Well, I don't like to make a fuss. I mean, I'm not that sort, am I? I get on with my work here and I try to be useful, and I don't like raising alarms about every wee thing. Plenty of things round here that I can take care of without calling for help. But I think, the last, I don't know, week, maybe longer, this place has been watched.'

Now he had Nate's interest. 'Watched? How sure are you?'

Gregor puffed out his cheeks. This was his moment in the spotlight and he wanted to play it right. He wanted to sound like the sort of gangster that Nate Colgan spent his days hanging around. He wanted, as everyone did, to make a good impression on the people who seemed to matter.

'I can't say a hundred per cent. It seems like it to me though, so I'm fairly sure. I've seen the same car with someone in it. I thought it was suspicious the second or third time I saw it. The one time I went out and went over to the car though, there was nobody there. So, I don't know, I can't be a hundred per cent, but sometimes, you know, you just get that feeling. You know what I mean? The feeling that you're being watched? I got that.'

Nate doubted very much that Gregor was familiar with that feeling because he doubted Gregor spent very much of his life under other people's microscopes. He also doubted that someone watching the place would make a point of parking the car in the same place every day. It sounded false.

'So you went over and there was nobody in the car. But every other time you've seen the car there was someone else inside?'

'Well, I don't know about every time. I can't vouch for that. Look, Mr Colgan, Nate, I only want to give you the best information so you can take educated steps. I only want to tell you what you can use, what matters. I can't honestly stand here and say that every single time I've seen the car there's been someone in it. I wish I could, but I can't. Sometimes there was a person sitting in the driver's seat, on their own. Maybe, I don't know, sometimes there wasn't.'

'Uh-huh. Yes or no would do.'

Gregor did well to keep the scowl off his face. Wasn't easy, this big ape had no right speaking to him that way in his own office. Okay, fine, he didn't have much practice speaking to people like Nate Colgan, but he knew what manners looked like. Gregor had met Jamieson's right-hand man, John Young, had spoken to him personally, and Young had been far more polite than this. Just because Gregor was sitting in a book-makers all day, that didn't mean he wasn't important. How would the Jamieson organization function without people working down the chain like him? Men like Colgan ought to have a little more respect.

Nate was silent for a minute or so. Put the bag down on the floor and gave this suspicious car a little thought.

'It's been parked in the same place every time?'

'Just about, yes. Yes.'

The same car in the same place almost every day. That just didn't seem likely. It didn't sound like the sort of thing any decent scout for a job would do, if indeed it was a scout and he was any good at his job. You use different cars, you park in different places, and you use a couple of different people if you have the numbers.

'You sure it was the same person you saw each time?'

'I think so, yes.' Making a real effort to keep his answers brief now. A petulant effort that Nate didn't care about.

The same person in the same car in the same place. It was either the world's dumbest scout or not a scout at all. One last question.

'This car. Was it there over the weekend?'

Gregor paused. 'I don't think I noticed it over the weekend, no, but that doesn't mean it wasn't there, does it? I'm off Sundays, and there have been days I didn't notice it through the week as well.' That answer was a little longer, trying to be persuasive. The drama was rolling slowly away from him.

'And is it out there now?'

'Not now, no.'

Nate nodded. 'I'll think on what you said; see about confronting the person if they show up again. For now, I need to use the safe.'

Gregor was standing guard out in the corridor while Nate opened the safe. He had two packages this time, larger than usual. Money had come in that wasn't budgeted for, although Nate wasn't entirely sure where from. It was his job to protect it, not earn it. Could have come from anywhere in the organization. After Angus Lafferty 'disappeared' they were left with all sorts of business problems. He had been their importer and they needed a new one, one who knew his place, but Lafferty also had a good collection of legit businesses that filtered money smoothly. The organization wasn't able to keep a hold on all of them, so it was getting harder to clean money, getting harder to deal with the unexpected windfalls any well-run organization should expect to get.

He placed the two packages in the safe. There had to be thousands in each. He was no expert on the weight of money, but if it was in large bills to reduce the size of the package then there could be a good twenty-five or thirty thousand in each. Even in mixed bills you were still looking at a lot of money for someone to walk away with. The packages were very carefully sealed, if anyone tried to open them, it would show. The anyone they feared being Gregor. Nobody, Nate included, was willing to entirely trust some random bookie with their cash.

Gregor was standing out in the corridor chewing a finger when Nate emerged. The bag over his shoulder still looked as full as it had going in. That was because Nate had put a bundle of books in there as well, this way anyone who cared to watch him going in and out wouldn't notice a difference.

'You'll look around though?' Gregor asked. 'I'm not being a wimp here, I'm just asking, because, well, if this place gets hit, I get the blame.'

Nate looked down at him, saw the fear in him. Fear of failure, fear of letting Jamieson down. Fear of catching the violent blame if Jamieson was pissed off about it. It was good that he was afraid, made him more alert to genuine problems. He was only half-right about where the responsibility would fall. Yes, he would get some of the blame if the place was targeted. It was his business; he had a duty to make sure nothing went wrong here. But the person who would carry most of the blame would be Jamieson's security consultant. Mr Nate Colgan.

'I'll check around,' Nate said.

Gregor was obviously just relieved that he had passed the message on. Now he could say, if something did go wrong, that he had done his bit, he had warned someone clinging to a higher link in the chain. In Gregor's mind, it became that more senior person's problem to deal with. Wouldn't provide much protection for a man as junior as Gregor, sure, but it was something.

Nate left the bookies and made his way out to the car. Slung the bag onto the passenger seat and looked up and down the street. Nothing stood out. There were people around, but it was a sunny afternoon and this was a fairly busy commercial street. At a glance there wasn't anything that looked like a threat. Nobody hanging around a doorway, nobody sitting in a car. There was nothing that should make a smart man nervous. Nate drove away. The day was too short and he was too busy to hang around chasing the ghosts of Donny Gregor's limited imagination.

That ghost, it gnawed away at him though, chewed on the back of his mind just long enough for Nate to need to do

something about it. Gregor was no squealer; he didn't go running for protection every time some bastard looked at him
funny. As far as Nate knew, this was the first time he had ever
raised a security concern. Might not have been much to raise
a concern about, but it was still the first time his bottle had
rolled off its shelf and hit the floor. Which led to a different
train of thought. Maybe Gregor was involved in a set-up.
Maybe he was giving out this info because he was planning to
clean the place out and pretend someone else had hit the
bookies in his absence. He wouldn't be the first who tried that
little trick. Jesus, first person you look at when money goes
missing is the person who was supposed to be looking after it,
that's just common sense. Never trust a man who's already in
the industry.

Problem with that theory was that it didn't add up. Gregor
wouldn't have thrown out something that vague as a cover for
an inside job, you need detail to protect you. Something that
points a damning finger at a certain person, someone that's
already not trusted therefore easily incriminated. Gregor
would know people he could incriminate; people that the
Jamieson organization would be only too happy to blame. He
hadn't done that. Even he, desperate and not planning well,
would have more sense than to wrap his cover story in such a
thin blanket.

All of which brought Nate back to the realization that
Gregor might actually have been on to something. Perhaps

people *were* watching the place, getting ready to hit it, and maybe they weren't as dumb as Gregor made them sound. Let's say, just for the fun of it, that they were watching the place every day. It's a busy street, there's parking nearby and once you go too far down the street you don't have a proper view of the doorway. Not an easy target to watch without being seen. So how would you go about it? You'd park your car there, watch the place a little, and leave the car empty most of the day. Watch from a different spot, the car left unattended to make it look like the vehicle belonged to a regular Joe, using the parking space while they went to work nearby. It wasn't a bad little strategy, actually. Sort of thing someone who had really thought this through might go for.

Final question. Why would someone watch it that long if they were planning to hit the place? It's a bookies, there's not an awful lot to watch before you learn the routines. You work out ways in and out and you work out who's going to be there at certain times of the day or night. You suss out the basics and then you hit the bloody place, not much more to it than that. Gregor was talking like this super-spy had been lurking on his doorstep a long time. Probably more than a week, certainly since before the weekend. What were they waiting for? Hard to think of anything other than the two wads of cash Nate had just put in the safe.

# 6

Martin had the gun tucked into the side of his jeans. Wasn't where he wanted to put it, he would have preferred it in his inside coat pocket, but either the gun was too big or the pocket was too small. Wherever the issue, size mattered and this was bad planning. He thought he had used the coat before, back home, on jobs. He was sure a gun that size would fit in the inside pocket, but this one didn't and it was too late to go buying a new coat. Too late because the job had started.

He was in a back alley, walking tight against a tall wall, keeping himself wrapped in shadow. Hardly necessary, the place was almost pitch black, but shadow is always a welcome accomplice. There was little light in the alley, which made it more difficult to count the buildings as he made his way down. Had to make sure he found his way into the correct one. Breaking into the wrong building on his first job in the city would make Martin Glasgow's new punchline.

He pushed open a metal gate and stepped silently inside. Looked like the right place. Martin fiddled with his balaclava, making sure it was properly in place. Hated these things, how anyone could use them regularly was beyond him. Focusing on the wrong things. It was strange, his mind always raced when he worked a job, always wandered off into irrelevant areas, like it wanted to think about anything other than the rather important task at hand. Some people, back home, had said that they found an incredible focus when working jobs, like the rest of the world melted away and the only thing that existed was the target. That sounded like bullshit to Martin; his adrenalin pushed and pulled his mind in every direction it shouldn't go, and he had worked every sort of job you could think of.

There was a burglar alarm, but no chance that it would be switched on yet. The back door would be locked, but the building wasn't empty. There was a metal grill covering the front of the shop now that it was closed for business, and a metal gate covering the back door that was left open because people needed to leave through it. The manager was still in there, that was vital. Martin needed the manager to help him along. He crept up to the back door and paused, listening for anything that should worry him. There was a frosted window on the back door, no light visible behind it. One man, and hopefully only one man, was in the building. So just because you can't see anything, doesn't mean nothing's there. That's why Martin was standing in perfect silence, his ear almost touching the door, holding his breath. Nothing.

He took the gun from the side of his jeans. Hadn't been a problem having it there so far, but escaping with it would be more of a challenge. He would have a bag of cash to occupy one hand on the way out. Or at least, he should have a bag of cash, if this went as planned, and he would be in much more of a hurry. The thought of running in unfamiliar streets, a bag of stolen cash in one hand and a gun in the other. His mind racing ahead to all of those worst-case scenarios. Focus. Stay in the moment, that was what they said. Stupid thing to say, if he didn't look ahead, how could he see the trouble looming?

He held the gun in his gloved hand, the barrel pointing back at himself. One last look around before he made his first move. Once he started, there was no stopping until he was finished or flattened. From this moment on, everything had to be done at speed and without error. The intimidating first step, he thumped the butt of the gun against the glass. The glass cracked. Another thud, just as hard, in the same place. Holding the gun carefully. A small break, tiny shards of glass falling inside the two panes. Martin thumping again, breaking a proper hole this time, using the butt of the gun to smash a big enough hole to fit his small hand through. Carefully reaching in and turning the lock on the inside of the door.

Now moving fast. The door open and he was into the dark back corridor, working against the clock. Martin moved with the gun held out in front, the first thing that would be visible to anyone that stumbled across him. Pushing open a door and finding an empty storeroom. Round the corner in the corridor. The manager was bound to have heard that smashing glass, bound to have reacted to it in some way. Maybe calling the man who delivered the money, or grabbing a weapon of his own. Martin needed to get to him before he could.

It was these moments, late at night, that Gregor was starting to hate. He did it every night, alone in the dimmed room, sorting out the books before he went home. Doing it in small bursts like this meant not having to stay deep into the dark hours to do it all at the end of the week. He had more to compute than simply what had come in and what had gone out, he had to make sure there was sufficient leeway within those figures for creative accountants to flush a little dirty money through. Not much, because they were careful, but enough gaps for Jamieson's money men to fill in.

Sitting in the grim little office where he spent too much of his life. It was a step ahead of working the counter, a job he increasingly hated. If he could pluck up the courage, he would try and find a way to get out, start a new life somewhere else. Gregor didn't have the guts, and was smart enough to know he never would. Couldn't even fool himself into thinking there was better to come.

He was sitting at his desk, back to the door, tapping at his laptop and filling in boxes on a spreadsheet. There was a flicker in the back of his mind as he typed, the thought that he'd heard an echo that shouldn't have been there. He paused, leaning back in the swivel chair, rubbing his eyes. Heard it again, not an echo but a thud, coming from the back of the building. His heart began to sprint, Gregor holding his breath and praying that he wouldn't hear anything more. A louder thud, and the tinkle of falling glass.

His first instinct was that of a sensible man, the instinct to get up and run. This place wasn't worth the danger of facing down an attack. Before he'd got to his feet the realization that he might step out of the office and into the arms of the intruders. Then the memory of Nate Colgan, and the fear of what that man would do to Gregor for running. So he went for plan B, grabbing the phone. Colgan's number was stored on it. Sweating hands grabbing the phone, pressing the button to call him, holding the phone to his ear as he heard movement over broken glass.

'Hello?'

'Nate, it's Donny, they're here.' He paused as he heard someone push down the handle of his office door.

Pushing open the first door round the corner and finding a dim light on. A lamp on a desk, the middle-aged man he'd watched over the last week was sitting hunched, a phone in his hand. He wasn't speaking, had the phone away from his ear and was looking round at the door. Martin moved fast. Three steps to reach the man and one closed fist to punch the phone out of his hand. Picking it up, making sure the line was dead before he dropped the phone on the desk with a clatter. The man looked terrified already.

That wasn't good.

Martin needed Gregor to be useful, needed him to have his head screwed on, to work quickly and calmly if this was going to be the fast job intended. The fact he was sweating and panting before they'd even started didn't bode well. Martin made sure he could see the gun, but was careful not to point it directly at him, that would invite further panic. The man was sitting down at his desk, a few folders, a bundle of newspapers and a laptop in front of him. Martin reached out and closed the laptop, killing the glow from the screen and the possibility of a webcam. He looked around the office, no security camera visible. A few steps to the office door and he closed it. All done in silence.

It had occurred to him, many times, that the silence was almost as incriminating as talking. If he had a local accent then he would surely talk, blab out instructions without fear that his voice would give him away. Which meant the people investigating this would realize that he wasn't local. Of course, if he talked, they'd be able to narrow their search down much more. Still, silence wasn't a perfect solution.

And it wasn't the police he was worried about; their forensic minds had no part to play in this. They would never even find out that this robbery had taken place. There would be no crime reported, he was sure of that much. Even in his worst moment of panic Gregor wasn't going to do his civilian duty and call the police to report a crime. He would have been using that phone to try to call the people who worked for the Jamieson organization. They would send their toughest round to try and find out what had happened. These would be brutal men, men determined to send a message to any potential future robber by visibly annihilating this one. Martin had seen the sort before. Had seen, and delivered, the sort of punishments that this crime would inspire. These were punishments to fear.

He and Gregor were alone in the office, the door closed, the world reduced to the shape of the walls around them. Martin stood, looking down at the sitting Gregor, trying to judge the prospect of this man doing something very stupid. The bookie had his mouth open, one elbow on the table with his hand reaching up to his forehead, his other hand on his lap. That was the one Martin needed to watch for trouble. The hand on the forehead was the purposefully visible distraction; the hand on the lap was the one most likely to make a grab for something sharp or heavy.

Martin stood right in front of him, closer than was really decent. Time to establish power, quickly, if he could. He reached down and grabbed Gregor by the collar of his shirt and forced him to stand up. It would be wrong to say Martin lifted him, Gregor weighed significantly more than the younger man, but he got him up. Ran a hand down each side, checked his pockets and his trouser legs. There was nothing there that posed any threat. Martin shoved him back down into the seat, using more force than he needed to because he wanted Gregor to realize that this was a man casual in his approach to violence. Make the person understand that the default setting is aggressive, so if they step out of line they can expect a severe reaction.

Now it was time for the note, the simple instruction he had written out on Joanne's laptop and printed. He had read it again and again, making sure that it was acceptable. Martin was painfully aware that his sentences were shaped differently to those of a local person. Without realizing, he might misplace a word or emphasize something that nobody speaking English as a first language would. That's why he had kept it so simple, why he had been so careful with the wording.

OPEN SAFE. TODAY'S MONEY FROM JAMIESON.

That was it. That was all it said, all it should need. It seemed simple and clear to him, seemed like the sort of thing a local might write to get their point across with the least fuss. Close enough to a good effort that it wouldn't identify him, anyway. He took the note from his pocket and passed it down to Gregor.

Donny Gregor sat there, in his chair, note in hand, looking up at Martin. Didn't react, didn't move, didn't even read the note at first. Sat there with his mouth still slightly open, apparently frozen in time by the shock of the event. It might have been fear, that can do silly things to smart people, but Martin suspected otherwise. His instinct told him that this was a man deliberately killing time. He needed to understand that he was killing something that didn't belong to him.

Martin swung the gun lightly, last thing he wanted to do was knock the man out before he'd opened the safe. He caught him, just solidly enough, on the lower jaw. Gregor went into full stuntman mode, rolling off the chair and onto the floor, clutching his mouth and groaning like a train had just ploughed through the office and into his face. Martin groaned in disgust, just a little. Not because of the inconvenience, you don't expect your victim to bend over backward for you when you're trying to rob him blind. He groaned because of what this told him. Gregor was wasting time because he knew someone was coming. There was an ugly little plan lurking in the wings of this pantomime. The line on the phone might have been dead by the time Martin got to it, but that didn't mean there hadn't been life in it a few seconds before.

Martin knelt down beside Gregor and shoved the gun at his face. He wanted to get it in Gregor's mouth; nothing scared a person more than tasting the gun that might just kill them. He missed the mouth; Gregor seeing what Martin was trying to do and quickly getting back up to his feet, hands raised slightly. All thoughts of procrastination swept aside. The reminder that the gun existed had him scared enough to cooperate, he'd done all he reasonably could to waste time. Cooperation wasn't enough for Martin now; the bookie had to be taught that you don't piss off the guy with the gun.

With his free hand, Martin grabbed a fist full of Gregor's dark grey hair and shoved him towards the desk. He wanted to run his face into it, but he didn't have the strength to force him down in one movement. He settled for shoving him against it and reaching down for the note that Gregor had oh-so-deliberately dropped. Martin picked it up and slapped it onto the desk in front of Gregor, made him look at it.

'Yes, the safe. Yeah, I will, okay, I will.'

This was overdue, the victim trying to strike up a conversation, trying to coax Martin into saying something. Anything at all would be a start, because Gregor understood that he would need to give details to his employers. Get him to say something and then try and get him to say something incriminating, some hint of identity. Possible with most robbers because most weren't all that bright, but not going to happen tonight.

Gregor moved around the side of the desk and knelt down beside the heavy safe that was bolted to the floor. He worked slowly, looking up at Martin.

'The thing is, I don't, uh . . .'

He stopped when Martin took a step towards him, pointing the gun directly at his head. Any attempt to pretend that he didn't know how to open the safe would be met with a bloody reaction, he had to understand that.

'No, okay,' Gregor said, his hands shaking as he turned

back to it. 'It's just that, uh, I don't, you see, I don't know what money is from Jamieson and what isn't. See, I don't know. It's all just money, isn't it? If it's Jamieson's money you're after and not mine. I don't know.'

This was rambling bullshit and didn't concern Martin much anyway. If they couldn't work out what was Jamieson's and what was Gregor's then Martin would quite happily take it all. Simple problems usually had simple solutions. The idea of taking only Jamieson's cash was to make sure that every penny stolen was unreportable to the police. But money was money, and the fact that this was a Jamieson business should be enough to make sure the police were never alerted.

'It's, uh, dangerous, as well,' Gregor said. 'You know, stealing from here. You're, you're taking a hell of a risk, I'll tell you that for nothing. A hell of a risk. Wouldn't want to be in your shoes when they come looking for you.'

Martin was fed up with him using repetitive mumbling to strangle more time. He reached out a boot and gave Gregor a kick in the small of the back. Enough to make Gregor jump, to make him screech like a small animal. He leaned in close to the safe and worked at it silently until the door opened. He stood up straight, stepped back away from it, watching Martin.

He had his hands up now, aware that they had reached the part in the process where he couldn't protect the money any more. Gregor had done as much as his employers had any right to expect of him. He had called in a warning; he had wasted time to the point that it provoked violence against him and could have gotten him killed. They had no business expecting any more of him. Now he would play sensible with this gunman. He would stand with his hands up, he would keep his mouth shut, he would do as he was told and he would make sure he didn't get shot.

Martin pulled the plastic bag from his pocket and kneeled down beside the safe. He had his back slightly to Gregor, which was a risk he was willing to take. He wouldn't have done this with a brave man, but it seemed Gregor had now abandoned that pretence. There was cash in the safe, wads of it exposed and wrapped in elastic bands. That was the takings, the money of the gullible, rather than the money of the guilty. There were two packages, well wrapped, just the right size to be stuffed with wads of cash. Could have been something else in there that he didn't want. Drugs, maybe. Something valuable to Jamieson and useless to Martin, but that was unlikely; it had to be the excess cash. Had to be. Martin opened the plastic bag and shoved the two packages inside.

He stood up and looked back at Gregor, thinking briefly about tying him up. No, don't make it any worse for either of you. Tying him up gives the bookie something else to complain about and would give Martin more work. Remember how much time has already been wasted and get the hell out.

\*

'You needing help with anything tonight?'

'Not really,' Akram said. 'Picking up a vanload, moving it.'

'Anything interesting?'

'Nothing I want to chat about with you, little brother.'

Akram smiled with his mouth and frowned with his eyes, surprised and not sure if he liked what he was hearing. Wasn't like Usman to be so willing to help, not these days anyway. Used to be, back when Usman was a kid and Akram was getting into the business. Back then he was making money and his little brother wanted a piece, he couldn't shake the bastard off. Now Usman made a point of not showing an interest, always insisting that he had his own jobs to work, his own money to make. Part of maturing had been proving himself to his big brother.

'I'm bored,' Usman said, sitting on the couch in Akram's house.

'Yeah, I got that. It's contagious as well.'

'Huh?'

'You're boring the shite out of me. And you need to get out as well. I'm going to be away a good while.'

'Big delivery, huh?' Usman asked, getting up and edging towards the door.

Akram looked at him and didn't say anything. Three years older, thirty years wiser, that was what he told himself. He loved his little brother, trusted him, respected him as well, let's not make any mistakes on that. If he was working a job that required people he trusted absolutely, his brother would make the list, somewhere near the top. He was tough and capable and his instincts under pressure were excellent, better than people with far more experience and bigger brains. Never assume that a man hardened by experience will maintain ironclad instincts when the heat is turned right up. Some people melt, but not Usman.

Akram didn't need that sort of support tonight. He was moving a van load of designer drugs to a warehouse operated by James Kealing, the buyer of said party drugs. There was little threat; he had done this umpteen times before. Plus he had other people he wanted to keep onside, guys he needed to keep happy by employing. Might not need them much now, but you wanted plenty of good people around you when times got tough, so he needed to show them loyalty in the good times. His brother he could rely on without using him often.

'You know, you should be helping me out more . . .' Usman started to say, as his brother shoved him out the front door and closed it behind him.

Usman looked back at the closed door and smiled. His brother would be running around, phone clamped to his ear like it always was, organizing and blethering away. Akram would remember his brother being there that night, pestering him for something to do, getting on his fucking nerves. He would be convinced that Usman had left the house and gone straight back to his flat.

It was the silence that gave them away. Gregor had stopped talking, was even breathing quietly now, determined to do nothing to upset Martin. Martin, with the bag at his side, was still for just a second as he dismissed the thought of tying up the bookie. That was when he heard them, the movement out in the corridor. The rustle of clothes and the step of a heavy man. Big men trying to be quiet.

Martin looked sharply around the room. No window that he could fit through, the only one in the office was too small and too high up. He would have to go out the door, knowing that they were on the other side. He would have to confront them. That was where Gregor was going to play a part. A hopeless gamble, a huge escalation, but they hadn't left him a better choice.

He took a step to Gregor and grabbed him again by the collar of his shirt. He pushed him in front as a shield, held the gun to the back of his head, making sure Gregor could feel it. The bookie started to whimper, unsure why his life-expectancy had once again plummeted. Martin pushed him forward, towards the door. Gregor opened it. He stopped, whimpering even more loudly when he saw the two large men standing either side of the door.

Nate he recognized, the older man he didn't. Both were

armed, guns held firmly and clearly. They were just standing there, waiting for the robber to come out. And the robber had a gun to the back of Gregor's head. The more guns in this building, the more chance of him being shot. He couldn't stop himself whimpering again.

It was Nate who took the lead, broke the silence. He looked at the short man in the balaclava and spoke in his low, nerveless voice.

'Two guns against your one. And you need to remember that we really don't care about this guy. You can go right ahead and shoot him if you want. He's no protection for you.'

Both ends of the corridor blocked and a paper shield. That left Martin with just about nowhere to go.

He was in the driver's seat of the car at the bottom of the bookies' street, waiting and watching. No gun for Usman, no balaclava either. A man sitting in a car with a balaclava on is going to stick in the memory of any gawper that wanders past. Take nothing that you don't think you'll need. He sat and watched the place, slumped down in the seat so that nobody would spot him. Nobody including the occupants of the car that came quickly along the street and stopped outside the front door of the bookies.

Two men got out, action-packed exits from an everyday saloon car. One man he didn't recognize, the other was Nate Colgan. Didn't matter who the other guy was, Colgan was a devil's handful all on his own. Usman watched in the wing mirror, afraid to move. The two men looked up and down the street, trying to spot a getaway car. They didn't see him; they were more interested in sweeping into the building that housed their money. They went across the pavement and Colgan kneeled down in front of the metal grate that covered the front entrance to the building. He had a key of his own. He unlocked it and the two of them slowly lifted up the grate. Taking an end each and pushing upwards at a crawl, desperate to be silent, to make their visit a surprise. Once it was up, Colgan unlocked the front door and the two disappeared inside.

Usman didn't waste a second. Not one. He was out of the car as soon as Colgan and his cohort were out of view, running round to the back and opening the boot. Taking a small claw hammer from the toolbox he kept in there. A hammer that was always intended more as a weapon than a tool. He closed the boot of the car as slowly as he could, grimacing at the thud it made and looking across to the door of the bookies. Nobody came back to the door, stuck their head out to investigate the noise. With the hammer in hand, he started running.

Felt like it took forever, running round to the next street and along the back alley, praying that Colgan and his mate would be slow about this. Praying they would take the cautious approach, try and maintain their stealthy advance through the front end of the building. Praying they would try and be clever, while Usman pounded concrete. Still had to try and be quiet. His only chance came with silence.

Usman reached the back door and paused, just for a second. The window was broken but the door was still ajar, which meant Nate hadn't thought to come check it. Usman pushed it slowly, listening for a creak, trying to check for anyone standing just inside. He had the awareness to look down for broken glass, making sure he didn't crunch onto any. One stride over the glass, then another, and a third to take him up to the corner. He stopped and leaned back against the wall at the corner, listening to others talk.

Usman wasn't sure which one of them it was. He'd seen Colgan before, he'd been pointed out from a safe distance, but he didn't know what he sounded like. This was a deep voice, rumbling along with a threat so casually full of itself that you knew it was backed by years of experience. Telling the other half of the conversation that their captive wasn't worth anything so they might as well give up now. That menacing growl painted a vivid picture in Usman's mind. A picture he hadn't seen yet, and wouldn't until he turned the corner; but he now knew what to expect. If the two armed men were facing him then he was in trouble. If they weren't, this might have a chance.

He spun off the wall and round the corner, taking a step forward and making his split-second decision. He could see all four of them in front of him in the dim light coming from the office. Martin and Gregor in the doorway, Martin with the gun to the back of the bookie's head. A big guy that he didn't recognize on the far side of the office door facing Usman, which meant the one closest to him with his back turned was Colgan. That thought ran through his head as he raised the hammer, gripping it tightly. He was about to crack Nate Colgan on the back of the head with a hammer. Nate bloody Colgan. Only the meanest bastard in the city of Glasgow, if you believed the well-informed rumours. A man everyone was rightly terrified of and here was Usman about to try and make a dent in the back of his cranium. That thought, the vision of a bloodied and furious Colgan looking for revenge, ran down from his mind's eye and caught a hold of his arm. It was the one thing that made him hold back just a little as he swung the hammer down. He saw the guy he didn't recognize open his mouth to shout a warning, but it was too late. The hammer cracked against the back of Colgan's head and the big man went down hard.

It was split seconds, that was the thing. The attack happened so fast that if you weren't moving already, you weren't going to get the chance. That was what caught Gully out, a man not as quick on his feet as he used to be. He saw a shadow move behind Nate but by the time he opened his mouth, Nate was falling forward into him, eyes closing. Gully still had the gun Nate had provided for the night in his hand, but before he could raise it the short man in the balaclava had changed his target and was pointing his gun at him. There was nothing sensible Gully could do but give up gracefully. The taller young man who'd come in behind Nate was now down on his knees, picking up Nate's gun. That changed the equation again, and once the maths was against you, experience said you just tried to find a safe exit. These kids were here for cash, not for kills. The one with the hammer had been quick to step back to the darkness of the corner as soon as he had Nate's gun in his hand, trying to get out of the light and out of view. Gully paused, just for a couple of seconds, just for show. Let them see that you're not rushing to give up, because an old pro never puts down his gun in a hurry. Then he dropped the gun on the floor in front of him. A short pause was good form; a long one could be suicidal.

The last man left in that corridor with a puzzle to solve was Martin. He still had Gregor standing and whimpering quietly between him and the exit. The bookie could become a problem, hapless as he had been so far. Let him go and that's two against two, and while it's still two guns versus zero, you don't give your adversary any boost. Better to deal with him, adhere to the old principle of not leaving an enemy standing behind you. Martin pulled back his gun, twisted it in his hand and brought the butt smashing down into the back of Gregor's head. A little harder than he had intended, his adrenalin getting the better of his judgement. It was harder than Usman hit Colgan with the hammer, nothing restricting Martin's effort. Gregor fell heavily forward, landing face-first on top of Colgan's legs.

Colgan wasn't out cold. He was already groaning, trying to move like he wanted to get back up and take another swing at a fight he'd already lost. Gregor was out though, and by lying on Colgan he was holding him down. Gully was standing watching, making it clear that he didn't think interfering was worth the wage he was getting.

Martin stepped out of the office and knelt down carefully in front of Gully, trying to keep half an eye on the big man. He picked up Gully's gun with the same hand that was holding the bag of stolen cash, struggling to hold the gun and the thin plastic straps of the supermarket bag at the same time. He took careful backward steps, gun raised in his right hand, pointing at Gully. Once he was back at the corner, beside Usman, he passed the spare gun across to him. Usman now had a gun in each hand, two more than he'd started with and two more than he should have needed for a job so carefully planned.

Now they moved fast. Assume that those two big guys would have the will and the means to chase them down, assume that they would be able to move fast so you had to move faster. Clattering out through the back door and into the alleyway. Sprinting now, feet thudding and bag bouncing, no more stealth. They were down the alleyway and out onto the street, still running. Usman was the faster, taller, thinner and more desperate, running from the job with a gun in each hand, one coupled with a bloodied hammer, and his face visible to the world. The big guy, the one they hadn't clobbered, must have gotten a look at him, even if it was dark in there. He wanted out, wanted away from here. Martin was struggling to keep up, the two packages in the plastic bag jabbing against his thigh as he ran.

Usman reached the car, dropped clumsily into the driver's seat. He had the engine going, starting to edge slowly out of the parking space, reaching across and pulling the handle on the passenger door. He crept out onto the road, inching forward as slowly as he could bear to go, watching Martin sprint up to the passenger door. Martin flung the door open, dropped inside and, before he had closed the door behind him, Usman pulled away with a screech and the car raced down the street. Not subtle, no, but certainly fast – and fast mattered more.

# 7

It was a success. Okay, it hadn't worked entirely according to the plan Usman had spent the best part of a year visualizing, but when do jobs like that ever? There might be a little bit of cleaning up as well, hiding stuff, dodging consequences, but that was okay. They could ditch the guns easily, that was nothing. No, Usman was convinced that it had been a success.

He parked the car outside the flat in Mosspark where they'd met to discuss the job, certain that nobody had followed them. They hadn't said a word to each other on the drive back.

'We sticking to the plan then?' he asked Martin. 'Count the money now, split it, go our separate ways for a while?'

Martin looked at the ceiling of the car, stretching his neck in the process. He didn't know, was the answer. He couldn't work out, on the spot, whether they should rethink the plan in relation to the danger they were now in. You could have called it a good plan if the job had gone well. There was plenty flesh on the bone: good preparation, well-equipped and armed with all necessary knowledge. The job had gone ahead, but thinking about it on the drive back to the flat hadn't convinced him that it had gone well. So, in short, he didn't know. When he didn't know what to do next, he figured it was better to stick to the plan.

'We do what we said,' Martin told him.

They both got out of the car, Martin carrying the bag, handles straining under the weight of guns and money, as they went through the close and the main door, up the stairs to the flat and in. It was cold, but it was quiet and it felt safe. Little chance of anyone guessing they were there. Martin went through to the living room and put the bag down on the floor, sitting heavily in one of the chairs, feeling his last reserves of energy deserting him. There had been times, back home, when the moments after a job were the most exhilarating. You knew you'd pulled off a dangerous task, you had your score and now you could enjoy it. You partied and you burnt off the adrenalin that raced through you. Those were the moments you lived for as a young man. This was different. This was a botched job in a strange city with a man he didn't know he could trust.

Usman came bounding in from the kitchen, the exhilaration clear on his face, his mind still up in the clouds somewhere. The goofy big grin was back. He had a bottle of beer in each hand, passing one to Martin and dropping down onto the couch.

'Think we should be celebrating a wee bit, don't you?'

'A job is not finished until we know we are safe,' Martin

told him, surprised by the miserable tone he was using. This wasn't him playing up to Usman's image of him, this was Martin feeling down. He had never thought of himself as depressing before, but here he was, killing the mood.

'Come on, we fucking nailed it back there. All right, okay, I know what you're going to say, I know. You're going to say that we claw-hammered Nate Colgan into the carpet and we battered a bookie, and that other guy saw my face. You're right, that ain't great, none of it. But, you know, we got the score. And we'll get away with it, trust me. They have nothing to chase after. We did good.'

Martin didn't say anything to that, just sat and watched Usman drinking in large gulps, the grin getting ever wider. Usman's comedown was still a long way off, although Martin felt determined to bring it closer.

'I thought your people didn't drink?'

'What, Scottish people? Mate, you have been grossly misinformed,' Usman said, enjoying his moment. He leaned forward and pulled the bag from the floor; plonking it on the coffee table between them, the guns and hammer clanking together. 'Let's see what we've got then.'

He took the three guns and the hammer out first, placing them carefully on the table and looking at them.

'We need to clean them,' Martin said. 'You did not have gloves on when you handled two of them back there. Then we have to get rid of them as soon as we can.'

Usman nodded. 'Shame we have to ditch them, there's good money sitting there.' People paid a good price for a weapon, and Usman hated to swerve a good price when it was right in front of him.

'We have to get rid of them. Nobody can know that we ever had those extra guns. Or our own gun.'

Another nod. 'I know, I know. You leave them three wee beauties with me and I'll get well rid of them. No risks.'

That had always been the plan. Usman had assured him that he knew how to get rid of dangerous and unwanted items, said he could ditch the gun they had bought for the job without difficulty. Now there were three, which made the task three times harder. Or maybe not; if he really did have an excellent site for ditching the guns then three would be little more of a chore than one.

'Right, time to get counting.'

Usman got up and went across to the window, pulling the thick curtains shut, swinging a hand to swipe at the dust that fell off them. He switched the light on, a bare bulb. They both wanted to do this quickly and without error. Also made it easy to take a good look at each other, the jolly Usman and the miserable Martin. The strain was written in bold over Martin's face. So this guy wasn't going to be a barrel of laughs then. Fine, okay, a prancing personality wasn't the most important thing. The most important thing was that he was good at the job.

'You want to take one packet and I'll take the other?' Usman asked him. He was quieter now, going for a calmer approach. If the other person was on a downer then you showed them respect. Usman knew he could grate if he got his tone wrong and that would scupper his hopes of working together again.

Martin nodded and Usman passed him a package.

'We will need knives.'

'Will we?'

It didn't seem to matter to Usman if they ripped the packaging; it was the contents they wanted. Anyway, no arguments, so he trudged to the kitchen and found one sharp knife and a whole drawer full of blunt ones. This flat wasn't well stocked, too rarely used for anyone to spend money on it. Usman had the keys for twenty-four hours, and it might be weeks before anyone else used it. He rifled through another drawer and came away with a pair of scissors that would do as a substitute. He went back into the living room and found Martin sitting exactly where he'd left him, his bottle on the table, unopened.

He gave Martin the scissors. He was already miserable; let him have the awkward tool. Usman took the knife and began cutting at the edges of the thick brown Sellotape.

'Jesus, did they not want to get back into these things themselves?'

Martin didn't say anything, nipping tiny cuts carefully with the edge of the scissors. It took them each a few minutes to get through the various layers of paper wrapping. Usman was the first to get his open, the contents smiling back at him. Blocks of cash, bundled together individually and then tightly packed together with thin elastic bands. He started to laugh.

'Look at that. Fuck's sake, man, will you look at it? How much you reckon is there?'

Martin looked, genuinely trying to work out a number in his head. He closed his eyes.

'I don't know. We will have to count it anyway. Is all the money the same?'

'Same notes. Uh, hold on.' He turned them all over, checking back and front of each. 'Nah, they're not. These blocks are all twenties, these are all tens. Shit. Imagine if they were all fifties, huh?'

Martin said nothing, cutting away at the last of his, not wasting a thought on what might have been. He found the same prize waiting inside his parcel. Bundles packed tight, some twenties, some tens. Nothing else.

Usman took a swig from his bottle. 'Now we count?'

'Now we count.'

It took over an hour. Wouldn't have taken that long for people who were used to handling this sort of money, and it would only have taken minutes if they had a counter to use. They couldn't have gotten a hold of one without someone getting suspicious, wondering why either of them suddenly needed to count cash. So every note passed through a human hand, carefully logged. It meant loose bundles being counted, not always accurately and having to be counted a second time. It meant a bundle falling on the floor and spilling everywhere, picked back up and counted again. It meant Usman going back to the kitchen for a second and third beer, the one thing he had made sure was stocked, and then to the toilet. Then Usman asking if Martin minded if he smoked, and going to the toilet to smoke because of the glare he got in response.

'I have sixteen thousand pounds, exactly,' Martin said when he had finished. He had tied his bundle back together into a neat block.

'Uh-huh.'

Usman finished counting and looked across. 'I got sixteen grand, exactly. So I guess we're getting sixteen grand each then.' Said with a grin. Surely now that the miserable little sod had sixteen grand sitting in front of him, begging to be a part of his life, he would be a bit more cheerful.

He wasn't. Not outwardly, anyway. He was just sitting there, original bottle still untouched, looking at the wads of cash. Six wads of twenties and four wads of tens, ten perfect little bricks of wealth. He was looking at the money and looking back at Usman, making him uncomfortable. There was something in the back of his mind, something pushing its way forward.

'The first time we met, you told me there would be fifteen thousand pounds for me.'

'Yeah.'

'How could you know?'

Usman shrugged a little. 'I didn't. I was guessing, that was all. I said you'd make about fifteen grand because I figured that was a reasonable shout. I was right.'

Martin said nothing for a few seconds, letting the silence get uncomfortable again before he broke it. 'I don't think you were guessing. There is no reason that you would guess fifteen thousand. You would say, maybe, a few thousand, or ten thousand. There is no reason why you would decide that fifteen thousand would be the right amount when it could have been anything.'

'You ain't very good at having a good time, are you, pal? I'm starting to work out why they ran you out of Poland.'

'I was never in Poland. I am Czech.'

'Yeah, well, you ain't welcome somewhere, I know that much, and I think I know why.'

'You knew,' Martin said, pulling at a thread he was sure he had a good grip on.

'Knew what?'

Martin leaned back and sighed. He wasn't looking at Usman when he spoke next. 'You knew how much money would be there. Somebody told you there would be that money, that amount. I am sure of this, so don't say no. You knew.'

'And if I did?'

'If you did it's dangerous for both of us. If you did then someone told you, and the person who told you knows that you know. It means someone will be able to point a finger at you for doing this job.'

Usman leaned forward, hands together. 'Listen, right. One of those guys in there tonight saw my face. I mean, it was dark, maybe he didn't get a proper look, I don't know, but some dangerous bastard had a chance to see my pretty face. They had a chance to see the car as we were driving away as well, if they ran to the front door and looked out for us. There are loads of ways that they could identify that it was me. Not you, me. You're safe, right. You're off the hook no matter what. You had a balaclava on, you didn't say a fucking word and we didn't use your motor. I'm the one that's swimming in the shit here, if that guy got a look at me or the car. I ain't worrying about it, I'm a good swimmer. Look, I'll work this out if I have to, but you got nothing to worry about.'

'You knew.'

'Fuck's sake, man, you're like some gif on repeat. You knew, you knew, you knew. Fine, right, I had an idea. Of course I fucking did. You think I would go in there not having a good idea what we were going to take out? All that risk and we might come out with four pound twenty and a bundle of fucking betting slips. I knew that was where they put their money. I knew who to look out for. Yeah, I knew there was a deal going down that was going to be a one-off payment for them, something they weren't expecting either. I had heard whispers about it. Rumours, you know. This business runs on the bloody things. Nobody knew that I knew. I wasn't supposed to know. I thought they'd have more than that, if you want to know the honest truth. I thought we were looking at a clean fifty grand, but they must have split the money up, hidden some of it away some-place else. Or maybe there were more people getting a cut of it than I realized. Anyway, I knew the deal they were doing and I tried to cash in. That a bad thing? Having all that information and doing something with it? We cleared thirty-two fucking grand off this job.'

'I did not say it was bad. Not if you're sure they can't work out that you knew. Trace this back to you,' Martin said, waving a stubby finger at the piles of money.

'Look, they had this deal. Something to do with importing, came about after Angus Lafferty pulled his disappearing act. You know about that?'

Martin shook his head.

'Right, well, never mind then. Point is, I heard a rumour about the deal when it was in its early stages. I had known about them using the bookies for awkward cash for a while and I was waiting for a big score to come along before I tried to work the place over.'

Martin wasn't here to argue. Seemed stupid, sitting here

and creating conflict when they had sixteen grand each to walk away with and plenty of bigger issues to worry about.

'We must not be in touch with each other for some time. Weeks should be, at least,' Martin said sternly. 'Be careful with the money; don't let people know that you have it. And then we can be in contact again.'

None of this was news, just common sense. Usman nodded, the grin starting to spread across his face again as Martin stuffed his money into the plastic bag to take home with him.

'And then after all that time away from dear old me, you'll want to do another job together, right? Another big score.'

Martin looked at him. 'Let us wait and see what happens with this one first. If nobody has taken my kneecaps away from me then I might want to work with you again. Only if you have a good job for us to do though. I have no interest in small things.'

Usman was grinning. 'Of course I got some big ones lined up, of course I do. Here, now, let me give you a lift home, you can't go on the bus with sixteen grand of Peter fucking Jamieson's cash in a carrier bag, can you?'

Martin shook his head. 'You have drunk too much. If the police stop you, we will both be in prison. I would rather take the bus or a taxi.'

'No way to either of them,' Usman was saying. 'Buses have got security cameras on them and you don't know that a taxi driver isn't keeping an eye out for you. Some of them work for Jamieson, right. They might have word out to look for a miserable wee Russian. I'm telling you now, the safest way home is in the passenger seat of my car. I drive better with a drink anyway, makes me less, what's the word, complacent. I have to go do something about the car anyway, change the plates or something, take the heat off it. And I got to get rid of these guns as well, might as well be now. Come on, I'll drop you off first.'

There was no argument, only the realization that he needed his own car if he was going to do this again. Martin wouldn't do another job in this city until he had one. They walked out of the flat, Usman locking the door with its only key, his money safely inside.

# 8

'Oh, for fuck's sake. Ah, Jesus.' Nate was grumbling as he tried to get back to his feet, unsteady and angry. A hand against the wall, struggling to get up. Something was on his legs, pressing him down, he wasn't sure what. He had to twist round onto his backside to see Gregor sprawled there, unconscious or dead. There was no sign of Gully. Nate kicked Gregor off, showing little pity. The bookie didn't make a sound, just rolled on the floor and lay there.

Nate got onto his knees, touching the back of his head and feeling the sticky wetness in his hair. There wasn't much blood there, but a head injury was always enough to make you nervous. Not as nervous as Gregor was making him, looking like a dead man on the floor. Nate, still on his knees, shuffled across to him. Gregor was breathing, his round mound of stomach slowly rising and falling. Nate leant down and gave him a gentle slap on the face. That got a groan in response, which was all that Nate needed to hear. The man wasn't dead, wasn't dying and this disaster hadn't just turned into a complete catastrophe.

Nate had to put his hand back against the wall before he could stand up. Bloody hell, the back of his head hurt when he moved. Felt like the skin had been ripped, the sort of pain you get from a glancing blow, where someone hesitates just enough to not hit you cleanly. Could have been a hit with a sharp object, but there would have been a deeper cut and more blood if that was the case. Nate had experience of every kind of punch, kick and weapon attack that was ever likely to be dished out; he could tell in an instant what this was. It was a different wound from Gregor's. Nate's was no big deal, painful and annoying but once the shock wore off he would be fine. Couple of stitches might be needed, but nothing more gruesome. Gregor had been knocked out cold, Nate hadn't. Gregor's was a vicious blow to the back of the head, there could be something more serious and long-lasting there.

Never mind Gregor, he had to find Gully. There was no sign of him at all; he must have gone after the pair of little shites that were responsible for this. Could be dangerous, he might need some backup. Nate stumbled forward, stopped, shook his head and started again. He felt lightheaded, damaged. He wasn't used to the feeling of vulnerability that came with it, or the feeling of defeat.

Gully stepped in through the back door just as Nate lurched round the corner. Glass crunched under his foot, he looked down and grimaced, then across to Nate.

'You finished your siesta?'

'Fuck's sake,' was all Nate could manage. 'Bastard snuck up on me.'

'You okay?'

Nate nodded. 'Not sure about our friend back there though, he's still half asleep. What did you see?'

'Got the car number plate. The one who hit you was a Pakistani boy with a hammer. Face wasn't covered, so I'm guessing he was supposed to be the driver for the other one. They got our guns.'

That didn't matter; Nate didn't like the bloody things anyway. The expense would be covered by the organization, and it would save him going to the effort of returning them. What mattered was that Gully had seen a face and had a car they could track down.

Gully led the way back round the corner to Gregor.

'Try and wake him up,' he said to Nate, 'and I'll find somewhere to write down that number before my ageing mind forgets it.'

Gully went into the office, found a pen and a sheet of paper and scribbled down the plate details, taking a glance at the open safe as he did. Smart little bastards, he thought to himself. Nate knelt back down beside Gregor. He was starting to get concerned; the guy had been properly unconscious for nearly a minute and he wasn't waking fast. That was always bad news. He slapped him gently again, the extent of his medical expertise.

'Come on, Donny, talk to me, you clown.'

There was a mumble, Donny trying to say something, slurring his words badly. Gully came back out and stood in the doorway, looking down at them both. Nate shook his head.

'I think we're going to have to get a doctor onto this one. He was out for a while. Concussion, or something like that. Could be serious. We can't afford to have him dropping dead on us. This is a big enough fuck-up already without a body.'

'We got a company doc or will I run him to the hospital?'

Nate had to think about it. They had a company doctor, a pill popper who technically wasn't a doctor any more, but he seemed to know what he was doing and he could at least give them a better idea of whether they needed to get Gregor to a hospital.

'Company doc first, see what he says. I'll write you his address. Don't know what state he'll be in mind you, this late at night. Get this one round there, I'll phone the doc up and warn him you're coming.'

Nate went past Gully into the office, wrote the address down.

'What about you?' Gully asked him, taking the sheet of paper with the address and passing the one with the number plate to Nate.

'I'll stick around here. Tidy up this mess. Work out what the fuck we're going to do next.'

'You don't need the doc?' Gully looked a little concerned;

he'd witnessed, suffered and inflicted enough head injuries in his time to know you didn't take them lightly.

Nate shook his head. 'I'm fine. Will be, anyway. You need a hand getting him out to the car?'

Gully smiled. 'Nah, I got him. All this loose muscle is still technically muscle. Plus I'm the only one here who had the good sense not to get my skull caved in.'

'Aye, that was clever thinking.'

It took some effort to get him off the floor, but Gregor was able to move slowly with plenty of sturdy support from Gully. They went out the front door, taking the shortest possible route to the car, and drove away.

Once they were gone, Nate went out and locked up, pulled down the shutter and made his way round the back, going in through the still open back door. He was inside the bookies, on his own. He wanted to punch a wall, but all that would achieve was the unwanted attention of people in neighbouring buildings and some cracked knuckles. So far this had been an almost silent night, the only noise coming from the cars coming and going. He went back through to Gregor's office and knelt down in front of the safe. He had a horrible feeling about what he was going to see when he pulled the already ajar door open. No surprise, the two packages of cash were gone, the bookie's own money still there.

He sat in the chair at the desk and tried to get his sore

head working. Think, you dumb fucker, how do you catch the people responsible? Is it possible to cover this? It was mere damage-limitation, he knew that much already. The job of defending the money from a known attack had failed. They could get the money back and punish the people who had stolen it, but they had still failed to protect it in the first place and it was that failure everyone would point to. That's what would become public knowledge, unless the punishment they brought about was so severe that it overwhelmed people's memory of the original crime.

Shit, he wasn't thinking straight, working out punishments for people they hadn't even identified yet. They had to *find* the pricks before they could make them suffer. They would. They could trace just about any car, work out who was using it, then go after them. There was a chance here, a slim one, that word wouldn't get out. Gregor would keep his mouth shut and only an act of crass stupidity would open it. He hadn't lost any of his own money, no reason for him to mention tonight if they could keep him out of the hospital.

Shit, phone call. He got out his mobile and scrolled down to the doctor's number. Nick Hall. Once Dr Nick, but not any more. He had been off on medical grounds for ages and eventually his colleagues managed to persuade him that there was no job for an addict like him to go back to. Not that it changed his life much; he had been working as a doctor for the Jamieson organization since before he went off work sick.

'Nick, it's Nate Colgan. What state are you in?'

'What state am I in? I'm fine. Why?'

He sounded fine, but that didn't mean anything. Nate had met the doctor a few times, sometimes when he was popping and sometimes when he wasn't and there was little noticeable difference. The guy was a pro at covering his addiction, a hardcore user who had learned how to always appear normal. Then again, Nate figured, if anyone should be able to cover a habit, a doctor should be. Or maybe the pills he was guzzling just didn't have a dramatic effect; Nate had heard conflicting stories about what the guy was into.

'Someone's coming round to yours with a patient right now. Can you see them?'

'Yeah, sure, I'm alone.'

'Gully is bringing him,' he said, then realized that Dr Nick probably didn't know who Gully was. 'It's a head injury, so we're not sure how serious it is. He was out cold for over a minute, groggy when he left here to go round to you. Have a look, see what you can do, and if they guy needs to go to the hospital then so be it.'

He hung up and looked back down at the safe, reached out a foot and kicked the door shut. Stupid bloody thing. He'd have to spend some time scouting somewhere better to store money from now on. He had mentioned already that they might need better stores, but there was always too much else to worry about, too much else that had to be organized. This wasn't a criminal organization any more; it was a tower-defence strategy. Trying to build ever more effective defences before the enemy strikes, always worried that there might already be an enemy inside.

All this because the boss was in jail. Everyone afraid of making big moves without his permission, the natural order of the business thrown into chaos until he got out. And Nate, catapulted into the position of security consultant. The man people within the organization looked to for protection, the man who was supposed to keep the likes of Donny Gregor safe from harm. Protect the money he earned and hid in his safe, more to the point. The money was always considered more important than the person who earned it.

If word got out about this job, Nate would look like a failure. If word got out that he was there when it happened and botched the whole fucking thing . . . Fuck's sake, his reputation would be circling the drain. Didn't matter how powerful your reputation was now, it only ever took one screw-up for it to collapse to rubble. Nobody would call him a failure to his face, nobody in this city would fucking dare, but they'd think it. He would lose respect. But word of the job getting out was still an if.

If this had been carried out by someone working for another organization then word would undoubtedly spread fast. They would want the world to know the joyous news that they'd hit a Jamieson business and got away with it, adding bad PR to the pile of money already gone. But if it wasn't someone from another organization, that was different. If this was just a random opportunist then it made sense that the attackers would be desperate to keep it to themselves. Only if they were tremendously stupid would they even think of spreading the word, inviting hell to fall down on top of them. So the two guys work on their own, they hit the place and then they lie low, they tell no one. They don't risk Nate discovering identities and chasing them down. Well, he was going to chase them down anyway, but he'd appreciate them keeping their mouths shut in the meantime.

# 9

It was very late when Martin made it back home. Usman had dropped him down the street and let him walk the rest of the way, accepting that it didn't make sense for the car to be seen stopping outside Martin's house in the dead of night. A glance at his watch, five past two, he was going to have to explain his late arrival. Part of him wanted to explain it in honest detail; he wanted Joanne to at least ask where the hell he had been.

He was still clutching the bag with sixteen thousand pounds in it that was going to have to be hidden somewhere in the house. He would have to tell her about it, if she asked. He was afraid too that she wouldn't ask. It was stupid, but as he put the key in the front door and went inside, he was afraid that she wouldn't care enough to ask.

The house was silent and dark. He went through to the kitchen, thought about putting the bag with the cash into the large cupboard there. No, too public. Needed to be somewhere that no visitor to the house would enter. Only he and Joanne ever used their bedroom, which was why he had to put it somewhere there. So he went quietly upstairs.

\*

She wasn't asleep, she was just pretending to be. Joanne rolled over and stretched, making it seem as though he'd woken her when he entered the room.

'You're back.'

'I am.'

She put on the bedside lamp and sat up, watching him. He already had the wardrobe door open and was down on his knees. He opened the now empty shoebox the gun had been in and forced the bag of cash inside. It burst one of the sides of the box, but it went in. He placed the lid loose on top of it, it wouldn't fit with the side burst, and put the now empty carrier bag on top of the box.

Joanne was watching him when he closed the wardrobe door and turned around. He stared at her, waiting for her to say something more. If she cared she would say something, he had convinced himself of that.

'Didn't think you were going to be this late,' she said, looking at him with an impenetrable expression. He'd never been this late before, but she knew he'd never worked on something intense like he had that night.

'I didn't think I would be. I would have said. I didn't mean to keep you awake.'

She smiled a sort of dismissive smile, her way of saying that if she wanted to sleep she would sleep and him not being there wouldn't change it. That self-confidence felt a little bit false and they both knew it. Martin went over and sat on his side of the bed, not making a move to undress. He looked at Joanne, almost forcing her to say something.

'You were working?' she asked.

'Yes, I was working. I was. It was a big job. I made some money.' He almost added the words 'for us' to the end of that sentence, but that would have been unfair. He had chosen to do the work, trying to imply that she was part of the reason for it was just delusional.

Silence. He had set the question up for her, but she wasn't responding. Joanne knew she just had to ask him what it was exactly he had been doing and he would spill his guts all over the bedroom. If she told him to stop working, he would stop. If she said she was disgusted with him and wanted him out of the house he would fight for the relationship. It was entirely up to her what happened next.

'Martin?'

'Yes.'

'What's in the box?'

Finally. Now she was asking something that forced them down the dark road towards an honest conversation.

'Money. Quite a lot of money. It is what I got for the work I did tonight.'

'How much is quite a lot?' She was on a roll now, correct question after dangerously correct question.

'There is sixteen thousand pounds there. In cash.'

Still no reaction. She sat looking at him with the same

mildly quizzical expression, the look of an intelligent person putting the pieces together. There was no shock, no gasp and no horror. That was the most important thing. Sixteen grand meant he had done something significant, and she was smart enough to grasp that straight away, but it didn't shock her.

'So you made sixteen thousand pounds for one night's work?'

'I did, yes.'

This time she looked away from him, looked down at the wardrobe and then at a random place in the middle of the bed. That warned him that the next one would be a big question.

'What sort of thing does a fellow have to do to make himself sixteen grand in one night?'

He looked at her, made eye contact. He was enthusiastic with his answer. 'I want to tell you. If I tell you, you might hate me.'

'I won't hate you.'

'Okay then,' he said, nodding. 'I will tell you. Tonight I worked with another man to steal that money. We took it from a bookmaker's shop. We broke in and we took the money from it. That is my half of what we stole.' He had been speaking quickly, excitedly, his desperation to share with her obvious.

Joanne looked at him. She was expressionless for a while, then nodded. 'Okay. Did you . . . did you kill anyone?'

'No, I did not,' he said. He was 95 per cent sure that he hadn't. He had hit the bookie hard on the back of the head, but it would be bloody unlucky if he died from that. Not impossible, that was why he couldn't be 100 per cent, but he was confident enough to say no to Joanne.

'Was it dangerous?'

He paused, considered how much he wanted to tell her, and then aimed for the truth. 'There is always some danger. Of course. Every job has that. But it was well planned. We knew what we were doing. What we were going for. So, it was dangerous, yes, but most jobs are more dangerous than this one.'

She gave a little laugh that was close to a snort. Martin's attempt at honesty was wrapped in vagueness.

'Should I be worried about the police battering down my door?'

'No,' he said forcefully. 'The police will not even be called by the people we took this from. I can say that with a guarantee. Okay? The police, they will never even know about this money.'

Now she was frowning. 'Why would the bookie not report this?'

'Because it was not legal money. It was not legal before we stole it and it is only a little bit less legal now.'

'By which you mean it was already stolen money?'

'Not stolen. Well, maybe stolen, maybe not. Just not legal, I know this. I don't know where they got it from, but it was illegal earnings. It was for a criminal group, it was their money. They were hiding it there. Then we took it.' His language skills were faltering a little under the pressure of her growing frown.

'So you're saying that the police won't come looking for it but some bunch of gangsters might? Gangsters big enough to make thirty-two grand when it suits them? Jesus, Martin, that's worse.' Her voice got lower, more exasperated as she went on.

'It is not worse. You are wrong. They don't know it was me; there is no way that they can know it is me, okay? There is no way for them to reach your door,' he said, trying to convince himself as much as Joanne. There was Usman, out there drink-driving with three guns in his possibly already identified car. There were ways. 'You think I don't know how to do this sort of thing properly? I know. I am doing what I am good at and I am making a lot of money for it. I want to bring money in. I don't want to be sitting here while you earn the money. Nobody would want that. I want us to be able to live properly. To go on a holiday. To have a car each. To have some nice things in the house. I don't want to be rich, but I want to be okay. This is how I do it and I do it very well. I am good at my job. They do not know it was me and they will never know it was me.' He had been speaking faster and faster, the intensity rushing out of him.

'All right, okay. I'm not saying you're not good at whatever you do. I just . . . don't want you ending up in jail.'

He leaned across the bed and kissed her hard on the

mouth. 'You tell me to stop doing this and I will stop doing it. Right now I will stop. I will find some other job.'

'You want to keep doing what you're doing?'

'Yes,' he said, not even stopping to think about it. This was all he had ever done. There were probably plenty of other things he could do well, but none that he had any interest in. This was it for him, the only job he wanted and the only one he'd ever really tried. Big jobs with big scores and fast money. Nothing else could beat that.

Joanne breathed in heavily. 'Right. Then we need to lay down some ground rules. I don't want to know details of anything you do. I don't want to know anything else that incriminates me if you get caught. I'll play the ignorant little housewife. Maybe, if there are ways of helping you with the money that don't get me into trouble, I'll help, but I am not going to prison because I know more about your work than I should.'

He nodded slowly. A little disappointed, but he understood. He had hoped he would be able to talk to her about his job, get her opinions and tap into her local knowledge. That was always the ideal relationship, someone who understood the business enough to give you an opinion worth listening to. It wasn't fair to expect that from her, she'd never been around the business before and had more sense than to wade into the deep end on his account.

'Okay, I will tell you nothing.'

She sighed again. 'Not nothing. You can tell me when you're working. You can tell me . . . I don't know, you can tell me when there's something I really need to know. I don't want you going out of here on some big, dangerous thing and me not knowing. Sitting here wondering why you haven't come home, jumping to conclusions. Just, don't tell me anything that could get me into trouble, okay?'

'I would never do that,' he said, leaning across for another kiss.

Martin undressed and went through to the bathroom. Joanne's reaction had been as good as he could realistically have hoped for. Of course she knew that he had been a criminal before, and she must have known that he was doing some criminal work in the city. How the hell else would he have made any money at all? She accepted it. She would go on accepting it so long as he didn't implicate her in anything.

That, right there, was the problem. He would never deliberately incriminate her, but he had glossed over tonight's job. It hadn't been the smooth process with no blowback he had suggested. He had gotten the money and done nothing that would reveal his identity, but Usman had been seen by one of them. There was a good chance they had seen the car as well. Those two things would give them a real good chance of tracking Usman down. If they tracked down Usman then they had a pretty good chance of tracking down Martin, too. If they tracked down Martin then they tracked down Joanne. They would use her against him. He knew these kinds of people; he had *been* these kinds of people. There was nothing they wouldn't do to punish him.

He went back to bed and lay down beside Joanne, his arm draped over her. They didn't say anything else. It took her a while to get to sleep, he could tell. Took Martin much longer. Running through the job in his mind, feeling the force of the blow against the back of the bookie's head in his fingers. The fear of a knock on the door. No, not a knock. The fear of some-one coming in through the bedroom door having already silently broken into the house. They were capable, and it's how they would approach it if they knew where he was. A new fear that he hadn't felt back home, back when he didn't have anything to lose.

# 1.11 a.m.

It's the cramp that's getting to him now. He can't stretch his legs. His throat is dry and he's coughing, swallowing in the hope of generating some saliva. There are tears in his eyes. He has to stay calm, keep his mind on what's coming next, he knows that. No way of getting out of this in one piece if he panics, starts thrashing around and injures himself. Stay calm, be patient. He's put other people in this position often enough to know how a smart man ought to handle it. Pulling against the plastic cords isn't helping and needs to stop, the cut on his wrist is only getting worse. Stop moving; conserve what little energy is left. But the cramp in his leg, he has to do something about that or he won't be able to move on it. He's pushing the chair back, slowly and carefully. It's scraping on the concrete floor, filling the silent warehouse with jarring noise. He's moving slowly; if he goes fast, he'll tip it over. Slowly back until the cord tied to the metal hoop in the floor begins to resist. That's as straight as he can get his legs, as much relief as is possible.

Martin's thinking a little more clearly now. The pain has taken a step back, letting his mind take a step forward. Thinking about Joanne. She'll be at home, waiting for him, worried that he's not going to return this time. She knew he was going out on a job and she understood that it was riskier than normal. They had agreed that he would tell her when he had something big on. Let her know that he was going out but without giving her any sort of detail. He told her there was a job, that it was dangerous, little more than that. He told her he would be late. She nodded along, didn't say anything. Didn't ask for any more detail, which he was relieved about; but he should have been home by now. She would be worried. That's what's causing him the most concern. The thought of her at home, on her own, worried that she might never see him again.

Nothing he can do now but wait. His mind is drifting, taking him back to other dark times. Taking him all the way back to a time when it was someone else tied up in a warehouse. Remembering the things he did to that person. Wasn't just him, there were other people there as well. People he hardly knew and didn't care a damn about. Can't even remember their names now, if he was ever told them. They were paying him, that's why he was there. He was the hired help, willing to do whatever he was paid for.

The victim, what was that poor bastard even there for? It was six or seven years ago, they were in some old warehouse in Brno. It was . . . no, he can't remember. Come on; don't let your mind leave you. You need to be sharp for this, you need to be alert. If you forget stuff, get sleepy, there's no way of getting out of this, no way at all. Think, that guy, the sad soul in the ware-house.

He was middle-aged. Soft as well, definitely not a fighter. Didn't seem like the sort of guy who would have survived as long as he had in the business. He was crying a lot because he knew what was going to happen to him. Martin was there to knock him around while the employers watched. They didn't want anything from him, information or apologies; they just wanted to see him suffer. He had upset them and he had no way of redeeming himself, so he got punished.

It took ages, that's what Martin remembers now. No tools, just knocking the guy around, trying not to break his own fin-gers as he did so. Just to make the guy suffer and make the people who paid him feel tough. It was pathetic, on reflection, but a lot of the jobs he did back then were. Knock some guy around, chase down someone who doesn't realize he needs to run from you, go send a bloodstained message, this person needs to die. Never a good explanation for why, just money and a target. Every person was a walking price-tag and when someone wanted rid of them enough to meet the price, they became a walking target.

That man in the warehouse. Martin spent a couple of hours on him. He was unconscious for the last ten minutes or so, which was probably a good thing. He had been uncon-scious before during the beating, but Martin had stepped back and given him time to come round. This time he wasn't coming round, he was either dead or dying. That was when they got out a can of petrol and poured it over him. One of them lit a match, threw it down. There was a whoosh as his clothes went up. Martin stood back, waiting for the man to scream or roll around, but he didn't. Hopefully he was already dead, or close enough not to suffer from the burning. That was tacky, unnecessary, a gangster wanting to do something dramatic, like killing him wasn't enough. They left him there, a charred corpse stuck to the floor. Pasted down by his own melted flesh. Maybe someone else came and washed him away, because Martin never heard the police mention the body.

Matej Dobek. That was the name of the man who hired him for that job, the man with the match. Can't remember the victim's name, pretty sure he was never told it. Often wasn't, on that sort of job. Matej Dobek. He was scum, a real bad one, taking pleasure in the power he could buy. But Martin can remember him, what he looked like. Shoulder-length black hair and dark eyes. Smiled a lot. Happy with the horrors he created. He can remember the conversation he had with Joanne in the kitchen before he left the house. Remember what she was wearing. He told her he would be back in the early hours of the morning. Maybe it's still the early hours; maybe she isn't worried at all.

He's thinking about Joanne because he wants to think about her. Thinking about her is nice, pleasant, makes him feel better. It's a distraction; it's a lack of focus. It won't be long now, they can't be far away. He has to clear thoughts of Joanne and thoughts of the past out of his mind. He has to think about himself, his situation. Think about Usman. Think about the next hour. His life until now doesn't matter; whatever remains of the rest of his life doesn't matter. It's the next hour. In that hour, everything will be decided.

# 1.29 a.m.

He went home to be sick first, which wasn't part of the plan. Threw up in the toilet, slumped onto the bathroom floor and waited for his heart rate to return somewhere close to normal. Lost all track of time. The whole thing had taken a lot longer than he'd expected, should have been finished by now. He should be drinking to forget, but he isn't. Usman's glancing at the clock in the car and realizing that he should have been done at least an hour ago.

They'll be pissed off with him, but it's their own fucking fault. They should have been there. Fuck's sake, it was their idea so they should have been present. Their sort of job as well, not his. They should have done this bit, instead of forcing him into it. It was something he'd never done, never even considered, and they knew it. He's an organizer, a planner. Yeah, he's got the balls to carry out a job as well, do some of the donkey work, but it's not his strength. That's why he hired Martin in the first place; he needed someone with expertise to do the dirty stuff.

Shit, van drifted onto the wrong side of the road there. Too nervous, too exhausted. His arms feeling weak and boneless, his head swimming. There was so much adrenalin at the time, enough to carry him through the first part. Taking the crowbar and smashing it into the back of Martin's head. Afraid of not hitting him hard enough so hitting him too hard instead, lacking the practice required to know how to judge it. Did it though. Did it because he had to, because they'd given him no choice. Did it because he wanted to, too. This was his chance, his one chance to get away from the danger of everything he'd done before. Get a bright new start.

He couldn't find the place. It was a pub in the city centre they'd given him the address of, but he'd never been there before. They told him to come along a back alley and in through the back door, which would be good advice when he found the bloody place. He wasn't supposed to be this late; they had assumed the pub would still be open by the time he got there. It won't be now, although there might still be a few stragglers out on the street. He needs to find the place and get out of the van, get some fresh air on his face. The way he's driving, he's likely to get pulled over. No matter how badly this has gone so far, that would be more of a disaster than he could ever explain.

He knows he's in the right area. Usman's been round here before, although he's not sure which is the right building to aim for. There, that's it, that's the place. A rush of relief now that he's seen it. There are still a few people on the street, although they all look the worse for wear and wouldn't remember him even if he drove along the pavement and over the top of them. Has to find the alleyway, park somewhere nearby. Can't go in the front, even if there's nobody hanging around it. People might not notice him driving past but some inconveniently sober passer-by might remember seeing him banging on the front door. Take no risks, so he's round the corner, onto a slant. Pulling over to the side of the road and stopping. The van's rolling back, a moment of baffled panic. Shit, handbrake. He just can't get his brain in gear. Getting the handbrake on and hoping nobody saw that little brain-fart of his. These little things, that's what people remember. You won't remember everyone you pass on the street, but you'll remember the idiot who didn't put his handbrake on when he parked his van on an incline.

There's nobody else on this street that he can see. Paranoid about being watched, worried that the only reason he can't see them is because they're hiding. He's looking at the gate that leads into the alleyway. They told him about it, described it to him in what seemed like stupid detail at the time. Doesn't feel so stupid now, actually makes perfect sense. They knew what he would be feeling, how much he would struggle to keep his focus and hold his nerves down. Men with their experience understood exactly how it would be when he made the drive back to pick them up.

Usman's opening the gate and slipping inside, closing it quickly behind him, the metal scratching on the cobbles and making him shudder.

A feeling of relief. He's off the streets, out of the public's view. Then a new fear as he's walking along the alleyway. Nobody can see him here. If this was ever going to be a set-up, this is where it would happen. But it won't, it can't. They've all come too far and worked too hard for this to be anything other than legit. Still frightening, that thought that everything you've done was for nothing, just a game other people are playing to bring you down.

Usman's walking the alleyway in the dark, reaching the metal gate they had told him was the correct one. Something else they described to him in what had seemed like absurd detail. Not absurd any more, he'd forgotten to count the gates on his way down and it was only the description that told him which one to open.

He's in the courtyard; a small, ugly cobbled place that even in the dark looks like it could do with a good scrub. Useless for anything other than storage, and apparently not much use for that either because the place is empty. Usman's walking across to the back door. It should be unlocked, unless they've given up on him and gone home. What if they have? Oh shite, what if they have? They would be so pissed off with him; he doesn't know what he would do. He's got his hand on the handle of the door and he's pushing it slowly open. It does open, thank fuck. Another relief.

The pub is silent, another unsettling reminder of how late he is. He's in a corridor, it's dark. They said go in, along the corridor and the stairs will be on your left. He's walking, one hand reaching out to feel the wall next to him. There's so little light, he's worried about crashing into furniture and making a fool of himself. They could have left a fucking light on for him, but no, they didn't think of that. They have no sympathy for him, that's the thing. They think this sort of thing should be as easy for him as it is for them. Well, it isn't. Wouldn't be easy for them either, he's betting, but they don't have to do it. *He's* doing it; he's lived up to the pressure and there's only a bit left to do.

He's found the stairs, making his way up. They might not be here, maybe they just left the door unlocked because they didn't have a key and they've fucked off home. Nah, they'd have a key. Two guys as organized as them, they wouldn't be here without having the full run of the place. At the top of the stairs he sees the door facing him, a crack of light underneath it. So they're definitely here. It's only occurring to him now that this is the actual point of no return. He'd thought cracking Martin on the back of the head and tying him to that chair had been the clincher. It had felt like it, but no, this is it.

He'd gotten him into the chair with a struggle, Martin not responding. Tied his hands behind him, pulled the cords as tight as he could to be on the safe side. Martin mumbled something, sounded pained. Maybe Usman had tied them too tight, but that was too bad. He wasn't going to loosen them once they were on, wasn't going to give Martin any chance to get out. Hurried to tie his feet together and bind them to the metal hoop in the floor that he hadn't initially remembered to check for. Thank fuck it was close to where Martin had fallen or he would have had to drag him halfway across the warehouse floor to get to it.

And that was it. Martin was tied up and in place, ready for the finale. As he started to come round and move his head, Usman stepped back away from him. He was looking around, not saying anything, still looking groggy. Usman stepped further back, towards the door they'd come in through. He wanted to say something, tell Martin that it wasn't personal, something like that. Words, when stacked against betrayal, felt inadequate, so he said nothing. He turned and walked to the door. As he was pulling it shut behind him, he was sure he heard Martin say something, some loud mumble that echoed just a little. Didn't catch what it was, didn't go back to check.

But he could have gone back, he's realizing that now. They were behind time already, even before he decided to go home to be sick. Further behind time after that, and after him struggling to find the pub. But he could still have backed out. Could have gone back to the warehouse, cut the plastic strips and told Martin he was sorry. Told him that their partnership was obviously over, but that nothing worse would happen. Explain it to him. Having a basic conversation with Martin could sometimes be so misery-inducing as to push you beyond the limits of your tolerance, but he was smart. He could be made to understand. Once Usman opened the door in front of him, it would be too late.

The door's opened by itself. The handle jerked back out of his hand and Gully is standing there looking at him. They're about the same height; Gully wider, older and visibly more relaxed. He's nodding, holding the door open for Usman to come in. Nate's sitting at a small circular table in the middle of a narrow room, the table and a couple of chairs the only things in it. Three beer bottles and a pack of playing cards on the table. They've been bored, waiting for him, watching the clock and wondering what the hell's taking so much time. Usman's stepping inside and Gully's closing the door behind him.

They heard him come in through the back gate, it scratched loud enough on the ground to announce his arrival. Heard him, or maybe saw him if they were watching from a window across the hall. So that was the point of no return. Feels a little better, finding out that it passed without him realizing, that it was never actually in his hands.

Gully's standing behind him at the door, not making a move to sit back down. Nate's looking at him, looking annoyed, but that expression isn't much of a departure from his default.

'Problems?' he's saying in his usual growl. That man just can't seem friendly.

'No,' Usman's saying, 'no problems. Just, uh, just took longer than I thought it would. We were slow going in, that's all. Cautious, you know.'

'And it went okay?'

'Went as planned, yeah,' Usman's saying, nodding. Doesn't want to think about that plan. Stupid plan that he couldn't understand to begin with. They should have been there. 'He's there. On the chair.'

Nate's smiling just briefly at the rhyme. Looking past Usman at Gully. Gully's nodding, time to go and get this finished. It should have been done by now, instead of the two of them sitting there playing cards badly, throwing their careful plan out of timing. Moving a body is always a delicate business, dangerous, you need to get it just right. Timing is everything, making sure you're on the road when nobody else is, making sure you get back home and out of view before anyone has the chance to notice you're not where you ought to be. This was in danger of keeping them on the road late enough for other people to turn up. Get moving, fast.

Nate's getting up from the table, walking across to Usman. 'Right. Let's go, get this done. Sooner the better.'

Usman's nodding, trying to look like he agrees. 'Sooner the better.'

# 10

'Come on, man, you can't tell me it didn't work out. And you can't tell me that you wouldn't like another good score.'

Usman was grinning, nodding his head in vigorous agreement with himself. Seemed to think that if he nodded enough, Martin would eventually feel compelled to join in. They were sitting opposite each other in the same flat in Mosspark that Usman had used for persuading and planning last time. Martin hadn't been there since the night of the job at the bookies when they'd counted the money and gone their separate ways. They'd spoken only once in the two months since then, and that was over the phone.

It made sense for them to keep their distance, although it made more sense to Martin than to Usman. It was Usman who'd gone in without a balaclava and it was his car they'd fled the scene in. If either of them was going to be caught then it was going to be him. Better not to be in close contact. Better not to let anyone know they'd had previous contact.

'So you haven't had any trouble?' Martin asked him.

Usman behaved like a man without a single damn problem to his name. The one phone call they'd had was casual, an attempt by Usman to make sure that they didn't drift apart when they could still be useful to each other. Now this, a call asking Martin to come round to the flat, telling him that he had a proposal he wanted to put to him. Trying to make it sound an everyday sort of conversation.

'Trouble? Me? Not a bit, nah. I told you before; it went as near to perfect as it needed to. I know it wasn't *actually* perfect, don't give me that grim-reaper look, I know. Hey, I was there, you might remember. But it went well, you got to say. Two fucking months ago, Martin, two fucking months and not a word about it. No trouble, nobody chasing us down the street with an axe in their hand, money still safely tucked away. Might not be perfect, but it's good enough, ain't it?'

There was some gloss on that. For the last couple of months Usman had kept at least one ear to the ground, listening for any mention of the raid on the bookies in Coatbridge. Barely a whisper, just some very loose gossip that didn't mention a robbery at all. Overheard a conversation which mentioned that the guy who ran the bookies for Jamieson in Coatbridge, Donny Gregor, had been replaced. Maybe temporarily, maybe permanently, the guy didn't know. Something wrong with his health, so the rumour went, so he was being sidelined. Usman figured that might have been an excuse. Hoped it was.

He listened out for any word of Nate Colgan as well. Expecting to hear that the thug was looking for him. That he was hunting him down and planning to rip him apart and feast on his innards. Didn't hear anything. Colgan's name got a couple of mentions, but never in connection with Usman or the bookies, just the sort of mentions one of Glasgow's meanest bastards would always get. One was in connection to the fact that he seemed to be doing work with Gully Fitzgerald these days, which gave Usman the identity of the other person at the bookies.

Gully Fitzgerald, another sharp-toothed monster to be scared of. Maybe not as scary as Nate Colgan these days, but still a beast in his own right. There was no good news in finding out he was the second man, but at least Usman now knew who to run from should their paths cross. He'd shared the info with Martin during the phone call three weeks before this meeting.

'You've heard nothing about them looking for us since?' Martin asked.

'Not a damn thing. I mean, they wouldn't advertise it, would they? They don't want people knowing that we ripped them off in the first place so they're keeping it under their hats, right. But they must have been looking, the amount of money we swiped from them. Even people rolling in it go looking for thirty-two grand when they lose it. First couple of weeks they'd have been sweating blood to find us. After that, I don't know, I figure maybe they eased off a bit. Those guys, they're busy men, always got new trouble to chase. Not like you and me, growing fat on our cash reserves. Working for Jamieson, they'll

136

have all sorts of brilliant distractions to get them away from us. So, I don't know, I figure they'll have moved on.'

Martin was incredulous. 'Moved on? You think they would ever just accept losing that much money?'

Usman raised a hand. 'Nah, nah, not accept it. Don't get me wrong, they'll still have one eye on the prowl for you and me. If we do anything stupid, catch their attention, give ourselves away, then they'll come right after us, don't worry about that. Those two, Jesus, they'll always be on the alert. But they'll have a ton of other stuff that they need to get on with as well. An organization that size, those two are going to be busy with that other stuff, course they are. And, as well,' he said, raising an arm and his voice in enthusiasm, 'the fact that their boss is in the jail works for us as well. They're stuck defending themselves from all sorts of attacks, other arseholes trying to pick away at their business while they're weak, so they can't just focus on a one-off hit like ours.'

Martin didn't look enthusiastic, but then he didn't ever look what you could call enthusiastic. Usman was just about getting used to that now. Wasn't so long ago Martin had been sitting in this flat, saying that he wasn't going to get involved in the hit on the bookies. Sat in the exact same chair, looking miserable and saying that it was a bad idea, that he wouldn't do it. Changed his mind quick enough though, announcing that it could be done if they did it his way. Usman was happy to go along with him now too, convinced that he could win him round to another job.

'We don't need to do another job,' Martin told him. 'You shouldn't be greedy.'

'Greedy? Me? You're calling me greedy? I'm not greedy, I'm just opportunistic. Ain't the same thing. Some of the jobs I got all worked out, they aren't jobs that we can just turn up and do whenever we feel like it. Some of them need to be done at certain times. Might be months before another one comes along, you know. That's just taking your opportunities when they're there. And you have to look at it this way as well, right: it's not about doing two jobs in three months. Stop looking at it that way. This is about getting the jobs when we can, cos we might go a year without getting any money. You aren't going to live on what we made from the bookies forever, are you now? I don't know how stingy you are, wee man, but sixteen grand ain't good living for long.'

Martin shrugged. Usman's argument was a no-brainer and they both knew it, but two months was too soon. Two months after you piss off one of the biggest organizations in the city and you want to go back to work. Two months after you piss off two of the most dangerous men in Glasgow. Common sense, gathered from spending years being the man who chased others down, was screaming for him to lie low a little longer.

'We cannot attack another business of Jamieson,' Martin

said. 'And we should not be attacking anyone until we're sure that we're safe.'

Usman groaned. Getting through to this guy was like headbutting your way through a wall only to find some dick had built another wall behind it. There was a part of him that wanted to ditch Martin, find someone that was easier to work with, which was just about everyone. An easy life, who wouldn't want that? But there was a smarter part of him that realized this was exactly what he needed, someone to hold him back when he was straining at the leash. Someone who took a totally different approach to him. Maybe it wasn't so much fun, but Martin looked at the world from a miserable starting point and that had real value when you needed every angle covered.

'We won't be attacking another Jamieson target. Wouldn't go near that bastard a second time, not for a long time, maybe not ever. But I got a target that's safe. And, I think you're wrong about keeping your head down this long. You keep keeping your head down and people start to wonder what you're hiding from. I see a guy refusing work and I start to think he must have done a job recently, must be in that cooling-off period, you know. Then I start to try and work out what that job might be. Come on, I'm right, you know I am, don't you?'

Martin just shrugged.

'So you'll hear me out?'

'No,' Martin said. 'I do not think we should do another job

together so soon. Maybe it is time for work, but not together. If you want to do a job with someone else, you should. If this job has to be done soon then do it. But I don't want to be involved. I will work with you again, in the future, but not now.'

Usman looked crestfallen. He'd finally found himself a man he could work tough jobs with, found a bloody gunman, for fuck's sake, and now the bastard was playing hard to get. He wouldn't beg though, that would just make matters worse. Martin needed to be convinced that Usman was serious and it was hard to gain that respect when you were down on your knees.

Martin got up from his chair. 'When more time has passed, and it's safer, then I will work with you again.'

Usman watched him turn and walk out of the flat. Let him go. Growled at him a little for being a fucking robot, and went to the kitchen for a beer, because there was nothing much he could do about it. For now, anyway.

Martin walked out through the close and onto the street. He'd parked his car down the road, a suitable distance from Usman's regular haunt. New car, bought a couple of weeks before, making them a two-car household. Only cost him a couple of grand, it was seven years old and it had 65,000 long miles on the clock, but it was in decent condition, and it was important to have it. Meant that Martin wasn't dependent on buses any more, so he could learn individual streets that bus routes didn't cover. Also meant that, if he needed to, he could work a job at any time without ever having to use Joanne's car.

He was happy with his decision to refuse Usman when he got back to the house. Content that keeping the younger man at arm's length for another few months was the sensible thing to do. He still had money in the bank, Joanne was bringing money in, there was no reason to roll the dice just because it suited Usman. Patience was the greatest safety net he had. He parked the car on the street and walked round to the back of the house like he always did. It was a habit they both had, using the back door and just leaving the front door locked.

He heard the voices shouting from the corridor as he approached the back door. Joanne and Skye, reaching volumes their lungs were struggling to maintain. Joanne was loud, but in control, Skye was basically screaming. Martin hung back, knowing this wasn't a fight he should wander into the middle of. Joanne was his girlfriend, but Skye was a bucket full of muddy water. Martin had been prepared to try and be some kind of father figure, a friend at least, but she had no interest. A handful of cringing conversations had been the extent of their relationship to that point.

'You'd rather have *him* here than me, your own daughter.' The 'him' was said with a degree of hatred that Martin didn't deserve. This time, at least.

Joanne knew what her daughter was trying to do, trying to

make her feel guilty about her relationship with Martin. Not going to work. 'Yes, I would, because he treats this place properly. You need to get your head in order, Skye. You're a grown woman.'

'I just need a place to stay. I thought my own mother would give me that much. Some fucking mother, rather have your little toy-boy instead.'

Feet stamping up the stairs, not hanging around to face the reaction.

'Come back here. You're not a child, Skye; you can't walk away from this.'

A door slamming. Skye in her bedroom, apparently back in the house for keeps. Joanne stood at the bottom of the stairs, hands on hips, trying to stop herself from shouting something regrettable. She wouldn't go chasing Skye up the stairs, not her style. She walked through to the kitchen, saw Martin waiting, and sat across from him at the table.

'You hear that?'

"Enough of it,' he said. 'What happened?'

'She's been kicked out of her flat.'

'Why?'

Joanne shook her head. 'She didn't say. Skye being Skye. Didn't pay her rent or picked fights with people. That's her.'

'So she's coming back here?'

Joanne sighed. It had been going so well, her and Martin finding a groove that made them both happy. Having the house to themselves was key to it. They had their own little world inside these walls that locked all the problems of reality out. Now reality had come storming back in, screamed its way up the stairs and slammed its bedroom door shut behind it.

'If she needs money . . .' Martin said, trailing off because he knew what the reaction was going to be.

'No. She has to earn her own way. She has to learn that she can't just come running back here every time she falls out with someone. She's behaving like a child, and that has to stop.'

Martin nodded. He clearly didn't agree, but he nodded. She wasn't his daughter, she wasn't his responsibility and he didn't have the right to insist. Only Joanne had earned the right to make decisions about Skye.

'There must be something we can do,' he said.

'To get rid of her?' She smiled a little when she said it.

'Not to get rid of her, but . . . well, getting rid of her would have to be part of it, yes.'

Joanne smiled. She wasn't picking Martin over her own daughter; it wasn't like that at all. Skye needed to find her own place in the world. It was doing her a favour to push her towards it, even if it would take years for Skye to understand that.

'You have to decide,' Martin said. 'Is her learning to pay her own way the most important thing? Maybe, I don't know, there are other things as well. Life is not just about what's best for her. We have to think about ourselves sometimes. Maybe, if we gave her the money to pay a – what's the word, you pay some money up front for a place to live?'

'A deposit? Jesus, Martin, we don't have the money for that. We've only just enough for us.'

'But if we did, maybe we could spend it on that. I mean, we could own the place, and let her stay there. We own it so it's worth money to us, she lives there. *If* we had money for a deposit, I mean.'

Joanne looked at him. 'You really want rid of her.'

'I really want us to have our space. It is not a fault of hers.'

'Okay. In theory, if we had that sort of money, that would be an idea. A bloody expensive one, and one she doesn't deserve at all. And it would leave us having to pay a mortgage, have you thought of that?'

He'd been thinking of it since he heard Skye screaming. That job at the bookies was to fund life with Joanne. Life was about her, about them, being together. He didn't want to make sacrifices, take risks, but he wouldn't always be able to avoid them. The most professional thing to do was accept a lack of finance, but that meant Skye in the house. Professional-ism meant a damaged relationship, and he couldn't let that happen.

'We have two incomes, we could manage that. I will get the money to pay the deposit. In the next few weeks, I will get the money. And I will keep earning money after that so we will be able to pay for the mortgage. It will be an investment. Years from now we will be glad we made it when we could.'

The investment he meant wasn't in the property, wasn't in Skye's future either. They both knew what it was. It was the investment in their relationship. The idea that this was the rest of their lives, and that was something they were willing to work for.

Her name was Alison Glenn. She worked in a bar on Hope Street, a legit place where she put in long hours and got short pay. Usman had been in the night before; chatting to her and then strolling slowly back to his place with her. They'd vaguely known each other for a couple of years through mutual friends, been to a lot of the same parties, had gone out a couple of times before. Always back to his, not hers. She lived with a bunch of other people, crushed into the only space they could afford.

They were in bed, in his proper flat, the one he actually called home. It was small but it was neat and it was filled with expensive things that he could afford. He wasn't stupid with money, said he had been brought up to be smart about it, always made enough to cover his costs and leave a little left over after every job. She liked that about him, the sensible side that balanced out the party boy she had thought he was when they first met. He was slowly building up a nice little nest egg, ready for the deluge that rainy days brought in his business.

145

Alison was comfortably smart enough to understand what his line of work was.

'And they're opening another bar right across the street from us,' she was saying, halfway through a conversation Usman was only halfway listening to. She looked younger than twenty-one. Her youth was in her large, dark eyes and small, round mouth. 'And JC says it doesn't even matter if they make any money because it's being run by a bunch of crooks.'

'Who the hell's JC?'

'JC Carson,' she said, like that meant something. 'My boss, I already told you about him. Well, he's not my boss I suppose, but he kind of is. He's the manager at Derby's.'

This wasn't Usman's idea of good pillow talk, but Alison was concerned about her job, so she wasn't giving him any choice but to play along. 'How does this JC Carson know that it's being run by a bunch of crooks then? They advertise?' He reached across to the bedside cabinet and grabbed his packet of cigarettes.

Alison waited, watching him light one for her and then for himself, then she spoke. 'He said it's being run by some guy called Marty Jones. This guy's some big gangster type, doesn't even need the place to be successful, can just keep running it and running it even if it's losing money because they use it to launder their dirty cash. It's the money-laundering they really want it for, shower of pricks. That means they can take business away from us and it doesn't even matter if they lose money, they can stick around way longer than we can, run us out of business, take all our customers. So now everyone's shitting it that we're going to lose our jobs.'

'Mm,' Usman said, taking a drag. 'Worst happens, you can always nip across the street and ask this Marty Jones for a job.'

'I suppose,' she said, taking the suggestion seriously.

'Better still,' he said, 'you can take the opportunity to find a better job altogether, something more long-term, you know.' That didn't get a response, but he was serious. Nipping across the road to meet Marty Jones was a bad idea for any pretty young woman. Usman knew who Marty Jones was. Knew he wasn't some big gangster type; he was a pimp and a fucking loan shark, exploiting as many people as he could get his claws into. But he was Peter Jamieson's pimp and loan shark, and that meant he was well protected. Jones must have been fronting the purchase of this bar for the Jamieson organization; no way he'd be doing it on his own.

Usman smiled. Maybe Jamieson's mob was only buying this place because of the job he and Martin had done on the bookies. Maybe he'd forced them into taking some serious action to make sure they had a better operation for cleaning money in a hurry. Then he stopped smiling. He didn't want that job to still be affecting them. It meant it would still be on their mind, still be costing them noticeable sums of money. There was nothing that would make them more determined to catch and castrate him than having to spend even more money covering up for what happened that night.

'Be nice to work somewhere where it doesn't matter if it's successful or not,' Alison said. 'No pressure. We're constantly getting hassle to try and get more people in, like that's *our* job. Up to the manager to get people through the door, but he's loading it onto us, prick.'

Usman murmured agreement; working without pressure sure would be nice. Not worrying about your partner being a suicide-inducing sod that doesn't want to work with you for months on end, no matter how good the job. Not worrying about your targets tracking you down and putting a bullet in the back of your devilishly handsome head.

'It's all right for you,' Alison said. 'You don't seem to have a care in the world. Always got enough money and I've never seen you work a day in your life.'

Usman nearly swallowed his cigarette. Not a care in the world? What a bloody cheek. He wasn't going to lie there and give up the mountain of cares he had, but he wasn't going to let this pass unchallenged either.

'I think you'll find that I got a lot of things to worry about. Got a lot of work to do as well. Tough work, right. Real tough work. Sort of thing you wouldn't be able to do yourself, no offence. You wouldn't fit into my shoes, nuh-uh. I got all kinds of stuff going on. Just because I don't broadcast it don't mean I'm not working, just means I'm subtle.'

She burst out laughing. 'Subtle? You? Come off it, you're as subtle as a firework, you. I know what you do, Usman; I've always known what you and your brother do. It's no big deal, not to me. But don't pretend that selling knock-off booze and stuff like that is proper work. It's not. Only reason you do it is so that you don't have to do proper work like the rest of us. And what have you done for the last month? Nothing that I've noticed. And I mean proper work.'

Usman started to huff and puff, stubbing out his cigarette in the ashtray he'd taken from the bedside cabinet and placed between them on the bed. He tried to think of something he'd done that could pass for gainful employment. Keeping your head down after a job wasn't a good explanation, not to someone you didn't intend to tell about it. You had to have an excuse handy, and he was starting to realize that the one he'd planned didn't quite convince.

'I've been doing stuff. Stuff for Akram, and, uh, setting some stuff up for myself. You know how it is. A lot of my work, it ain't stuff that shows a result straight away. I'm setting stuff up. Putting stuff in place so that I can score off it later on. Playing the long game, so I am.'

'Sure you are,' Alison said with a smile that dismissed his answer as a joke.

'I am,' he said, starting to get worked up now. He didn't like having to cover his tracks, because he didn't like doing anything he was hopeless at. 'I got something I'm working on right now. Not right now as in right this second. Right this second I been working on you,' he said, trying for a cheeky grin.

'A lot of effort, not much of a score,' she said with a shrug and a smile. 'But if you're working on something, you're keeping it well hidden.'

'Of course I fucking am,' he said, louder than he intended. 'That's the whole point. I keep everything I do well hidden. That's the nature of the business, ain't it? That doesn't mean I don't have anything to work on. I have something. Something pretty big as well. Full of concerns and worries, full of the bastards. It's very complicated stuff, right, and I'm facing it alone because the guy who's supposed to be doing it with me is backing off, scared of the heat. It's a fucking nightmare, right, so don't tell me I don't have any worries. I got worries all the way up to my sweaty armpits. I might have to can a big job because of that prick. That's a pretty big worry right there. A big score down the crapper, that is.'

His tone had been getting more serious, even a little bit annoyed, as he went on. This was something that had gotten under his skin and killed the mood in the bedroom. Alison hadn't intended to provoke such seriousness. She stubbed out her cigarette and ran a hand down his chest.

'I wasn't saying you didn't have any worries,' she said. 'Forget it.'

Usman started laughing. 'I'm sorry; I didn't mean to get

like that. Just me running off at the mouth. Forget I said it, okay? I ain't got any problems, not real ones.'

He put an arm round her, and eventually they both fell asleep.


Usman woke first. It was early, or earlier than usual for him anyway. Half eight on the clock, and his mind and body protesting that this was no hour to be awake. Alison was sleeping with her back to him. He got out of bed and wandered through to the kitchen, standing at the sink and letting Martin's contagious misery wash over him. He was going to have to try and do this job alone, there was no other choice.

That fucking Martin Sivok. Polish or Czech or Russian or whatever bastard faraway country he had slinked in from. Leaving Usman hanging out to dry like this. A pro like Martin should have known that doing one job meant you were on the hook to do more. Should have known that he wasn't always going to get to pick the timing either. If you team up with a guy who's organizing something then you have to accept that he has more control of the timing than you do, should have made that clear. Usman frowned. Should have said Martin was working *for* him, not with him. Made him a partner instead of an employee, that was the mistake.

Now he had this job with a tight time-limit on it. He was sure he had a week, maybe less, and then the chance would be gone, perhaps never to return. If it came along again in the future it wouldn't be in its current form, not with the same certainty it had for Usman now. He didn't have anyone else he could use, and it sure as hell didn't feel like a solo gig. Go back to Martin, talk to him again, offer him a bigger cut. Something, anything, to get him on board.

# 11

He was in a pub in Anniesland, tucked away at the back in the dark. There was hardly anyone in there yet, and there wouldn't be a lot as the evening went on. Slowly but surely this dump was running into the ground, where it belonged. That emptiness was why Aiden Comrie used the place as often as he dared. Use it before the bank and a health and safety officer get into a race to shut it down.

He didn't know much about the girl that was buying, apart from the fact that she was a she and her name was Sarah something-or-other. He had picked the meeting place, the time, everything about it. He felt comfortable, felt in total control, even if this was a big deal. Big deal for him, maybe not for her. She was just an employee; here to do someone else's work for them.

She worked for the Allen brothers. They had a good operation, selling mostly outside of the city but increasingly willing to move in. They had lurched in after the Jamieson arrests, looked like they were working with Don Park back then. That changed, they backed off, scared away to the safety of their usual haunts. Word was that Jamieson's men hadn't even chased them out; they just chickened out of trying their luck.

But they were back again, like a bad penny, with an impressive drug network in tow. This meeting was a part of their moving in; part of striking up an agreement with Chris Argyle, the man Aiden was working this deal with.

If he could get this right, work it clean, then he had a chance to get well in with Argyle. Aiden had set this deal up for Argyle; he had done some street work for the Allens back in the distant past. He knew they weren't brothers, they were cousins, but nobody cared. A couple of drug dealers, a double dose of hard work and trouble, that's what they were. Everyone called them brothers, it was just easier. Aiden knew them just well enough to pitch an idea to them on behalf of someone else.

That someone was Argyle, an importer and another tough bastard. Smoother than the Allens, understood the need to make people like and respect him a little bit more than the gruesome twosome ever did. Argyle told him that he'd be happy to try and make a deal with the Allens, if Aiden was so sure he could set it up. Argyle importing, them selling, everyone making money. It made sense, they were a good fit, but there was other stuff going on in the background, Aiden was smart enough to know that. The politics of the business. There was talk of Argyle getting close to people that were moving against Jamieson while he was in prison, something like that. It was all kind of confusing, people getting into bed together and not bothering to tell the workforce. Didn't matter to Aiden. What mattered was this deal and what it would do for him.

Moving a lot of gear from Argyle to the Allens, Aiden as the middleman. A lot of gear meant a lot of money. A first step to big things.

As soon as she came in through the front door he wished he'd made more of an effort. Aiden was short and stocky, receding brown hair and tattooed up both arms. A man in his early thirties who could pass for older, younger if he had a hat on. He was wearing jeans and a hoodie, scruffy trainers that had walked through a lot of puddles. He was dressed to do a deal in the arse-end of a crappy pub, not to make a good impression on an attractive young woman. He regretted that, and the fact that he didn't have time to slip his wedding ring off.

Sarah wasn't looking to make a good impression either, the fact she did was accidental. They didn't get a lot of blonde twenty-somethings in that pub; it really wasn't a blonde twenty-something's kind of place. Grey sixty-somethings, if anyone at all. She was wearing jeans and a plain top, but her jeans were tight and she was tall and pretty, so creeps like Aiden Comrie went slobbering after her anyway. She picked out Aiden in a heartbeat and walked confidently over.

'Aiden,' she said, sitting across from him. Said it like they'd known each other all their lives. You wouldn't guess this was their first meeting after one phone call.

He looked unsettled by that, a person so confident when

she'd spoken to him. She didn't know him, the familiarity was false and anything false was worth being wary of in his line of work. But it was only one word, and she was so casual with it.

'Sarah, right?' he said.

'That's right. So you have something interesting to tell me then?'

She smiled when she said it, politeness that could, to a stupid person, look flirtatious. Someone as dumb as Comrie, on the other hand, might think it was her way of getting rough, tough criminal types to melt and tell her what she wanted to hear. It wasn't. He was planning to tell her what she wanted to hear anyway.

'I have a proper deal, a right proper deal,' he said. This sounded better in his head, sounded more formal in there. Out in the open it sounded amateurish, like he wasn't educated. 'See, I have an importer who can provide every single thing your guys want. I got the full range at my fingertips, always at the best price.'

'We know that,' she said, cutting him off before he could say everything he'd so carefully planned out in his head before she came in. These were things he wanted to say, not things she needed to hear. 'We don't doubt the variety or the quantity. We know you have serious backing, don't worry about that. The issue here is whether what you're offering is of the quality we're looking for, and whether us working together will be a suitably painless experience.'

Okay, the conversation had skipped ahead, but it only took him a few seconds to work out where they were up to. Sarah was in a hurry, wanted to get out of this tip. Spend as little time as possible in the company of the middleman. She needed to do this deal as much as he did though, and that gave him a sense of power. Her superior attitude made him hate her a little.

'You already know we got the quality. You want to do a deal then, a test period, see how it works?'

'Exactly. Are you sure that you can cover a month's supply for us?'

Aiden laughed. 'You don't need to worry about that. Could cover that and then some. You got a list?'

She took a slip of paper from the pocket of her skinny jeans and passed it to him. He didn't even look at it, didn't need to. Unless the Allens had suddenly gotten into some weird exotic shit, there wasn't going to be anything on there that Chris Argyle couldn't handle.

'We'll want it soon,' she told him. 'Within the week.'

He shrugged. Should have looked at the list maybe, some stuff was harder to get, could take more than a week. He couldn't tell her that though. Treat everything like it was no big deal, leave her thinking this was easy for him.

'I look forward to seeing you at the handover, Sarah.' Dropped her name in there all casual, the way she had with his when she came in.

She gave him a look that a beautiful woman would give a pathetic thirteen-year-old boy and got up. 'We'll be in touch,' was all she said, and she left the pub.

Might not have been the most flawless performance of his roller-coaster career, but he had what he needed from her. The list had probably been written up ages ago, as soon as Argyle and the Allens first made contact. It would be a long list, and it would be a deliberately challenging list. If they could get through it all without any fuck-ups then it would be very profitable, too. That was the important bit.

The meeting had turned out to be a best-case scenario. Worst case, she came into the pub and he had to try and persuade her to do any deal at all, which would have been tough. Snobby bitch like her wouldn't have let herself be persuaded by a proper working-class guy like him. Instead it was the most they could have hoped for. Her coming in with a list prepared meant that it was always going to be a brief meeting of intermediaries, which meant Aiden got to go back to Argyle or one of his people with good news. That made him smile. This would be his success.

He took the list out of his pocket and looked at it. Mostly bog-standard, with a couple of designer items near the bottom that seemed to be there as a test. Wouldn't be a problem, Argyle had connections in Holland that could get him a lot of that synthetic stuff. Looked like a tap-in to Aiden, an open goal with the Allens getting an assist. They were making it as easy as they could for this deal to succeed. He put the list away and sipped at what was left of his drink.

He left the pub ten minutes later. He had given Sarah a head start, just in case anyone was watching the place, just in case anyone was watching her. Nobody was watching him, he was sure of that. Aiden had been in the business long enough to know how important he wasn't. He was a middleman, probably lower end of the middle ranks. Maybe, just maybe, the Argyle deal would give him the chance to step up to something better, be the senior figure he knew he was capable of being, but he wasn't a man who had ever been important enough to be a target for others.

Usman had watched him go into the pub. He waited at a safe distance, watching carefully. He wouldn't go in; any customer would stand out in a nearly empty pub. Didn't need to get that close anyway to work out what was happening here. He saw Sarah McFall arriving. She was the link, the one he knew to watch out for. Her ex had drunkenly spilled the beans about her working for the Allens, about her trying to make some sort of deal between them and Argyle. The guy was the kind of self-righteous, bitter loudmouth that was always fuelled by alcohol and inspired by being deservedly dumped. He told a friend of Usman everything and the friend passed the info on.

So he watched her go in, admired her from a safe distance.

She was smarter about looking for tails, checking the street before she went inside. Aiden Comrie had wandered into that dump without so much as a glance up the road. Complacent halfwit, thinking that because nobody had bothered to keep tabs on him before, they wouldn't start now. People don't start paying attention to you when you become senior, they start watching you when you're on the way up. Sarah was smarter; she looked both ways before she leapt. Usman was playing it carefully; he was comfortably out of view when she looked.

They didn't take long in there. She was out first, moving quickly to her car and driving away. Didn't look thrilled with the world, but you wouldn't after spending a few minutes with Aiden Comrie in that hole. Her being unhappy didn't mean the deal was dead, or even floundering. The one to watch was Comrie, he was the weak link here. If the chain is the Allens, Sarah McFall, Aiden Comrie and then Chris Argyle, then the weak link is pretty damn glaring. You follow him and you wait for that moron to give you an inevitable opening.

Aiden Comrie left the pub about ten minutes after Sarah McFall. He didn't bother looking around on the way out either, having not gotten any smarter in the twenty minutes he'd been inside. He walked with a sort of waddle, a short and broad guy with his arms out from his sides, taking up more of the pavement than he needed. He walked like he was fat, which he wasn't. Could be tough, Usman reflected, to take down a brawler like Comrie. Following a dumbass is easy enough.

Working a job against said dumbass is only easy if his body is as weak as his mind. There was no evidence of that; Comrie could probably fight his way out of being cornered by a lone attacker. Usman waited for the target to get into his car, watched him drive to the end of the street before he followed.

# 12

Her shift at the bar started at six, so she needed to make this quick. Alison knew the way; she'd been in the pub she was going to before, although she hadn't worked there. One of her flatmates had told her who to call, given her the number and a few details about the person she was talking to. She knew a lot of people in the business, the flatmate. They didn't talk about it, not a subject you casually raise, but Alison knew Heather was connected. So she asked, and Heather delivered.

'I had a word with BB, and he told me this is the guy you want, if you're sure.'

Heather Cannero was tall, pushing six foot, and Alison always had the sense that she was tough, a fighter. No reason for that assumption, other than Heather being very tall and quite broad-shouldered. She was always tucking her curly brown hair behind her ears, which annoyed Alison for some reason, and because of small things like that they had never been especially close. But she knew people on the fringes of the criminal world, had done since childhood, and had gone out with a few of them.

'Who's BB?' Alison had asked her.

'Oh, he's a sweetie. Works for Billy Patterson, I think.'

'Who's Billy Patterson?'

Heather smiled. 'Bad people, be glad you don't know. Works for Peter Jamieson.'

'Him I have heard of.'

'Good. Well, BB says this is the man you want to go talk to. Nate Colgan. I don't know what he does exactly, but I know he's got a big reputation, a man to be scared of. BB says he's the man. And he's expecting you to call now, BB told him you would, so maybe you have to. They know you know something. I don't think Nate Colgan is the sort of person you disappoint.'

Which sounded ominous and unusually dramatic for Heather, so Alison called Nate Colgan. She got a very brief and rather grumbly set of instructions in which he informed her that they had to meet face to face and told her where and when, as well as how to get there without anyone seeing her. All seemed pretty over the top, but he insisted and he didn't sound like someone who wanted to be argued with. So she found herself, a little after five o'clock, on a busy city-centre street, looking for the gate to an alleyway.

She found it, looked up and down the street in a cartoonish way that would have been suspicious to anyone who was watching her, and went inside. She was on a narrow path, high fences from the backs of the buildings on either side of her. She counted her way down to the third gate and pushed it open, recoiling at the clatter it made on the cobblestones of the little courtyard. She moved quickly across the courtyard and in through the unlocked back door of the pub.

There was plenty of noise coming from the front of the building. People shouting orders, the general murmur of badly constructed conversation and too-enthusiastic laughing. The stairs were on her left, as he'd said they would be. She went up, knocked on the door at the top, heard a shout for her to enter.

Nate was sitting at the little round table, looking miserable. Glancing at Alison Glenn didn't help his mood, a pretty young girl who made him feel instantly like an old man. It was the place that depressed him though. This pub, which was becoming a regular haunt for meeting people he didn't much want to meet, was one of the last places he wanted to be. This was where Kelly's ex-boyfriend had been killed, and Nate had been part of the clean-up. You don't go back to the scene of a bad event, especially when it becomes personal. Recently he'd cracked, asked Kelly out, begun the process of turning it into a proper relationship. She'd stayed at his place a couple of times, he'd been to hers, they'd been out to dinner and the cinema, doing all the things normal couples do. It was uncomfortable, because these things always were for Nate, but it was nice too. He was part of something enjoyable and exciting, and he liked that. Falling hard for Kelly and feeling the sort of things that other, weaker, people felt. Bringing her into his life and knowing that she could be used against him. And here he was, back in a place of bad memories, because he didn't have anywhere better. Not for meeting this girl, anyway.

Information. She said she had some, suggested it would be valuable to him. Everyone thinks the information they have is the most valuable thing in the world and they can't all be right. She looked like a kid, and he knew she wasn't an insider, so the chances of her knowing anything worthwhile were slim, but you still had to meet her, hear her out. One of Billy Patterson's debt collectors had put her in touch with Nate, vouched for her as useful. That meant nothing.

'Sit down,' he said to her as she closed the door.

She walked quickly across to the table and sat, nervous already, perched on the edge of her chair. She was here to ask for a favour, and Nate wasn't the sort of guy who handed them out freely.

'I'm told there's something you wanted to tell me,' he said. The usual opening gambit, make it seem as though she has to tell him everything first and only then can she ask for a reward. It was all part of the haggling process.

'Um, yeah, there is,' she said with a mumble. 'The thing is, there's something I wanted to ask you first. I work in a bar, Derby's, do you know it?'

Nate nodded. She was very pretty, which was distracting. That was what made her dangerous. If she ever learned how to use that distractive power in Nate's industry she could be quite a weapon, and quite a target, too. Jesus, when did he start looking at young women as nothing more than weapons to use against others?

'Well, the rumour is that it's struggling. I'm worried about losing my job, and I know that your boss is opening a place across the street. I figured, maybe, if I could get a job there, that would really help me.'

Nate shrugged. 'It's not up to me to hire staff for a bar. That would be up to the bar manager. You would need to talk to whoever that is. How do I know you're any good at your job?'

She was flustered. She might have met people in the business before, but she had never met Nate Colgan. This was a step into a world where every conversation was a battle, people trying to hold back as much as possible.

'I am good at my job. Really good, I would say. I know the business and I know how to do a good job. All I'm looking for is, like, a recommendation. If you recommended me then that would be worth something, right?'

Nate very nearly smiled at that. Smart girl. He either had to agree with her or pretend that his recommendation meant nothing. He couldn't very well do the latter, even a novice like Alison could find out that his word carried weight in Glasgow. It was why BB had passed her along to him.

'If I recommend you then you will get the job,' he said to her. Not bragging, his tone was flat throughout. 'But I will not recommend you for no good reason. You want a recommendation, you have to earn it. You tell me what you came here to.'

'You know Usman Kassar?' she asked him.

It took him a few seconds. He knew a Kassar, but it wasn't Usman. A lad who had done some work with the organization, mostly with Kevin Currie and his counterfeit-goods business. 'I don't think so.'

'Oh. Well, it's him I have information about. Do you know Akram Kassar?'

That was the one. 'Yes.'

'Well, Usman's his little brother. He's a nice guy, kind of harmless. Bit flashy, you know, but decent enough with it. People think because he's all flash he isn't smart, but he is. I know that he works in your business. I don't know exactly what he does. I can't give you that sort of detail. But I know that he did something a couple of months ago that made him a lot of money. Enough that he hasn't had to do anything since. And I know that he's working on something right now and I think it must be pretty big. I know that he works with another person, and that this other person doesn't want to work on this new job with Usman. He's annoyed about it, so . . .' she said, trailing off. It didn't sound like much, when she said it out loud. Not quite enough to fill the empty little room, take the cold out of the air around Colgan. She felt like she had overreached herself.

Nate was looking down at the little table. Didn't say anything for about twenty seconds, seemed to be considering issues far bigger than anything she'd said.

'I'll find out who's running the bar, make sure that your name is top of their list,' he said eventually. 'They'll contact you, so don't go chasing after them. They'll set up a way of making it look like they headhunted you. I expect you to do a good job for them. Don't make me look stupid. And when you have any more information that might be useful to me, I expect you to get in touch.'

'I will,' she said, nodding her head. That line about not making him look stupid had been said with a hint of venom so slight that she had to stop and think about it, make sure she'd heard it right. As soon as she realized she had, it scared her.

She didn't want to leave until she was sure that he was finished. 'Can I go?'

He looked at her with a rather sad expression. She didn't know he was thinking about Kelly and the fragility of any relationship you thought you could trust. She was about to start explaining that she needed to get to work when he spoke.

'Yes, you can go. The same way you came in.'

She got up and left quickly. There was something about this man that was hard to explain. He was intimidating, but not threatening, like it was just natural for him, a man who couldn't help but scare people. Never mind that, she had gotten what she came for. She would get a job at whatever they called the swanky new place across the street, and the people who hired her would know that she had gotten the job through the one and only Nate Colgan. That was the clincher, the thing she hadn't mentioned. It wouldn't just get her the job, it would make the job secure. Whoever was bar manager wasn't going to sack an employee who had been recommended by someone so senior.

Nate knew all that without her pointing it out, but it didn't matter. The girl had given him information that made her valuable, she was worth putting into a position where she would have to pass along any other information she gathered. They were only buying the place and using it because they needed somewhere else they could clean money through. They had taken their eye off that particular ball when Jamieson went inside. Used to be his right-hand man, John Young, who handled that sort of thing, and Young was inside as well. The guy who took over from him, Stuart Crockley, picked the wrong fighter in the internal squabble that got Nate's former protégé Ronnie Malone killed, and was now outside the organization. Money laundering, always a challenge, had become a fucking great chore.

As soon as she began to talk about Kassar, the pieces started falling into place. He knew of Akram, the older brother, knew he wasn't going to work a job against Jamieson. But the little brother, that one had flown right under the radar. Worked a job a couple of months ago that paid well. Worked with another person. That ticked a couple of key boxes. Nate needed to find out who the other person was and needed to find out more about Usman Kassar. Most important thing was finding out what this new job was. He wasn't going to find out on his own. He picked up the phone and called Gully.

# 13

There was a definite hint of smugness in his voice, a little relief as well. Usman was doing his best to hide that, but he wasn't an actor, or not a good one anyway. He knew he was radiating relief, even on a slightly iffy phone line.

'I want to hear every detail about this job first though,' Martin told him. 'Every single thing.'

'Of course you do, sure, and I want to tell you every wee detail. I wanted to tell you a couple of days ago but you buggered off back to miserable-land. You want to come round the flat and talk about it?'

'The same flat?'

'Yeah, the same flat.'

'Is it safe to always be using the same place?'

Usman, walking along the street outside his brother's house as he talked, sighed right into the phone. He hadn't actually thought about that, but it wasn't a bad point. He didn't use the flat often, but when he did it was either to meet Martin or set up some other kind of criminal work. A pattern was developing and patterns were treacherous, they gave the game away.

'Yeah, you might be right, I suppose. We can use it again in the future, but maybe not this time, eh? What about your place?' Usman knew Martin was living with a woman, he knew they had a place of their own. It made sense.

'No,' Martin said. A little word with a lot of force behind it.

'All right, okay, never mind then. We can meet up at my own flat then. Breaks the routine, and we can talk properly, in peace.'

So Martin was going round to Usman's flat. They sure as hell weren't going to use Joanne's house, it was bad enough to have his criminality in her life without bringing it all the way into her living room. And it was still her house, not theirs. He hadn't earned the right to call it his yet, although his sense of home was growing within it. But they couldn't use it for a meeting when Joanne might come back and catch them. Worse still, Skye might be lounging around the place now. Then the explanations would really have to begin.

But he didn't want to meet Usman at Usman's own flat either, that felt like it was escalating the relationship. The place in Mosspark had been a good meeting place. A flat that didn't belong to either of them, where they could meet without being seen and without seeing much of each other. It was business, and nothing else, there was no danger of getting any little glimpses of personal life. Martin didn't want any personal element to worm its way into this. He didn't want a friendship. This was business.

Usman's flat was up in Maryhill. That meant a drive with the satnav on, taking instructions from a detached voice with a lot more confidence and a little more knowledge than he had. With a couple of wrong turnings it took a lot longer getting there than he had expected. He was half an hour late.

The flat was in a small block, new and well-kept. Not private though, in terms of getting in and out, a front door the whole street could see. If someone was keeping an eye on Usman's flat then they were bound to notice Martin showing up looking shifty. As a matter of routine he looked around, but he couldn't see anything out of place. Wasn't sure he would recognize if there was, given that he had never been here before. He rang the bell at the front door and Usman buzzed him in. Usman was waiting in the corridor up the stairs for him, front door of his flat open.

'Come on in, man,' he said. He was dressed in a T-shirt that looked like a manic child had scrawled all over it and a pair of baggy jeans with a long silver chain hanging off the pocket. Martin said nothing, went inside.

Inside was the flat of a man who earned. Every little thing looked new, shiny and expensive. Even the artwork on the walls looked like it would cost enough money to make the seller laugh behind your back on your way out of the shop. It was a young man's flat, full of gadgets and bad taste. When he had a partner, had kids and responsibilities, things would change. He would learn to save; he would learn that there was no shame in having the second most expensive version of something.

'You want a beer or something?' Usman asked him, leading him into the living room.

Martin sat in the leather recliner Usman had intended to use. 'Nothing. Just information about this job and a lot of it. What it is, when it's happening. I want to know everything.'

'Right,' Usman said, sacrificing his own beer and sitting on the couch. He had Martin on the hook and he wasn't going to give him any chances to get away. 'You can take your jacket off, man,' he said, 'unless you're planning on doing a runner.' Try and get the little bastard comfortable.

So much for giving the impression that he wouldn't stay long. Martin took his jacket off, put it over the arm of the chair. He was impatient, his instinct told him he shouldn't be here. Not just because it was Usman's home, but because it was only a couple of months after a major job with him. Martin didn't know Glasgow and its industry well enough to take any sort of risks, and here he was taking a sizeable one. Maybe back home he would work a couple of jobs in quick succession but that was different. He knew the business there, knew how people would react and what toes he could afford to dance on when. The politics here played a different tune. Here he still had to learn.

'Right,' Usman said, clapping his hands together. 'This one's a tiny wee bit complicated, so if there's anything you don't get, you just butt right in and ask me, okay?'

Martin smiled. This wasn't going to be nuclear physics; it was going to be a job. There was no way it wasn't going to be some variation on a job he had done before. There were only so many ways to make money ripping people off, very few deviations from the norm, and none that he hadn't at least tried before.

'Okay, here's the thing. There's this guy called Chris Argyle. You heard of Chris Argyle yet?'

Martin nodded and shrugged at a name he remembered only vaguely. Moments like this, he realized how little he did know. He heard names occasionally, but they weren't repeated often enough in his company for the memory to stick. That was becoming a problem.

'Well, Argyle runs a pretty major importing business. The guy's growing fast, a real player these days. Not young, I don't think, but he got into it late. People want him on their side, right, cos everyone wants the growing power on their side, you know. Now, I think – and I just think, right, I don't know for sure – that he's moving towards working full-time with a guy called Don Park. You heard of Don Park? Doesn't matter, he ain't a big deal in this job. We need to be more worried about Argyle, he's the one we're screwing here. So this Don Park, he's a sort of rival of Peter Jamieson's. It's complicated, because Park doesn't run his own organization, but he kind of does. The guy who controls the organization is old, on his way out. Guy called Alex MacArthur, you might have heard of him. Dying, is what I heard, but that might be bullshit. People always gossip about old folk, saying they're half-dead and all that. Park's going to replace him one day anyway and everyone knows it. So Argyle's helping Park by setting up a deal with the Allen brothers. You heard of them?'

Too many names. 'No,' Martin said.

'Okay. They run a dealing operation, street-level stuff. Quite a good operation though. But they've always been careful; made sure they didn't get into any battles they couldn't handle. They stayed outside of the city, most of the time. Worked their own patches. Thing is, I know they're brewing up a deal with Argyle. He supplies, they distribute. Simple enough, but if Argyle is working with Park then it means the Allens are taking sides.'

'Against Jamieson,' Martin said, getting the hang of it.

'Exactly. *Exactly*. So there's a lot of people with an interest in seeing that little venture fail. Big people.'

'So if we do something against Argyle, there are many others to take the blame.'

'Yes, you've got it, wee man, got it in one go. No one's gonna finger us; they'll be too busy chasing after Jamieson's men, or some other organized mob. Whole list of better candidates to get through before they'd even think of little old you and me.'

'Which means nothing if there is no job,' Martin said. He was here for detail that hadn't yet been forthcoming.

'Well of course there's a job. I wouldn't have called you up if there wasn't a fucking job. You'll no get me crying wolf, I'll tell you that. I have a job. All planned out. See, this is a big step for them, the Allens especially, and they're not working face to face. They're using other people to set up the first deal for them. What do you call them, intermediaries, right? Third parties. Keeping a layer of someone else's flesh between them this first time. Cash handover for a large supply.'

Martin leaned forward in the deep chair.

'Thought you might like the sound of that,' Usman said with a smile. 'I know who's doing the handover on each side. The Allens have got a woman called Sarah McFall working their end of it, but she's no good. Too sharp. She knows what she's doing. We won't get it easy off her. The guy Argyle has working his end for him, that's our target. Aiden Comrie. Been a street dealer for years. Must have lucked out and made some sort of connection with Argyle to be able to work a deal this size. This is way over his head. Guy's a bit of a moron; he should be easy to pick up. He's the man we go for.'

'So he will have the drugs?' Martin said with a frown. He didn't want drugs. Stealing drugs meant selling drugs, and selling drugs meant multiplying the risk many times over. He wanted money, and nothing else.

'He'll be handing those drugs over to the lovely Sarah. As soon as she fucks off out of our way, we pick up Comrie and the money.'

Martin paused. 'The man and the money?'

'Yeah, see, I been thinking about that. We need to buy ourselves a little bit of time, right. I been thinking about it every which way and I reckon we need to take him too. Maybe, I don't know, we need to kill him. Maybe not. Depends on how we work it. You would be more of an expert on that than I am so you can probably make your own mind up there. But there's going to be a shitload of money and some serious people waiting for it. If we nick it and run, he only has to make a phone call and we have a hundred mad bastards chasing after us. Everyone Argyle has working for him, for a start. Maybe a bunch of Don Park's men as well. That's more shit than I want on my fingers, you know.'

'So we take him,' Martin said slowly. 'They don't know where he is. Don't know where their money is. They wait a little. Then they think maybe he has run with their money.'

'Exactly. That he's run off with it, or that he's crossed over to someone else with it. Even if they think it's been nicked, it ain't going to be us they blame, not if Comrie can't point the finger at us.'

'And you know that he will do this handover alone? If he has people with him . . .' Martin said, and shrugged. More people meant changing the approach completely, or abandoning it.

'Nah, they're working this alone. Just him and McFall so far. I don't see that changing. One on each side. Makes sense to keep it that way. Safer, stops anyone getting spooked by numbers. They might have other people nearby, wouldn't be surprised by that. People to drop them off and take them away. That's why we have to be fast and careful about this.'

Too many mights and maybes. Martin was shaking his head. 'You know where this will happen?'

'No,' Usman said. Didn't like admitting that. 'But Comrie's an easy tail. We follow him to wherever and we strike. It means being ready. Tailing him all the time, the both of us. It'll be soon though. A few days, at the most. They've already had one meeting. Next step is the handover, surely, so we got to be on top of this right now.'

Martin groaned a little. There were so many holes for them to fall through, so many assumptions that couldn't be shaped into fact. This was a job that invited failure. The odds of him being on his own, out of view, long enough for them to take him and the cash were not great. The odds of them getting him and the money out of view long enough to make this clean were worse.

'I know what you're thinking,' Usman told him, holding up both hands. 'I know. It ain't a perfect job. We might have to ditch the fucking thing before it even starts. He turns up at that meeting and there's three other guys there, we might have to walk away. That's the way the business goes though, right? This one's a bit of a gamble, but there's value there. I'm talking big money on this one, way bigger than the bookies. Think about what sort of money they'll be handing over for a big deal like this. Fifty grand, minimum. I ain't going to get myself killed over my half of that, but I'm going to have a look and see if it's gettable, you know.'

There was a slightly pleading tone in his voice by the time he finished. Trying to be reasonable, make it sound like there was nothing they disagreed on about this job. Martin didn't say anything, not for a long time. He was piecing it together, working out all the terribly sensible reasons that he shouldn't do it. Even if Comrie was alone, there was a chance the handover could be somewhere public. Not *very* public, not busy, but somewhere Comrie's probable backup could keep watch. If they were seen taking him there would be a chase on, which was the last thing they wanted.

But there was one reason to do it. Twenty-five grand, minimum. Put that together with the savings he already had and that would push them up over thirty grand for a deposit. A chance to have the house to themselves. An investment in the relationship. Putting roots down.

'We will start this job,' Martin said. 'Maybe we will not finish it. Maybe it will become as silly as it sounds right now. We watch this man, and if the chance is there then we do it. We don't force it, not if it's not going to be easy. Not if it's going to turn into the wreck it sounds like. But if it doesn't, if there is a chance that we can do it and do it well, then we will do it.'

Usman grinned. He had him. A risk this big and Martin was still on board. That meant he was determined, or desperate, to make the job happen. That was as much as Usman could hope for.

# 14

Gully had the unenviable task of watching the flat first. That was the problem with being the part-time, lower-ranking guy now, he had to take the shit jobs Nate gave him. No longer dishing out tasks like he had in the old days, working for the Knights. Back when Gully was the man.

He was there watching when Martin Sivok arrived and when he left. Gully didn't recognize him. No reason why he would, they had never met without Martin being in a balaclava and the short man didn't have a profile in the city. He was just some random guy going into the building that Usman Kassar lived in. But everyone going into that building was getting their picture taken, no matter how unlikely they seemed. Nate was very firm about that.

Nate was still mightily pissed off about the job at the bookies. It didn't worry Gully so much, these things happened in the business and time taught you to roll with them. His reputation didn't matter much to him any more either, and he wasn't going to lose sleep over Peter Jamieson losing himself some money. The man was rich enough to dry his tears with a fifty-pound note.

At times of failure Gully was more than happy to consider

himself part-time, semi-retired. Lisa, his wife, knew that he was doing some work again. She objected, as he'd expected. The silent sort of disgust she was good at. He understood it, understood her hatred of his old life, but they needed money, and he was good enough at this that he could make a living without even making an effort. Working with Nate, an experienced guy that he liked and trusted. It was easy.

Not for Nate. Wasn't easy for the security consultant when a place he was supposed to be protecting was knocked over by two persons unknown. Worse still when he happened to be there at the time and didn't do anything smarter than get hit on the head with a hammer. That sort of thing could put a dent in any reputation, even one as ironclad as Nate's. Nobody knew, yet, which was a relief. They could find out though, and Nate wanted this sorted before they did. If the world knew that two people had robbed the place while he lay on the floor and let them, it would be shocked. If it found out the two people responsible had already been punished with stomach-churning severity, it would not be surprised at all. Image protected, and image was vital for Nate.

Gully thought about the poor sod of a bookie, Donny Gregor. Took him to the doctor's on the night, the man struggling to stay awake and mumbling all sorts of rubbish. He had pretty bad concussion, apparently. Suffered from blackouts for a couple of weeks afterwards as well. Should probably have gone to a hospital and gotten proper medical attention, but he was too scared. Terrified of Nate's reaction if people found out about the job at the bookies because of his medical treatment. That's why he only got the half-arsed treatment the organization doc gave him, which didn't seem like enough to Gully, but you couldn't persuade the bookie of that. The business ran on people like Gregor living in fear of people like Nate.

After a day spent watching, Gully went round to Nate's house with the photographs. They sat and looked at them. It was strange, being at Nate's, seeing the few little items that reminded you of his daughter, Rebecca. She was eight or nine now, about the same age Sally was when she died. It was a strange feeling, not unpleasant, but not one he wanted to linger on. There were occasional signs of the woman in Nate's life as well, Kelly. Those were more amusing to Gully.

'About time you got yourself a woman to shave the sharp edges off you. Hell, you'll be cuddling those bastards from the bookies when you catch them, all happy like you are.'

Nate gave Gully a cold look.

'And all that bedroom business you'll be enjoying, that'll knock a man of your age flat. You sure you can handle this?'

Nate muttered something, pressing the buttons on the small digital camera Gully had used to make sure he wasn't spotted. Gully just chuckled.

'This guy,' Nate said, pointing at the picture of Martin. 'We know who this guy is?'

'Nope.'

'Looks quite wee, doesn't he?'

'He was, yeah.'

'Looks about the right size to be our man in the mask. If Kassar's working a job then this guy might be his partner.'

'Might be,' Gully said, 'or he might be some random wee guy who's having it away with the woman on the ground floor. Or maybe he's the brother of the guy on the second floor.'

Nate sighed. Gully was right; you didn't make flimsy assumptions on the basis of one photo.

'We need to sort this out, good and fast.' Nate spoke quietly, serious now.

'Need to decide what we want from chasing this Kassar boy first,' Gully told him.

Years gone by he would have agreed with Nate. You know one of the people responsible, you go round and you flash your brutality at him. In the process, you make sure he tells you who his partner was. It's quick and easy, little room for mistakes. It achieves your priority of punishing the people that made you look weak, but that's it, that's all you get out of it. Nothing more than damage limitation.

'So what do we want to get out of it?' Nate asked him. His tone suggested that he already knew exactly what he wanted, and that there wasn't going to be much room for argument.

Gully smiled. 'It's your call. The boy cracked your head, not mine. Mine's in the same glorious condition it's always been in. But you might want to think about what those two pulled off. They did a good job, you can't argue with that. They knew what they were after when they went in there, knew *what* would be there, knew *who* would be there. They pulled off a neat job. If we hadn't got there so quickly it would have been textbook. As it was, they still got out with the money when two old troopers like us were there to block them. I think that's something to consider.'

Nate looked at him with a slight frown. 'I'm not sure what exactly I'm supposed to be considering.'

'One of them managed to set that up. One of them was armed, which suggests a pro gunman to me, or at least some-one who could become one. A kid with a gun in that situation and he had the sense not to fire it. The two of them know their business. All I'm saying is that it's worth keeping that in mind when you go and talk to them. And there's another thing.'

'Oh is there now?' Nate smiled.

'There is, yeah. If their next job is against us, then we stamp on it. That's our job. But if their next job is against someone else, well, maybe we have an interest in letting them go ahead. Maybe we have an interest in helping them work jobs against other people. Weaken our enemies, that sort of thing.'

Nate didn't seem to like it but Gully didn't care, it made sense to him. You want to harm your enemies, that's great, but find someone else to do it for you. Don't put the full load on your own shoulders when there are donkeys nearby willing to take some of the strain.

Nate let Gully leave the house without committing to any sort of an answer on that score. The first thing he needed to do was get hold of Usman Kassar, sit him down and talk to him. Somewhere quiet, somewhere Nate could do the work he was so good at. He knew just the place, a disused garage he'd made use of once before.

That's what had the two of them sitting outside Kassar's flat the following day, watching the door. Nate was directing everything, asserting himself as the man in charge. It felt weird, being the senior man when he had Gully Fitzgerald next to him. Back in the day it had always been the other way round, the older man using his practised judgement in tough situations. Gully didn't make it difficult now, that wasn't his way, but Nate couldn't get the thought that Gully knew best out of his head.

'I don't think he'll run,' Nate said quietly.

'I'll not put my hard-earned money on it, if you don't mind,' Gully said with a smile. People were daft to begin with, so you make a daft person scared and you have no idea what reaction you'll get. The most sedate people in the world turned into runners. Lovers became fighters. Nate knew that too by now, all the people he'd encountered.

It was a little after nine o'clock in the morning when Usman emerged through the front door and walked down towards his car. Nate was in the driver's seat. He opened the door, stepped out onto the street and started to move towards the target. Gully watched him from the passenger seat. Settling in to play the role of appreciative audience, ready to participate should the cast go off-script and need help. Nate was quick for a big man, moved softly along the row of cars parked at the side of the street.

Usman had a bounce in his step as he made his way down the stairs and out the front door. This close to having the short-arsed gunman work the job with him. Still might fall through, but he was starting to think he was a little too lucky for that to happen. The job on the bookies worked. This job would work. Just needed a good pickup point for the dealer and it would be note-perfect.

He pulled open the front door and skipped out of the building.

He had a habit of walking with his head down, shuffling along the pavement and looking at his feet as he went. He'd moved through the gate and onto the pavement by the time he bothered to glance up and see what was around him. Cars parked along the side of the street as usual. Someone walking on the road, a big man. Usman assumed he was crossing. Took a split second to realize the man was walking along the far side of the cars to keep himself out of Usman's view. A big man hiding, getting closer, Nate Colgan. Nate fucking Colgan.

Colgan moved between two cars and onto the pavement. Usman stood and looked at him. He could feel a stupid look of horror spread across his features, but he couldn't seem to persuade his face to smarten up. Colgan stopped a few feet in front of him.

'Usman, I want you to relax. I want you to come along and talk to me about something. You don't need to worry about it, nothing bad is going to happen to you. It's just me and I just want to talk to you about a friend of yours, that's all.'

Usman nodded. The most dangerous man in the city had a damn good reason to hate him and he was standing in front of him, telling him to do something. Of course he was going to nod.

'I'm parked down this way,' Colgan said, gesturing towards the bottom of the street. He stepped back to let Usman move past him, Colgan tucking in behind.

Usman walked ahead, looking down the street and not seeing anything threatening. He could hear Colgan behind him, keeping close. They were about the same height, well over six feet, but Colgan was much heavier, more muscular. Usman was thinking about Colgan as he walked. Older than Usman by at least a decade, maybe a decade and a half. Wouldn't have a gun on him, wasn't that sort of madman. With a few seconds of a head-start, Usman figured he could sprint away from this guy. If he picked the right moment to run, there was a chance. Any chance was more attractive than the thought of being tortured by Colgan.

Usman looked at the pavement, listened to the footsteps behind him, and then bolted. Took long, leaping strides as he sprinted down the street, hearing the growl from behind him as Colgan started to run. The footsteps sounded like they were falling behind, Usman finding a turn of pace he'd never known he had. No way Colgan would have caught him, but Usman hadn't seen the extra man sitting in the car. He should have gone onto the road and across the street, moved away from the place Colgan had told him to go. He wasn't thinking clearly enough for that. He ran alongside the cars parked beside the pavement. Ran alongside the one Colgan had wanted him to get into. The passenger-side door of that car opened just in time for Usman to crash right into it.

Gully opened the passenger door a second time, just as Nate reached Usman and grabbed him by the collar. Then he opened the back door of the car for Nate to shove the boy in, Gully dropping in beside him. A panting Nate got into the driver's seat, fumbling the switch as he got the car started. Usman sat silently, looking sideways at Gully.

'Good to see you again, young man. Been a while,' Gully said with a smile, and Usman grimaced.

They drove in silence. Usman had nothing to say, the situation was bad enough without his mouth making it worse, something one wrong word could do. Nate was concentrating on driving and cooling his temper, annoyed with the boy for running and with himself for not keeping up.

The place they were going to use had been empty for a long time. Years, probably. Nate had said there was a garage and a workshop, and that the workshop would be ideal for this. It was out back, away from the street, away from where anyone would hear a scream. If the boy tried to break loose, run for it, he would have to get out of that room and through the garage to make it to the street. The place was shut up when they arrived, the garage door locked, but Nate had a key.

Gully watched from the back of the car, Nate unlocking the door and pushing it up and over. Gully kept half an eye planted on Usman, waiting for him to do something else stupid. If he was going to, now was his last chance. Once they were inside the decisions were all Nate's to make. But the kid didn't look like he was going to do anything, sitting there, looking more impatient than anything. Looking like someone with something to say and wanting his moment to come soon. Gully hoped that when he did open his mouth, something smart fell out. Nate was looking for punishment, but a smart person could protect themselves from that with the right speech. Last thing Nate was going to do was cost his employer money by putting punishment first.

Nate got back into the car, drove them into the garage. It was dark in there; even in the daytime it was a grimy little hole of a building that could crush the spirit of any occupant. Usman didn't wait for instruction, knowing how this would play out. He got out and stood in the garage, waiting for the other two to tell him where to go. Nate led the way through to the workshop in the back, Gully taking up the rear to cover the only exit. There was a small chair with its back missing sitting in the middle of the room, like it was waiting for Usman to come and fill it.

'Sit,' Nate said to him.

Usman did as he was told. Sat down, his long legs stretched out in front of him. He looked up at Nate and Gully. 'Can I explain?'

Gully hung back at the door and watched. It wasn't up to him to get involved in a conversation. Nate was every inch the man in charge. If Nate needed help, Gully was there to provide it.

'What is there to explain?' Nate asked him.

You had to know Nate well to hear the annoyance in his voice. It was always that low grumble, and because of that it rarely gave anything away, which might have been the point. It was the speed he spoke at that Gully noticed. Nate was talking faster than usual, wanting to dish out a slice of revenge to one of the few people that had ever gotten the better of him. Holding back, because holding back was the professional thing to do. For now, anyway.

'I did that job at the bookies in Coatbridge,' Usman said.

There was confidence in his voice, defiance. He was scared, just not scared stiff. 'I didn't want anyone to get hurt on that job, right? It was supposed to be clean and easy but then you two turned up. Not that I'm blaming you for turning up, that's your job, I know. It just, you know, shat all over my plan. Anyway, I did it, and I'm sorry about the way it went down. Didn't ever mean for you or the bookie to get hurt, that was a shame. But that was a one-off. I ain't targeting you, or Peter Jamieson. I just target easy money, that's it. You got to understand, this wasn't part of anything bigger.'

Nate shrugged. 'I never thought it was.'

'And I'm working a new job right now. Me and my partner, right? We got something lined up. It ain't against Jamieson. In fact, you ask me, you should want me and my mate to make this job happen. It could do your boss a pretty big favour, if you let it happen. We do the work, take the risk, and you benefit.'

Nate didn't say anything at first. Gully smiled a little, making sure nobody was watching him when he did. This kid was just smart enough to live another day.

'So what do you think is going to happen here?' Nate asked him. 'You think I'm going to let you go back out there and work more jobs, just because you tell me my boss might benefit from one of them? You give me your word and that's supposed to be enough? You really think that's how it works?'

'I think,' Usman said, 'that I got a job lined up that would stick a spoke in a deal that's going to make Don Park a lot more powerful. I don't think you want that. I don't think your boss wants that. And, yeah, I think you should let me out of here. Let me go do this job. We do it, and Park gets held back. We don't do it, he makes a shitload of cash, and he becomes more powerful, maybe big enough to go to war with your organization before your boss gets out of jail.'

Gully straightened. These were awfully dangerous words for a kid to throw around. Talking about a war between Park and Jamieson, that was sticking your finger into a wound the rest of the industry was trying to ignore. Gully might not have paid an awful lot of attention to the industry in the last couple of years, but he knew enough to know that the Jamieson organization was desperately trying to avoid war until the boss got back on the street. You go to war without a chief and you've got a lot of Indians running wild. Park was the guy they feared most, too. If he took control of Alex MacArthur's organization, which he would as soon as the old man wheezed his last, then he would need to prove himself. Pick a target and destroy it, just to show that he could. Jamieson would be top of that particular list.

Nate, still standing in the middle of the room, looked down at Usman. The kid met his gaze. He was scared but strong, sure of his footing. Nate glanced across at Gully. Gully shrugged just a little.

'Right,' Nate said, 'tell us about this job.'

# 15

He hadn't had the chance to go out to Argyle's big house yet, that was for senior guys only. One day. One day soon, Aiden figured. He had this invite along to the office to meet him, which was more than most people got. An ordinary red-brick building that could have been flats or offices or anything else inside. Argyle had offices in there, took up a chunk of the first floor. A proper place, legit, on the books, the sort of place a big operation has so that it can clean all its money and pay all its taxes. Might have been a small office, but it was big-time.

Aiden was excited about going there and he was struggling to hide it, he knew how much this meant for his future. This was Argyle pulling him a little closer. This was Argyle telling him to come in and see what real power looked like, bask in it. It showed the progress he was making, how important this deal with the Allens was.

Aiden was about twenty minutes early, so he hung around out on the street. Smoked a cigarette, then worried about going into the meeting smelling like an ashtray. He chewed gum to get it off his breath, and spat the gum onto the pavement. Then he started worrying that Argyle had seen him from a window, spitting gum onto the street. Bad enough that he would see him hanging around, like he had nowhere else to go. He decided to go inside, it was nearly time.

Up the carpeted stairs and along to the first door on his right, knocking and going in. It was a reception area, he felt stupid for knocking. They should have had the fucking door open then, so that people could see that it was a reception area instead of knocking like it was a fucking office. He felt his face burning red as the receptionist watched him come in and close the door behind him. He walked across to her desk, trying to act a little cocky.

'I got a meeting with Mr Argyle,' he told her. He went for confident and came across stupid, and he knew it.

The woman, she must have been about thirty, was dressed primly with hair and make-up like she was in the 1950s. She gave him a smile that said she was smarter than him.

'Just one moment,' she said, and picked up a phone. She didn't say anything into the handset, not at first. Then: 'Yes, I'll tell him,' and she hung up. Made him feel more powerful to know that she only had to pick up the phone and they knew who she was calling about. It felt good to be expected. 'If you'd like to wait just a moment, someone will be out,' she said, nodding across to a row of three chairs against the side wall.

Aiden stood there for a couple of seconds, looking down at her. Sit and wait. He looked round at the chairs, back at the receptionist. She had that smile again, the one that said she had just enough patience to deal with the stupid person in front of her. He walked across and sat down on the middle chair. Didn't know what to do with himself now. Thought about taking his phone out, make it look like he was an important person with loads of messages to handle in these spare minutes, but then thought that might look disrespectful. If Argyle came out to greet him and he was sitting there dicking around with his phone it might look bad. So he sat and stared straight ahead.

It took a couple of minutes of awkward stillness and silence in the reception room before a door to the side opened and a young man came out. It wasn't Argyle; it was one of his men. Aiden had seen this guy around before, knew he was someone quite important called Liam Duffy. Younger than Aiden, yet more senior and more confident. He walked straight across to Aiden.

'Good to see you, come through.'

Maybe this was a good thing, Argyle sending his lackey out to lead Aiden through to the big office. Made it clear that Aiden was now more senior than Liam Duffy when Duffy did the fetching. There was a little swagger coming back into his step as he walked down a narrow corridor. Duffy ducked sideways into a small office, held the door open for Aiden to follow him in.

It was a narrow room, cramped, a large table filling the middle, chairs round it. Duffy sat at the head of the table, invited Aiden to sit with him. There was no sign of Argyle, or anyone else for that matter.

'We have the stuff,' Duffy told him casually. 'All of it. You need to get in touch with Allen's person and set up a meeting place. We want this done as soon as possible.'

Aiden nodded, looked back over his shoulder at the door, and nodded again. 'Sure, yeah, no problem. I'll call her. No problem, yeah. Plenty of places we can do it.'

'You need to pick somewhere appropriate,' Duffy told him, cutting across him and talking loud. There was no hint of respect in his voice. 'If you need us to come up with a few ideas for you, we can. We have a couple of places you can use, but you'd need to get their person to agree to it.'

Snotty little bastard, talking to him like he couldn't handle a handover. Fuck's sake, how many had he done in his career already? Okay, fine, maybe none this big, but the idea was the same. You give them the gear, they give you the cash, you both walk away. This prick hadn't done half the handovers Aiden had. He knew places he could use; he didn't need some silly wee bastard drawing up a fucking list for him.

'I got places,' he said. 'I don't need any help with it. Don't you worry, I can handle all of that. Anyway, they ain't going to come along to some place they know you use. Got to be neutral territory, that's how it works.'

Duffy gave him a dirty look. To Liam Duffy, Aiden was some halfwit who got lucky, a street dealer who happened to be able to get in touch with the Allens. That made him briefly useful. Once this was over there wasn't going to be any room for a guy like Aiden Comrie in Argyle's set-up. Duffy, he'd worked for his position, taken risks and done things a man like Aiden would never be capable of. Made mistakes as well, because that's how the business goes, but he was still a mile ahead of Aiden at a younger age because he was a much smarter man.

'Fine, you find somewhere, but make sure it's somewhere proper. Make it somewhere with more than one exit, we don't want people coming and going by the same doors. And make sure it's somewhere you can hang around awhile without getting noticed. We'll be nearby, of course. Me and a couple of the boys. We'll collect you and the money at the end of it, get you clear and safe. You call them, you tell them it's time to organize this. You let us know exactly where and exactly when it is going to happen so we can get the goods to you. Hey, you listening to me?'

Aiden had turned to look at the door again. Thought he'd heard someone coming down the corridor, hoped it was Argyle coming to meet him.

'I hear you,' Aiden said with a shrug. 'Set it up, let you know, I get it, fine. It ain't brain surgery, is it? I done this before, loads of times.' He paused. 'What about the boss? Doesn't he need to know about this?'

Duffy leaned back in his chair, a smug look. 'The boss

knows. I already talked to him about it, and I'll talk to him about it again in a wee while. Don't you worry about him, you worry about yourself. Worry about getting this right. Maybe worry about me as well, because *I'm* your boss on this, okay?'

Aiden shrugged, looked at the table, tried to summon up a tough look to shoot back at Duffy and failed. So he shrugged again, which was less of a response than he had hoped to conjure. They were back to treating him like a street dealer. He had met Argyle himself to set this up, but now that it was in motion it was being handed across to some guy who hadn't even been in the business as long as Aiden, hadn't worked nearly as many jobs.

Duffy could see the disappointment in Comrie. He had been honest, but he didn't want to lose this guy. Comrie was an idiot, but he was still the best chance they had of clinching a deal with the Allens and taking another big step forward in the industry. So he had to reassure him, lie to him a little, pat him on the head.

'Look, Aiden, Chris is a very busy guy. He's in meetings all day today. In meetings most days. That's the way it is now, with all the work we've got to cover. There's so much happening, and so much we got to do to cover it all. He can't be hands on with everything the business does; he'd need to be in ten different places at once. So sometimes guys like me have to do some of the organizing. Chris is still involved, still in touch with all of it, and you'll have another meeting with him straight after the handover. That's when he'll really want to talk to you.'

That was enough to persuade the easily persuaded. Aiden looked happy, impressed by the suggestion of legitimate scale that Duffy had thrown at him, looking forward to the prospect of meeting Argyle again after the handover had been a success.

'Sure, yeah,' he said with a nod. Thinking that in a year's time it would be him sitting at the head of the table, him in the position of power.

Duffy didn't bother with a friendly goodbye, just took him to reception and let the dumbass leave. He walked back down the corridor, past the office they'd used and into the one at the bottom. This one was about the same size, but there was only a single desk in it, a chair in front and shelves behind and to the side. Sitting behind the desk was Chris Argyle, a man in his early fifties, looking younger. An energetic man, an inspirer.

'How did that go?' he asked Duffy.

'About as well as expected. He's going to set up the meeting himself, didn't much like being offered help. I don't know, I suppose he might have enough experience to avoid screwing up the location, but I won't bet on it. I'll get a couple of the boys on it; make sure we have the building well covered. If anyone can find a way to fuck this up it's Aiden Comrie. The guy doesn't have a clue.'

Argyle gave him a measured look. 'We wouldn't have a deal

without him. If he hadn't worked for the Allens before, we would have no connection with them. He's useful and we need to get the maximum profit from that. But you're right, of course, he is just a street dealer and he doesn't have the smarts to handle all of this. That's why I've got you looking over the deal. You keep this under control and we'll have nothing to worry about. He doesn't understand all the things that could go wrong but you do. You need to have it covered.'

Duffy nodded, left his boss to it. This was a big moment for them, a chance to clinch a key deal. Argyle's set-up was already big, already lucrative, and this was a chance to lock them into the kind of long-term stability that the organization craved. It was true that they needed Aiden Comrie for the set-up, but it seemed daft to leave him in charge of the handover. He was a liability.

Aiden was out on the street, taking a walk back towards the city centre and dwelling on that meeting. He would soon be as important as that arrogant shite Duffy. Would only be months before he was strutting around that office building, acting like the big cheese. Time would come when he might be able to push Duffy aside, make him pay for his attitude. Yeah, that would be pretty sweet, Aiden at the head of the table lecturing Duffy on how to do his job. Right now he needed to get back to his car, get somewhere quiet and private and make the phone call to Sarah McFall. He was looking forward to that. Get that pretty blonde on the phone; get her running around to meet him. He would insist on it being his location, wouldn't let her make the decision, no matter how much she argued. Aiden was going to be commanding. That would show Duffy who was really in charge around here.

Aiden was thinking too much about how he was going to handle the future, not focusing enough on the present. He didn't notice the guy on the other side of the street, walking slowly and checking his phone. He was a short guy, shaven-headed, didn't stand out at all. Looked casual, like he didn't have a care in the world, but if you were observant and a little paranoid you might think it was funny that he was keeping exact pace with Aiden. But Martin was good at that. Didn't matter where he was, he could blend into the scenery, make himself seem like just another guy on the street. It was easy for him to tail Aiden, and text Usman the details as he went.

# 16

It had been a day since they sat him down in that garage and he talked his way out of a grave. Maybe they wouldn't have killed Usman, maybe they'd just have battered him badly enough to make him a walking advertisement for their revenge. Whatever, he had got out of it in one glorious piece, which was a significantly lower number of pieces than he had feared when they'd bundled him into their car. But it had changed everything.

The first thing he had to do was make sure that Martin didn't find out. That was key, and he had made it clear to Nate Colgan as well. Wasn't easy telling Nate Colgan anything, insinuating that you knew better than him, but he had. If Martin found out, he was likely to run for the hills, or wherever Czech people run for. Colgan agreed with a half-shrug. So they were keeping Martin in the dark, and that was why Martin was out tracking Comrie, happily oblivious to the new people looking over both their shoulders.

It was never going to be the same. Not now that he had someone the size of Nate Colgan on his back. There was a reason every single person in the city was intimidated by that man. A good reason, a bloody one. Usman had heard enough skin-crawling stories to know he wasn't going to defy Colgan.

What the big man said went, which meant Usman had to tailor every job from now on to make sure it suited him, or at least didn't offend his sensitivities. Usman wasn't naive enough to think it would just be this job and then he'd be free to do as he pleased. Once Colgan had him under the thumb, he was never letting him out.

That was the punishment. Work every job as though you're an employee of Peter Jamieson without having any of the benefits of actually working for the man. That was the high cost of stealing thirty-two grand from him. Colgan hadn't mentioned paying the money back. He would have, if it had just been about the beating. Every penny would have gone back, maybe with a little interest tacked on to act as compensation to the bookie. Now they were letting Usman and Martin keep the cash, but Usman was going to have to earn it.

There had been a knock on his door a few minutes ago. Usman didn't think a lot of it. People were always coming to see him, his brother, friends, Alison, Martin. Could have been someone looking to set up a job and hoping he would work it with them, that still happened even while he was lying low. He pulled the door open to find Gully Fitzgerald filling up his doorstep.

'Come in,' Usman said quickly.

Gully smiled and stepped inside. He was on his own, dressed like a middle-aged man out for a stroll in the sunshine. He looked so innocuous, if you didn't know him. But there were stories about Gully as well; he had a reputation of his own to scare the children with. And it didn't matter how far removed he was from the worst of those stories; he was still a big unit. Broad, tough, ready to knock you around if you happened to annoy him. The smile was designed to make you think that nothing could annoy him, that you were always safe. But it was a trap Usman had seen others use before.

'Something the matter?' Usman asked.

'Nothing the matter with me,' Gully said in his usual cheerful tone. 'Just that me and Nate think now would be a good time to go over some of the details about this job of yours. See if there's anything we can provide that gives you a better chance, you know. Make sure you have a proper chance of making it happen.'

'I do,' Usman said, trying to get a little cheerful confidence into his own voice. It would be good to have matching tones, he figured. Cheerful attitudes walking forward hand in hand in the spirit of newfound friendship.

'Aye, well, you might. I'm not saying you don't, but we can help to make sure that this job happens, and happens properly. That's a help to you, wee man, and you shouldn't be turning help away.'

They had gone through to the kitchen because that's where Gully had wandered unchallenged without knowing where he was going. He was sitting now at the small breakfast bar, looking back at Usman who was still standing in the door-way.

'So,' Gully said, 'details.'

Usman sighed to illustrate his reluctance, and then gave every detail he could think of. 'We're tailing Comrie right now. He's at Argyle's office as we speak, I figure that's them either giving him the stuff or telling him to set up the meeting before they give him the stuff. So we're a couple of days away from it happening, tops. They won't want this dragging on, not when they've got a dipshit like Comrie handling the handover. Longer he's involved, better chance of the whole thing going tits up. Once we know he has the stuff, the two of us will track him constantly. They're going to do the handover somewhere private. So we'll go and watch. We'll try and make sure that we don't go anywhere near the Allens' employee, keep them out of it. Safer that way, you know. Pick up Comrie and the cash after the handover and take him away, out of sight.'

'Take him away and . . . ?'

'Kill him, I suppose. Would be better if we didn't have to, but I don't see a way around it. We want to get him out of there, give ourselves enough time for them to think he's done a runner, go looking for him. No way of taking him quietly with-out him seeing us. That means there's only one ending for him if we want to stay anonymous. Can't take him and then let him go, that doesn't help us, so we kill him. That's what

Martin used to do, back in the old country. He was a gunman, and a bunch of other stuff, so we can handle that.'

Gully nodded. 'You think you have a chance of persuading them that he's run?'

'If he does the handover alone, then disappears with the cash, yeah.'

'He might do the handover alone,' Gully said with authority, 'but he'll be watched. A man like Argyle isn't going to let some random dealer go off-radar with his gear or his cash. He'll be watched all the time. That's why you're going to need some backup for this.'

Usman began to look doubtful, then doubted himself instead. 'You think?'

'Aye, I do, son. So you'll need someone to watch the watchers, make sure they don't nip in and block you off. We can take care of that. You and your man focus on what you've got to do. Track him; find out exactly where it's going to happen. The second you know, you call us. I don't care if that blows your cover with your mate; you're not getting this done safely without us. Then you go and pick him up as cleanly as possible. Get the cash, keep it. Kill him. That has to be done, there's no way out of this job otherwise.'

Usman nodded. 'Sure, yeah.'

Gully got up and smiled at him. 'We'll be waiting for your call then.'

\*

He let himself out, strolled back to his car. Gully wasn't in any rush, never was these days. Nothing to run for. Back when he was young, man, he never slowed down. Life was lived fast enough to blur at the edges. Attacking targets and intimidating everyone. Never kept track of days because they buzzed past at such a speed. Living fast was the only kind of life that mattered. But life found a way of slowing him down eventually. Meeting and marrying Lisa, trying for a kid for years. Then Sally came along, and Gully started thinking about surviving, rather than living. The priority was making sure he was around to see her grow up; protect her from mean people like him. Then she was stolen away from him anyway. He hadn't been motivated to live fast since. Life blurred only because he drank so much.

He would go and see Nate, tell him about the meeting with Usman. Let him worry about the details; let him worry about the dangers. There would be dangers to the job as well, Usman was gambling on this one and even the best-case scenario involved some kind of trouble. If he didn't have Nate and Gully breathing down his neck, he would probably have a contingency plan to pull out of the gig. Let the deal happen without interference. Couldn't do that now, no way Nate would let him. Usman was going to have to go through with it, whatever danger turned up to join him, and Gully and Nate were going to make sure that he could. They would have to work security for this job, and keeping a gunman and a thief safe from some established dealers was going to be risky. Riskiest job Gully had worked in years.

He wasn't nervous. It was the politics of it that always got under his skin. Taking risks with your own life for the sake of some employer you hardly knew. Shit, Gully had never even met Peter Jamieson, wouldn't get the chance until he got out of prison. You weren't even taking risks to protect that employer, just to shore up the profitability of his business. That's all this was, taking lives so someone else could make money. It was always that way. Used to be that Gully could accept it when he was making some money for himself, when he was earning for someone he knew and cared about. Old Danny Knight had been a likeable boss, treated him well. Money didn't seem like enough any more. Still, he would do it, because he had told Nate he would.

Nate had known for a while that Chris Argyle was cosying up to Don Park. Holding Don Park back was a priority. If he had Argyle supplying him, at a time when the Jamieson organization was struggling to replace its former supplier, that would put them in a position of weakness. Then you pile the Allens on top of that. Argyle supplying Park, the Allens distributing for him. That was the sort of flow that turned drugs into cash quickly and effectively, a much better set-up than the one the Jamieson organization was limping along with. Simple solution. Botch their deal and strangle it at birth. Argyle loses money, big money. The Allens find out that they won't be safe working with Argyle and Park, but they don't suffer from the lesson. Might want to use them in the future, so don't burn that bridge. Argyle, and by extension Park, is the enemy. The enemy suffers. You look stronger by comparison.

Would have been exciting, once upon a time. Let's hunt down our enemies. Let's scupper their deals, cost them a lot of money and weaken their ties. We'll risk our lives and we'll piss off some very tough people at the same time. Young men would be excited by it. The drama of the fight, the money and drugs involved, the people whose futures you were changing. That's why young men were the absolute worst ones to do it. They got excited and they revelled in it. Jobs like this should be done by people who recognized their real value. People like Gully, who understood there was nothing to get excited about.

# 17

Aiden hadn't even seen the gear; Duffy had it in the car in a big holdall that would be handed over at the last moment. There were three of them in the car with Aiden: Duffy and two big guys who hadn't felt the need to share their names. They were sitting in the back, looking ready for a fight. Eager for one, it seemed like, all twitchy movements and beady eyes. That worried Aiden. They might not have thought he was very bright, but he was smart enough to know that they shouldn't go into this looking for trouble. This situation needed to be kept calm. Aiden, in the passenger seat, kept glancing back over his shoulder at them, and it was annoying Duffy.

'Forget them,' Duffy said quietly. 'They're here for the worst-case scenario, nothing else. They know it. You just focus on *your* job.'

They were parked at the bottom of the street. Down in Govan, watching a large building that used to belong to an engineering firm and was now being converted into something else. The place was empty while the work went on. The inside of the building was gutted; plenty of builders there through the week but none on a Sunday. The street was basically empty.

'You're sure about this place?' Duffy asked him. Wasn't the first time he had asked him either and it was starting to grate. It was also feeding the sense of looming trouble for the two jackals in the back.

Aiden had picked it and Sarah McFall had been happy to use it. It was a perfect spot for this gig. A big building, lying empty. It was on a corner, so Aiden could get in one side and Sarah the other without their chaperones bumping into each other, because she would have people along for protection too. Meant Duffy could watch the place without anyone seeing them.

'It's a good spot,' Aiden told him. 'You don't need to worry about that. Trust me, yeah?' Trying to sound calm, but his heart was racing already.

They were both watching the clock on the dashboard. The plan was simple, like the best ones always were. Sarah goes in first, bang on five o'clock. At ten past, Aiden goes in by a different entrance. They make the exchange once they are both inside. Each of them will be alone, a third person appears and they walk away, no deal. They check each other's bag, and, if everything is satisfactory, Sarah leaves. Aiden waits ten minutes and then leaves. Basic, simple, sort of thing that leaves little opportunity for error. Makes it a little harder for any random passer-by to spot something untoward. Gives both sides the chance to get in and get away without ever crossing paths. That, Aiden thought as he looked back over his shoulder again, was a particular relief.

Eight minutes past five on the clock on the dashboard. Aiden glanced at his watch, it said nine minutes past. That was late enough. By the time he got the bag out of the boot of the car and got inside the building it would be ten past.

'Right,' he said loudly, trying to project confidence, 'I'm away in. Give me ten or fifteen minutes before you panic.'

Duffy looked at him with scorn, didn't say anything. Aiden got out of the car and walked quickly round to the boot. His nerves dictated that he move fast, too much energy to look casual. He opened it and found a large blue holdall. First time he'd seen it. He had to assume that the contents matched everything the Allens had put on their carefully considered list. He lifted it out, a little surprised at how heavy it was, but it was the good kind of surprise. It felt substantial, felt like the sort of weight a big deal could be built upon. He slung it over his shoulder and closed the boot.

Aiden could almost feel Liam Duffy watching him as he walked up the pavement towards the building. Duffy wanted him to fail, he knew it. That's why he had those two brainless thugs in the back of the car with him. He wanted to see Aiden stumble so that him and his two mates could go running in and rescue things, like they were the heroes of all this. He was threatened, that was why. Duffy was threatened by the good work Aiden was doing setting all this up, handling the handover. Aiden knew it was fear that made Duffy hate him.

One of Argyle's lads had been at the building earlier in the day, making sure the entrance Aiden was planning to use was unlocked. The door had two large pieces of metal propped in front of it, the builders presumably thinking it acted as an extra layer of security. They were worried about people vandalising the site over the weekend, using the place for improper purposes. No fear of theft, anything valuable would have been moved to the security of their own yard on Friday afternoon. One of the sheets of metal had been moved just far enough for Aiden to slip in behind it. Meant that he could pull the open padlock from the door without being seen from the street.

The place was cavernous inside. A tall and empty building, individual floors removed and dividing walls cleared before new and suitably modern units were built for new businesses to occupy. There were holes in the remaining walls, the signs of an old building being upgraded for a new purpose. There was plenty of light coming in, easy to see anyone waiting inside as soon as you entered. The ground- and first-floor windows had been boarded up, but there were plenty on what had once been the third floor that hadn't. Sarah was standing over by a much larger door near the corner on Aiden's left. She had a bag at her feet, smaller than his.

Aiden smiled and walked across to her, working to keep the smile on his face. He knew it looked as nervous as he felt.

'Hi, Sarah. I take it that bag's for me.' He'd been thinking about what to say for a few hours, how he wanted every part of the conversation to go. He had run through it so many times in his head that any deviation would throw him off.

Sarah, wrapped up in a dark coat, gave the bag at her feet a little kick. 'Check it,' she said. 'I don't want your lot complaining about anything afterwards. Make sure it's all there.'

'Yeah, sure,' Aiden said, stopping in front of her. He pulled the holdall round and passed it to her. 'Same for you. You know, check it.' It was going as planned, although he had sounded a lot more assured in his head.

Sarah didn't respond to being told something she already knew. Aiden placed the holdall on the floor and unzipped it, looking inside. She was being thorough, taking out bags, checking everything against the list she had memorized. Aiden tried to copy her work ethic, but there was less for him to do. He opened the small rucksack she was using and saw three light brown paper bags inside. They should contain £71,000, he knew that. He wasn't going to kneel there on the dirty floor, the knees of his trousers getting manky, counting every fucking note. He opened all three of the bags carefully, making sure not to rip them. They were all stuffed with cash, he could see that. Plenty of it as well, all looking legit. If he was smart he could have counted the amount in each stack and multiplied it to work out what was in each bag, but his brain couldn't possibly move that fast when he was calm, let alone under pressure.

Sarah took three or four minutes going through the bag, checking everything with a due care that seemed to come easy to her. Aiden stayed down on his knees with the rucksack for as long as she did, thinking it made him seem as professional as her, and long past the point where he had anything to count. She zipped the bag, grabbed the handles, stood up and pulled it round over her shoulder.

'Right, I'm happy. You happy?'

'Yeah,' Aiden said, 'totally happy.'

She nodded, giving him another superior look. Sarah turned and pushed open the large door, slipping out into the street, leaving Aiden alone.

Usman had provided the van. Turned up to collect Martin and took him straight down to Govan. They had watched Aiden pick the location, waited until he was gone before they went in and scouted it themselves. A quick look around and then planning their next move. They had agreed they would watch the building instead of Aiden from now on, Martin bringing a gun and Usman the van. Now they sat across the road, down towards the corner, watching the entrance as Sarah McFall went inside.

'We wait for her to leave,' Martin said. Couldn't do the job with her there, so if he left first then it was just too bad, they would have to call the thing off.

'Aye,' Usman said, 'sure.' Didn't sound certain, but he was playing along.

They sat and watched the large door Sarah had entered through. It looked like a fire exit at the moment, leading out onto the side street. Chances were it would become a gleaming glass entrance for some of the companies that would work out of the site when the units were sold. Small hi-tech firms, start-ups replacing the old industry.

'Be ready to run in as soon as she comes out,' Usman said. Leaning forward in the van, his hand on the handle of the driver's door.

'Let her get away first,' Martin said.

The car she'd arrived in was parked up the street, two other people in it, waiting for her to return. They had to let that car get out of sight, and Martin knew they would have time. If she left first, Comrie would give her at least a five-minute head start.

'When she has left in that car, you drive up and park right beside the door. Even if we are not supposed to park there, you park there. Make it as close to the door as we can get.'

Usman nodded. That made a lot of sense, making sure the distance they had to move Comrie and the money was as short as possible.

McFall came back out the door and walked quickly down

to the car, a different bag slung over her shoulder from the one she had taken in. The deal was done, and the money was now in Comrie's possession. The car started before she reached it, pulled away as soon as she had yanked the passenger door shut. Usman drove the van quickly towards the side door, doing a sharp U-turn in the street and then stopping.

He had to give her ten minutes. Hang around in this empty building and wait for her to get away before he let himself be seen on the street. It was the polite thing to do, the professional thing. It was that sense of professionalism that Aiden was determined to develop. They'd respect him then. But ten minutes, on your own, in a completely empty building, worrying about the police barging in, that's tough. Hard to persuade yourself that nobody saw you coming in and called the cops because they thought you were a vandal or a thief. So he started trying to work out how long it would take the police to get there if someone was smart enough to think he was suspicious. Two minutes? Three? He glanced at his watch. Twenty-one minutes past five. Three minutes since she left. Another seven to wait. Okay, let's say five, round it down. No reason for Aiden to give her the full ten minutes when eight would serve the same purpose.

Aiden put the rucksack down on the floor again and unzipped it. Might as well have a look at the money for five minutes. It would be a fun and reassuring use of time. Good to see the success in paper form, hold it and smell it. There couldn't be many in the industry who managed to arrange and carry off a deal this big. This would always be on his CV, the man who brought Chris Argyle and the Allens together. He opened one of the paper bags and took out a couple of small bundles of cash, just revelling in the weight of wealth. He thought about pocketing one. No, they'd notice a whole bundle missing and they wouldn't react well to someone screwing them. Maybe slip a few notes out of a couple of bundles, make it look like the Allens miscounted. Was it worth it? It would make it look like the Allens weren't careful when they were paying their money, and that would piss off Argyle, maybe even jeopardize the deal. No, a hundred quid in his pocket wasn't worth that. He needed this deal to be a complete success. That would be worth a hell of a lot more than a hundred quid to him.

He heard a vehicle on the road outside and paused. Could be the police, or Sarah again. The door scraped behind him as someone carefully pushed it open. Must be Sarah coming back with the bag. Shit, must be something wrong with the gear, he thought. Might be time to work some damage-limitation on the pretty blonde. He stuffed the money back into the ruck-sack and zipped it shut in a hurry. Didn't want her realizing that he'd been thinking of pocketing some, even if he'd decided against it. He spun round and stood up in one movement, getting a smile on his face for her, ready to smooth over whatever complaint she had. But it wasn't Sarah McFall. It was two young men, their faces showing. The white one, he was shorter, and he was pointing a gun at Aiden.

It wasn't hard to keep everyone in view. The key was getting access to a building across the street from the handover spot. They had minutes to get in, get a good view of events developing. Usman had texted Gully with a location, told him that Comrie was already there but hadn't gone in yet. Nate and Gully rushed down in a transit van designed to fit right into this area. They knew that the business would have started by the time they got there, but the start didn't matter.

'There, that's the building,' Gully said.

Nate slowed down. There was very little traffic, hardly any cars parked at the side of the road. This was a place people came to work, and very few of them came to work here on a Sunday.

'There's a van up there,' Gully said, looking up the adjoining street. 'Arse facing us, can't see if anyone's in it.'

Nate kept going straight and steady, not accelerating much as they moved down the street.

'There,' Gully said from the passenger seat. 'Left-hand side, gaggle of pricks in a car.'

Nate drove past, neither him nor Gully looking down at Liam Duffy and the muscle he had sitting in the back of his car. Didn't want to alert them yet. Then they turned into the yard of another big building much further down the street. They were just about out of view of Duffy, but it didn't take much effort for Nate and Gully to get a look at the back of Duffy's car.

'Must have started the job by now,' Gully said casually.

Nate didn't say anything. *Should* have started the job by now wasn't the same as must have. The van on the adjoining street could have belonged to anyone. Could have been the Allens' people, or it could have been Usman. None of that mattered. What mattered was Usman and his pal getting their end of the job done properly. If they did, then Nate could make this a very bad day indeed for Chris Argyle. That's why they were watching Duffy, waiting for him to catch on to the fact that his pal wasn't coming back out of that building with the cash.

'I'll be taking that,' Usman said to Aiden, striding across and pulling the rucksack from his grasp. Aiden didn't do anything to stop him. 'Come on,' he said, shoving Aiden towards the door Sarah had used.

'What is this? Hold on, no, hold on,' Aiden said, trying to resist.

Martin moved a step closer, the gun pointing at Aiden's head.

'Whoa, all right, come on, fuck's sake. What is this, huh? What is this, guys?'

'Don't sweat it,' Usman told him, moving across to the

door and pulling it open. He seemed casual, talking in a friendly tone. 'This is just business, you know how it is. Business. We'll be done in half an hour.'

Aiden nodded at the word business. Sure, business, he was all about business these days. He couldn't work out what sort of business these guys had though. Were they working for the Allens? They weren't the two from the back of the car but that didn't mean they weren't working for Argyle either. Maybe they were going to count the money with him before it went to Duffy. But why the gun? That intense-looking little guy with the shaved head, still pointing the gun at him.

'Who are you guys with? Is it . . . ? Who?'

Usman stopped and looked at him. He was starting to lose patience; he wanted Comrie out of here by now. Look at this mug, desperate to believe the best of the situation he was in. Not smart enough to see the worst-case scenario standing right in front of him. He could be spun a story.

'We're working for Don Park. You know of Don Park?'

Aiden paused. It was hard to think fast under the pressure of a pointed gun. Don Park. He knew who Don Park was, of course he fucking did. He was the guy Argyle was working with on this. Hell, he was bigger than Argyle.

'Will I meet him?' Aiden asked hopefully.

Usman smiled. 'Not if you're just going to stand there. We need to be quick here, Aiden.'

Aiden nodded, obviously trying to play this right. Looked

like a man wanting to make a good impression on Don Park, boost his standing. He walked to the door, Usman ahead of him and Martin slipping in behind, lowering his gun but keeping the same focused look. Usman looked past Aiden briefly, got a slightly stunned shake of the head from Martin. This person was a clown. That didn't deserve a shake of the head in Usman's opinion; clowns were the very best people to steal from.

Usman stuck his head out the door, looked down to the corner on the left. If Comrie's backup were going to approach, that's the way they would have to come. There was nobody there. The light blue Mercedes van Usman had borrowed for the day was parked at the kerb in front of them. Usman stepped out and slid the large side door of the van open, smiling to Aiden as the dealer stepped past him and into the back. Martin followed Aiden, still shaking his head slightly. Usman closed the door.

Another look up and down the street before he got in the front of the van. Still nobody there. They were going to pull it off. They were actually going to get out of here with the cash. This was working. Maybe the dirtiest part was still to come, but this was the obstacle they were most likely to trip over. He jumped into the driver's seat and threw the rucksack into the foot-well on the passenger side. He started the van and pulled away, watching his mirrors constantly as he went, trying to make sure he drove at a speed that drew no attention. Looking for threats, and looking for allies as well. He didn't want either coming into view.

They were out of the van, at the edge of the yard, looking back up the street at Duffy's car. It was schoolboy stuff, sneaking around like this, trying to catch a glimpse of the enemy. Nate looked at his watch. Jesus, what was taking this long? That wouldn't have been Sarah McFall's van parked on the other side of the building. She would have used a car, made sure she had something that didn't in any way stand out wherever it was she was taking the drugs, rather than picking a vehicle for this location. That big van had to be what Usman was using. Get Comrie into the back of it, out of view of the passing world, and get away.

That meant they should be out by now. The time it took Nate and Gully to get down to this yard, turn the van to face the exit and then stand here gawping back up the street like a couple of old women was time enough to get Comrie out. Then it became a question of how long Duffy was prepared to wait before he went looking for awkward truths. A couple more minutes, at the most.

'If they let him go,' Gully said, 'this whole thing is fucked anyway.'

'They won't.' Nate spoke quietly.

'I don't know, that boy's a bit wishy-washy. He's only in it for the cash.'

225

'He'll do it,' Nate said. 'Not for the cash, it's about having to explain to you and me why he let Comrie walk away . . . There, they're getting out of the car.'

Gully looked up the street, saw the driver's door and the two back doors of Duffy's car opening. Nate was already round to the driver's side of the van. They waited about ten seconds, long enough for the three men to approach the door of the building, and pulled out of the yard. Shit, they were already inside, young men moving faster than these old men expected. Nate raced the van along the street and screeched to a halt outside the door of the building. Then they were out – and into the building in seconds, just quick enough to cut Duffy off.

Nate and Gully more than filled the doorway, both standing expressionless. Duffy stopped still, his breathing becoming heavier as his mind and heart raced. Nate and Gully didn't need to act threatening, didn't need to introduce themselves upon arrival. If you knew who they were then you knew what this meant, and Duffy clearly knew. His muscle did not. One of them started laughing at the older men blocking the exit. The other one pulled a knife from his trousers.

Gully, still expressionless, opened his thin jacket and took out a small handgun. He wasn't going to use it, not even as a last resort. He wasn't a gunman, never would be. He ruined lives, he didn't end them. Hated guns as well, they spoiled a good fight and got you into more trouble than you could handle. These kids didn't know any of that though, they couldn't see past the gun to the reluctance of the holder. The one with the knife dropped it with a clatter.

'Nate, right,' Duffy said. He was nervous, obviously, but holding it together. Talking with an authority he clearly found natural.

Nate nodded very slightly. 'Liam Duffy. How is Mr Argyle these days?'

'Always looking for good help.'

A good answer. Nate laughed. 'I'm sure he is. He could certainly use it. Fancy sending one of my guys in here with a big bag full of drugs to collect a big bag full of cash. Not the sort of thing a good employee would allow to happen.'

Duffy smiled, but it was a shoddy attempt at covering his nerves. His stomach was churning, failure punching him in the gut. Aiden Comrie, working for Peter Jamieson. His first instinct was that it wasn't plausible. That brainless nobody, working a scam this effective for a man as serious as Nate Colgan. No, that couldn't be right. But the evidence was looming over him. Comrie gone and neither the drugs nor the cash left behind. Nate Colgan and Gully Fitzgerald, standing in the doorway, gloating. The evidence was too much to argue with.

'So Comrie's with you, huh?' Duffy said. He could feel the nerves radiating off the muscle standing behind him. They were in a spot where they might get shot, and that scared the crap out of them. Best-case scenario, they were about to be associated with an embarrassing failure. This was, if they were lucky, a very bad career move.

Nate just smiled at the question. Stood there and smiled. Don't go into detail when detail could expose your lies. He wanted Duffy to think that Comrie had gone of his own free will, that they'd failed to spot the traitor in their midst. Never tell the world you killed a man if the world is willing to believe something else. It was too late for them to get him back now anyway, but Nate wanted to make this failure as big as possible. Make it as dispiriting and damaging as he could. It would make the deal between Argyle and the Allens shaky. The Allens get their produce but Argyle loses his money and won't get it back. The Allens get annoyed about being so close to a publicly botched job and begin to question the wisdom of working with Chris Argyle. But the big one, the one that matters most, is the unrepresented man, Don Park. He sees Argyle making a spectacular bollocks of a relatively simple job, finds out he hired a man who was working against him and got himself set up. That was going to damage the relationship between Park and Argyle, maybe irreparably.

'So, uh, what now, huh?' Duffy's asking. Showing weakness, giving all the power over the situation to the other side.

Nate shrugged. 'I think we're just about done here, don't you? Unless you boys have anything else you'd like to say, hm? Any message you'd like us to take back to our bosses. You already know the message you have to take back to yours.'

Duffy scoffed, a belated attempt to downplay the situation that fooled no one.

'Right then,' Nate said with a smile. 'Thanks for the cash, boys; you have yourselves a safe journey home.'

Nate and Gully turned and left. They made it look as casual a departure as possible, but both of them were alert for an attack. Not from Duffy, he knew better than to try and rescue a lost situation. One of the muscle might have been stupid enough to try their luck once they saw a back turned towards them. They didn't. Nate and Gully got into the van and drove away.

This had been Nate's gig. If there was someone to report to, to claim glory from, then he could do it himself. Gully was happy to be dropped off at home.

'Make sure you get rid of that gun,' was the last thing he had said as he got out of the van. He had put the small handgun into the glovebox, Nate assuring him that he was going to get rid of it before he did anything else. Guns were treacherous little bastards; Gully couldn't remind Nate of that often enough.

Usman drove for a couple of minutes, all three in the van sitting in silence. Nobody was following them, they were clear. He relaxed, took a quick look over his shoulder at the two men in the back of the van.

'Won't be long now, Aiden,' Usman said with a broad

smile. 'We'll get this done as quick as possible; no point making life any more awkward than it has to be. Just business, you know.'

'Yeah, yeah, business, good,' Aiden said, and he smiled.

He was a businessman now. Thinking about meeting with Don Park. What would he say to a man that senior? It was a chance to make a better first impression. This was a clean slate. Tell Park how much he'd like to work for him without coming across as a crawler, that was the challenge. He had another chance to impress a senior man, and his heart was starting to beat fast. First the Allens, then Argyle and now Park. Those kind of connections made him senior, too.

'Is this going to take long?' he asked the little guy with the gun, sitting in the back of the van with him.

The skinhead shrugged, like he didn't know and he didn't care. Another one who thought he was above talking to people like Aiden. Aye, fine, be like that, but his attitude would change when he was taking orders from Aiden, probably not long from now. That was a great thought.


Lisa was in the kitchen, sitting at the table with her laptop open. A short woman with short blonde hair, a brittle look. Gully touched her shoulder as he walked past, went over to the fridge and took out a carton of orange juice. He wouldn't be hungry; they'd had a big lunch. That was traditional, a big Sunday lunch. Lisa spent all morning cooking it. Get the family sitting down round the table for a roast dinner. Of course, the family just meant the two of them now, but they kept to the routine, all the family habits they'd developed with Sally over the years. It was a little part of clinging on to her.

'You weren't long,' Lisa said.

Gully was filling a glass. 'No, not long,' he said, which was as much as he planned to tell her about his working day.

She watched him walk over and sit at the table, that forceful look he got when he knew he wasn't entirely welcome. He was just getting in her way, annoying her, but he seemed to consider it a necessary evil. They needed to talk more, Lisa knew it. It went in cycles, sometimes they had a normal, functioning marriage in which they spoke to each other often and seemed to get along. Then there were the other times. Times that could last for weeks or months when they hardly spoke and everything they said seemed to annoy the other. At least this time they both knew what had sparked the fresh hostility, it was him going back to work. Lisa had told him so, and didn't think she should have to tell him again.

'Anything doing?' she asked him. There wasn't a hint of interest in her tone, but that didn't matter. Him sitting there had forced her to say something.

'Not really, no,' he said. He wasn't going to tell her that he'd been pointing a gun at a bunch of drug dealers, pissing off the sort of people who were stupid and violent enough to come looking for revenge. Lisa had no interest in the things that he did. 'What about you?'

Lisa looked at him with a frown. 'I've been sitting here doing nothing. You're the one who went running off God knows where.'

He nodded. 'It was nothing really. Just making sure of security somewhere. Done now. Good to get a wee bit more cash in the pocket. I was thinking, maybe we should look at booking a holiday for this summer. Don't want to leave it any later than this. We can afford it this year.'

She glanced at him and then back at the screen, reluctant to show any enthusiasm. She was thinking about Sally. Thinking about holidays they took with her and thinking it was wrong for them to enjoy a holiday without her. The last one they'd been on, the only one since Sally died, had been miserable, guilt smashing any enjoyment.

'I don't know,' she said. 'Maybe it would be better to stay at home this year.'

Gully nodded, didn't say anything. He had never been the sort of man to try and force his wife into doing something she didn't want to do. He would sit down at the table and nudge her into a conversation but he wouldn't go further than that. He understood that this was a slow process. He took a gulp from the glass, emptying it, and got up.

'Well,' he said, walking across to the sink, 'maybe we can

think about it for a week or two. Maybe then,' he said with a shrug, not finishing the sentence.

Trying to buy himself a little time, a couple of weeks to bring a little optimism back into their lives. Lisa stared at the screen of the laptop, considering whether a holiday might actually help them both. Not to forget Sally, they would never do that, but to live a life around the grief that her death had caused. Have a few weeks together, away from all the reminders, happy. The thought of being genuinely happy again. It seemed impossible.

# 18

Usman kept on driving. Aiden just sat there, watched Martin and occasionally looked out the front of the van. If there was anything going through his head, any thought that this might not be what they had told him it was, then he didn't show it. There was no visible sense of concern. No questions, no attempt to jump either of them and take control of the situation. He accepted it.

Usman checked the mirrors constantly. Making sure Aiden wasn't playing up, making sure they weren't being followed, increasingly confident that he had nothing to worry about on either score. Checking Martin as well, looking for nerves. There hadn't been any when he took a gun into the bookies, but he hadn't had any intention of using it then. This was different. This was Martin going into the job knowing it could only be successful if he pulled the trigger and killed a man. Every time Usman caught a glimpse of the gunman, though, there was no sign of nerves. No sign of anything. He looked the same as he always looked, disinterested, calm. That was Martin. The same old Martin.

'Not long now,' Usman said over his shoulder for the third

or fourth time. He was trying to kill the nerves before they could be born.

He had gone in with the intention of forcing the moron into the back of the van, and Comrie had removed that need. He had given them a hand, walking into it quite happily. This job would have fallen down if they'd been trying to catch a smart man. Even a dumb man who understood the danger he was in. They had lucked out.

They were heading out towards Bridge of Weir. Aiden wasn't too concerned by the change of scenery, city replaced with increasingly green landscape. In his mind, he was thinking that this made sense. A meeting like this, this big, you don't conduct in public. A man like Don Park will have all his meetings off the radar, somewhere that the chance of being discovered is as small as possible. Getting out of the city, that was getting way off the radar. That, somehow, just about added up to Aiden.

Usman pulled onto the track leading up to the farmhouse. The metal gate was closed. He stopped and got out of the van, moving quickly, worried that if Aiden was going to do something he would do it now. He didn't. Usman was back in the van and through the gate, stopping again to get out and close it. He drove slowly up the hill to the farmhouse.

It was a recently renovated building, and the barn across the yard was obviously new. The metal shined, there was no rust, it looked like a farm just about to open for business. Actually, it had just closed. The renovation of house and barn, the purchase of new equipment, had been made by someone with a dream of being a farmer. Reality bit hard. The place went bust before it really got started.

Usman parked beside the barn, out of view of the gate, switched off the engine and looked back over his shoulder again, smiling at Aiden.

'Right then, we're here. This'll be quick, just meet and greet and confirm the deal. Keep it quiet, no talking back, and don't go acting all surprised with things either.'

'Sure, no, I got it,' Aiden said with an authoritative nod. These guys were being more respectful than Duffy, treating him almost like an equal, so he was going to play at being casual with them. Agree with them; make this run as smooth as possible. Well, the driver was respectful anyway. The other guy, the one in the back with the gun, he was just silent. Looked bored and miserable. Maybe he knew he wasn't needed and that annoyed him. Well, it was too bad, because this was going to go the right way. Everything was going the right way for Aiden all of a sudden.

Usman got out of the van and slid the side door open. It opened on Martin's side, but the gunman nodded for Aiden to go first. Didn't bother Aiden. They were being cautious. Ultra cautious, in fact, and that was actually reassuring. People around Don Park probably always behaved like this with new people. Just something else to get used to when you're moving in these elevated circles.

'In the barn,' Usman said, leading the way across to the sliding double doors.

Aiden laughed, then stopped himself. If this was how Don Park did his security then good luck to him. Why not? Places people wouldn't ever expect you to have a meeting were the safest places of all. He walked behind Usman, heard Martin stepping out of the van. Usman fiddled with the lock and slid open one of the barn doors. He stepped through, waiting for the other two to follow him.

It was quite dark inside. There was one window but it was small, at the back of the barn, and didn't allow a lot of light in. The place was completely empty. The stalls that had been intended to hold animals were gone. Just the concrete floor, scratched as people dragged equipment and valuable metal away.

Aiden looked around, couldn't see Park, or anyone else, anywhere. That was okay, made some sense when you stopped to think about it. Get the less important people into the barn first, and then Park comes over from the house. Better that than Park waiting around in here when he didn't know how long Aiden would be. There was really no scenario here that Aiden couldn't find a justification for in his own mind. Everything was fine, everything was going to be brilliant, just play along with it.

The barn door scraped shut. Aiden turned round to smile again, keep it casual. He turned to see the silent one pointing a gun at his head. A flash and a bang. He never worked out what was happening to him, not even in that last second. He kept the smile on his face as he collapsed backward and crashed onto the floor.

It happened much faster than Usman expected. He was standing back by the door, waiting for Martin to say something first. He didn't. He stepped forward and raised the gun, Aiden turned round and Martin shot him in the head. It took three seconds, tops. The bang was louder than Usman had expected as well. He had ducked, trying to escape the sound. He gasped a few times, and saw Martin look round at him, expressionless. That forced Usman to stand up straight, try and match the cold and professional stance of his colleague.

'You have the tools to bury him with?' Martin asked.

'Yeah,' Usman nodded. 'I got the stuff, in the van. I'll, uh, I'll get it.'

He slid the door open and stepped out into the bracing air. Thank God for fresh air. He looked off down the track as he went back to the van, nobody coming. No way anyone was close enough to hear that gunshot, not with the sound kept mostly inside the barn; but someone might have seen the van, might be curious. He had explanations lined up. Working for an engineering company or the plumbers, come to do a repair on the property before it goes back on the market, something like that. Good enough at a pinch, but it wasn't going to explain them burying a body here.

While Usman got the gear, Martin was in the barn, leaning down beside Aiden. Checking for the kind of trouble that could spoil a good job. Good old Aiden, making this as easy as possible. His thick head had kept the bullet in. An exit wound would have meant more cleaning up; looking for bullet fragments and bits of skull. Now there was much less blood, too. The place wouldn't be forensically clean, but there would be nothing for the naked eye to see. He took a cloth from his pocket and wiped at the small stain on the concrete beside the body, then pressed it onto the entry wound. He slid his hand into Aiden's pockets. There was a wallet and some keys that would be ditched. The phone he found was much more of a problem. Couldn't have done anything about it while the dealer was still alive. Aiden had been dumb enough to take it with him, but not so dumb as to have it switched on. That was a start. The door slid open and Usman came back in with a couple of sheets and a couple of shovels.

'Put the sheets beside him, open,' Martin said. He was prepared to talk Usman through the process if he needed to. It didn't seem as though the younger man had any experience at this, so the gunman needed to find his voice. People with no experience always got jittery in front of the body, always made mistakes. People thought they were tough, thought that working in the business made them immune to the terror of this, but they were wrong. Death, when it was lying right in front of you, was always horrifying. Even to Martin, who had met it many times before. It was too big, too final, the consequences of being involved too huge, to ever stop being frightening.

That Usman didn't seem nervous was a testament to his acting ability. He moved quickly across, put the shovels down out of the way, and laid out the sheets next to the body. He did it quickly and quietly. Noticed the wedding ring on Comrie's left hand, cursed the fact that someone would be waiting for him to come home. Without being told, he moved to grab Aiden's feet and lift him up. Martin took the top end, where the blood was coming from. They placed him near the edge of the larger sheet, lined up straight and pulled it tight over the top of him.

Martin opened the back of the phone and took the SIM card out, doing his best to fold and damage it, make it unreadable. He put the phone down on the sheet and ground his heel into it, listening to the satisfying crunch of plastic. He would throw the SIM card out the window on the way back into the city. It wasn't perfect, or anything close, but it was the best of a bad situation. A compromise solution because this was a job done on the hoof.

They began to roll Aiden into the sheets. It wasn't as tight as Martin would have liked, but it was good enough.

'We'll take the shovels first,' Martin said. 'You show me where.'

Usman led him round the back of the house and down a small hill to a copse of trees. The trees looked young, relatively, and there weren't enough of them to provide a perfect shield, but it would do. There was no other building in view, little likelihood of being spotted. There was a longer-term worry. How long would it be before anyone stumbled across the body? In a place like this, it should be years. If they buried it deep enough, maybe decades. Not much chance people would be digging around here for housing or industry, so it should be safe long enough. But it wouldn't be as good as burying in proper woods, way off in a national park somewhere. There, you know the body will probably never be found, unless you make some stupid mistake. Here, a future farm owner could just decide to pull up the trees and build on the spot, however unlikely it seemed. That was the risk.

They found what Martin judged to be the best spot, as far out of view as possible, and they started to dig. It was tough, exhausting, neither of them used to that sort of physical effort. Martin huffed and made noises indicating misery; Usman didn't feel he had earned the right to complain, although the sweat was pouring off him and his arms burned. He hadn't pulled the trigger. Wouldn't matter much to a judge, but it mattered to him. Someone else had done the worst part, done it without hesitation, without thought, so that he didn't have to. Martin was a killer with experience.

'That will be enough,' Martin said.

It seemed deep to Usman. It had seemed deep enough for a while, but, again, he wasn't going to be the first to suggest it. The man who pulled the trigger called the shots. Martin was the calm one, the expert in this situation, and Usman would follow where he led.

They clambered out of the hole, making more mess as they did, and walked back up the hill to the barn. It was starting to get gloomy overhead. The cover story about being tradesmen working on the house would start to get flimsy if they were there late into the night. If they could fill the grave in quickly, they would be out of there in half an hour. That would do.

Aiden felt heavier than he looked. Usman took the head-end this time; it seemed like the decent thing to do. He was bigger than Martin, younger.

It was a struggle getting the body down the hill, and Usman wished he had picked out sheets that weren't a dazzling white. Hadn't thought about them increasing their chances of being seen when he took them out of his cupboard and put them into the van.

They weren't gentle with him at the grave. Dropped him in heavily, grabbed their shovels and started to fill in the hole. The truth was that Martin didn't have a lot of experience with burials either. Killing he had done before, but his usual routine was to pull the trigger and then make an escape. He'd only been involved in one burial before this and had no idea if what he was confidently claiming was the right way to do it was indeed correct. But the body was in the hole, the soil filled in and the turf back on top and that much felt right to both of them. There was, though, some extra soil in the grass around them and you could see that a rectangular hole had been dug here. It didn't look great.

'It will do,' Martin said quietly, and hoped he was right.

They walked back up the hill and put the shovels into the back of the van. Martin took a last look in the barn to make sure there was nothing they had missed, no visible blood spots or personal items that had fallen out of Aiden Comrie's pockets. The place was clear, and they got into the van. It was a relief for them both to get out of there. They shut the gate behind them, and Martin dropped the SIM card out the window at high speed as they made their way back into the city. They stopped in a garage on the south side to switch out of the van and into Usman's car.

'I'll come back for this later,' he said.

They drove up to Usman's flat and got the rucksack inside. They worked more quickly than they had after the bookies job, separating the cash into two piles and counting through it. Seventy-one thousand, two hundred pounds, exactly. Minus the cost of the gun and the unrecorded hire of the van, they were left with £35,050 each, in cash. It felt like an intimidating amount of money to carry around for both of them. They left the flat, Martin with his money bulging in a bag Usman gave him.

The van, the gun, the shovels, they were all Usman's burden to shoulder. Up to him to get rid of everything they had used on the job. That's how it was for Martin. It was a truth he learned early, you do the point and click of killing, other people usually do everything else. Usman dropped him off about half a mile from his house and Martin walked the rest of the way.

Joanne was in the kitchen. Skye was skulking about in the city somewhere, spreading her misery to the masses. Martin stuck his head round the door, didn't go in.

'I'm going up to change,' he said quietly.

She heard him going upstairs but couldn't hear what he was doing there. There was a good chance she would find out, see some hint that led her to work out what he'd been doing. She already knew she wouldn't make a fuss about it. A relationship built on desperate silence. In his world, it probably had a better chance than one built on the old-fashioned cliché of openness.

Joanne heard him coming back downstairs.

'Have you eaten?' she asked him.

'Yes,' he said casually, after a split-second pause to think about it. He hadn't eaten, but he wasn't hungry. Nowhere close to hungry. Never was after that sort of job. Killing a man took all his energy away from him. He just wanted to go and sleep, but he wouldn't, not with Joanne around. It would make her uncomfortable to see him behave differently from his routines, and he'd do nothing that made her uncomfortable. Nothing that might help her remember this day and his movements on it.

'Busy day?' she asked him. Looking at him with an expression that said she didn't really want to know. A look that understood that the truth should have no place in his answer.

'Quite busy. You?'

She smiled at his attempt to move the conversation away from his work. Joanne still got it. Martin did things he didn't want to talk about and that she didn't want to hear about. He made money in ways that he shouldn't. She could accept that early on, when she wasn't sure if this would last, but that acceptance would dim as the seriousness of their relationship became clearer. The more unmentionable work she thought he was doing, the more worried she'd get. At some point, she was sure, he would do something that horrified her. Or someone was going to do something to him that crushed her. The fear of that day arriving was beginning to make its mark.

# 1.29 a.m.

The pain in his wrists has dulled. The biting of the plastic strips has fallen into a steady ache that he can almost live with. Martin's legs are stretched a little, he's moving them as much as possible, getting the blood flowing. It's taken some of the edge off the physical pain. He knows what's happening. The dull aches will make it impossible to stand up when he needs to; will make it almost impossible to fight for his life. That's why he's moving, exercising, doing all he can to be ready for the moment they come back.

Think about the pain. Think about them coming for him. Don't think about her. Joanne. Sitting at home, waiting for him. Knowing that he's out on a job because this time he insisted on telling her. Worrying about what's happened to him. Then he doesn't turn up. She'll wait days, hoping, believing there's still a chance. Then what? Maybe she'll just give up on him, decide that he might have done a runner, or that he might have been killed on a job. What can she do about it? She won't go to the police, and he wouldn't want her to. That would get her into trouble for hiding everything she suspected about Martin since they met, and get her into trouble with the people responsible for this, too.

It's the uncertainty, that's what would do so much harm to her. Thinking that he might still be alive. That he might have run out and left her, his story about a dangerous job a lie to provide him with a route out of their relationship. That's the last thing he would want her thinking. It's felt as though they've been slipping apart lately. Not deliberately, neither of them seeking separation. Just the consequence of him working this job. A consequence of the decision that he would keep her in the dark.

Go back in time. Go back and tell her that he wants this to be a totally honest relationship, where nothing is kept a secret. He tells her about the attack on the bookies and how carrying that out brought him up against people like Nate Colgan. How being an enemy of Nate Colgan is the sort of thing that gets you killed in this city. She would have talked some sense into him then, would have made sure he didn't get involved in anything even more dangerous. Or maybe she would have said nothing. Maybe she wanted to stay out of it and no amount of honesty would have changed that. Joanne might have let him go ahead with the job on the drug dealer.

That job on the dealer. He knew. At the time, he was certain there wouldn't be a way of doing it that didn't end with him, Usman or both of them paying a price for it. It was a good score, sure. They got away with a little over thirty-five grand each. That was a terrific score, the best Martin had ever made for a single job and easily the best of Usman's life. Martin opened an account, filtered the money into it slowly, trying to keep it hidden. But it wasn't about the money. That was always going to be there, whatever kind of job this was. He knew it was wrong, the way it played out.

They could have killed the guy at the handover point. Keep everything the same up until the point the woman left, they didn't want any part of what she was carrying, too hard to sell all that stuff with Argyle and the Allens looking for it. Kill the dealer once he was alone, take the money and run. They couldn't have known exactly how it would work out, that was why Martin didn't say anything. They couldn't have known in advance that she would leave first, and leave them alone with Comrie. Once they did, they should have reacted. Had multiple plans ready to put into action when the moment came. You don't just stick to a single plan if something better comes along. They had the chance to go in there and kill him, leave themselves enough time to get away before Argyle's men came rushing in looking for him. It was possible. Argyle's men would have gotten rid of the body for them; they didn't want a police investigation either.

It played out wrong. The nagging sense of a job that should have been done better. No gunman wants that. No gunman can go through a job feeling he's botched it and not worry about it. He should have said something to Usman. Not at the time, on the job, that's not the point where you open an intense discussion on strategy. Once the job was set in motion, there was no time to stop and chat about it. They went into that building and got Comrie out. Once he was in their possession there was no safe way to talk. After they'd killed him they needed to go their separate ways, so he still said nothing. He should have created a moment, later, to investigate, to discuss what had happened.

He had convinced himself it was just something else he needed to get used to. You work for an organization and you keep your distance from them. You know that things are going on in the background that don't concern you. You learn to live with the unchangeable. When you're working with one other person, it can't be that way. There can't be secrets, surely, or the whole thing falls apart. But he told himself he could put up with it. Let Usman live his life and Martin could build something with Joanne without the work intruding. They had done the job, and they had made good money from it. There was nothing else Martin needed.

There was the distraction of Joanne to occupy his mind. Finding a place for Skye, getting her out of the house. It felt like the most important thing in the world to Martin, having the house to themselves, being able to build their relationship in peace. He was thinking so much about Joanne and their happiness that he didn't think about Usman. Didn't worry about what he was getting up to. The feelings he had, the unease, that didn't go away just because he was focusing on something else. Fine, just don't do another job with Usman. Simple solution.

A simple solution he wasn't able to follow. That's why he's strapped to this damn chair. Why he's looking across at the door, trying to work out which way they'll come in. The big door, probably. They'll have a van, one large enough for them to move a body easily. There'll be three of them. They'll bring the van in and close the door. Move quickly; get the job done and the body out. Make sure no trace is left behind. It'll be a few minutes from start to finish.

They should be here by now. Maybe . . . No, that's not realistic. It will happen. It has to happen. Maybe if it was just up to Usman it wouldn't happen. His bottle might crash when faced with a challenge as huge as this, something so much bigger than any he had encountered before. But it is really about Nate Colgan and Gully Fitzgerald. They decide whether this happens. They decide how and where. This is their job, nobody else's. Or Colgan's job, more to the point. He's in charge of all this. He won't let this opportunity for revenge slip away.

Martin's groaning without realizing he's doing it. Surprised by the sound of his own voice. It's the first thing he's heard since he scraped the chair back to stretch his legs. Pulling at the plastic cords on his legs again, just to see if anything's changed. It hasn't. Usman wouldn't have dared to get that wrong. Terrified of what Colgan would do to him if they turned up at the warehouse and there was nobody there. No, he has to sit here and wait. They won't be long.

# 1.32 a.m.

Nate's walking up to the van. Dark blue, smaller than the one Usman used on the Comrie job. It's parked at the side of the street. Usman's looking around but there's nobody here at this hour. Just a conspicuous group of three men getting into a van. Nate's getting into the driver's seat; Gully's holding open the passenger-side door.

'Jump in, squish across,' he's saying casually to Usman.

Usman's doing as he's told. Up into the van and watching Gully get in after him, struggling to fit. There's only just enough room for the three of them in the front, Usman squashed in the middle. That's no accident, he knows. He's in the middle so that he can't go jumping out into the street at traffic lights if he suddenly changes his little mind. He'll sit there and they'll drive to the warehouse and there's nothing he can do to stop them.

'Have we got a place lined up?' Usman's asking. 'For the body, I mean.'

Nate's starting the van, pulling out without even looking because there's nothing else on the road. He's ignoring Usman's question, just concentrating on keeping his speed down and his vehicle anonymous. Do nothing to attract the interest of the speed cameras.

'It's all sorted out,' Gully's saying. He seems relaxed, and he's always been friendlier than Nate anyway. 'You don't need to worry about that, Usman, my man. You get the target in place and you finish him off. We'll handle all the spadework; it's what we're here for.'

Nate is silent, focusing on a drive that doesn't need much of his attention. Usman's between them, wanting to talk, wanting reassurance. He's glancing at Nate, then at Gully. Gully's turning and looking back at him, nodding a little.

'Tough, I know,' Gully's saying with a shrug. 'This business, you know, it's full of dirty work. That's the thing about it. You want to get to the good stuff, to the jobs that you got all planned out already, then you got to earn it. Got to do shit like this to get the chance to do the jobs you really care about. That's this business for you. Not a lot of fun, huh?'

'No,' Usman's saying, and nodding along. It helps to hear words like that coming out of the mouth of a man like Gully. Implying that he had to go through this sort of thing too, back when he was Usman's age. Even if he's not being entirely honest, even if he's just trying to make Usman feel better, it's good to hear. Good that Gully is willing to make the effort to say it as well.

There's silence in the van for another few minutes. It's starting to feel uncomfortable again, Usman dwelling on things he doesn't want to acknowledge. He's taking a heavy breath and Gully's looking at him, realizing that someone needs to fill the silence. You work with a man like Nate Colgan and you get used to hearing nothing more than the odd growl. The silence becomes routine, comfortable. Eventually you forget that it isn't the same for other people, that a kid like Usman needs to hear any old noise that'll take his mind away from his grim situation.

'You've done a good job so far,' Gully's saying. 'Wasn't sure, when we started, that you had it in you, lad. Thought you might be a bit fly-by-night, but, no, credit where it's due, you've worked this well, better than I ever predicted. Hasn't he, Nate?'

Usman looked round at Nate. Warm words from Gully are pleasant, but Gully's a man with a pleasant natural temperature. Nate, he's different, ice cold. If he gives you a compliment then it's not just empty flattery, it matters.

'Yeah, he has,' is as much as Nate's saying, in his usual flat tone.

Usman's glancing back at Gully and Gully's rolling his eyes and smiling. Trying to make Nate's coldness seem like it's just typical old Nate, a man who doesn't know how to say thank you when the world does him a favour. Usman's smiling, because he wants to be reassured.

'You made plans for the next job?' Gully's asking him. Keeping him talking, trying to get the kid to focus on the next

253

positive thing on the horizon, instead of the dark stop they'll arrive at first.

'Yeah,' Usman's saying, eager to talk about it. 'I might need some help with it. I mean, it's more than a one-man job, so I'll need a couple of pairs of hands to help me out.'

'Don't worry about that,' Gully told him. 'If the job's good, you'll get all the help you need. That's how it's going to work now, the organization will be able to provide you with the manpower and the equipment you need. Bit of funding as well, if the investment looks like it'll pay off. Won't be blank cheques or anything like that, and you'll need to share the detail of the job first, mind you. We'll sit down and have a talk about it afterwards, next couple of weeks or so. You give us the kind of detail you think we need to know, we'll get you the people and the equipment to make sure it works.'

'Should be a good score,' Usman's saying, reaching out to that distant, bright light of the future. 'Will I be working with you guys on these jobs?'

Gully's shaking his head, screwing up his mouth. 'Doubt it. Don't know, mind you, could be on some of them. Suppose it depends on what kind of help you need. If you're looking for a couple of decrepit old shite-bags to help you out then we might just be perfect, eh? But I reckon the higher-ups will want you to have one or two people that you use on all the jobs. Your own wee crew, you know. It'll be less experienced guys, but they'll get their experience with you, and it'll give you a regular crew of people you know and trust to work with. Always better that way, always better. Got to have people you're comfortable with and that you trust. People that'll know to keep themselves available for you.'

'Sure, yeah, definitely,' Usman's saying.

That was the problem with Martin, you could never get comfortable with that bastard. He was so reluctant, always trying to find a reason not to work. You want to go into a dangerous job with someone loyal by your side, someone you like and someone you know will always be there to back you up. That wasn't Martin. It wasn't, and now it never would be. The thought of having his own crew, two or three guys that he always used, that he was in charge of and that he could trust. Maybe build it into a bigger group, Usman at the head of it. Man, that was a prize worth the pain of acquiring.

'Nearly there,' Gully's saying. 'You ready, lad?'

'Yeah, sure, I'm ready.' Usman doesn't sound convincing, not even to himself.

'Take your time with it, that's the thing,' Gully's saying. 'I see kids running into tough jobs and they want to get everything done right away, want everything over and done with as fast as possible. That ain't the way to do it, not how a pro does it. You got to take your time, let your nerves settle, let your mind get used to the idea of what you're doing. See, it's about hours on the clock. You know what I mean by that?'

'I'm not sure.'

'Well, the longer you spend working each job, the more experience you have of being in that world, that – what's the word? – environment. See, you rush in and just go boom, boom, boom, and you get every job finished in quick time. Problem is, you're going to end up going on a job where you have to spend a long time on it, where you don't have a choice, and you got to have the nerve for that. You got to be able to dwell on things, take it slow, make sure you pick the right option every time. That takes practice, and you won't get that if you're doing everything at a hundred miles per hour. Can't afford to make mistakes, and rushing causes mistakes.'

'Experience on the job,' Usman's saying, 'yeah, I get it. I won't rush it.'

'Good lad,' Gully's saying, 'good lad.'

# 19

He hadn't seen Martin for a couple of months. Phoned him, tried to keep in touch, but the gunman wasn't having it. No answer, no call back, just the two of them drifting apart. It wasn't what Usman wanted, not when he had other jobs lined up. There was profitable work to do and that work couldn't be done alone. But how do you persuade a man who doesn't want to be persuaded?

Forget about it for a while, that was his attitude. Live your own life, give Martin the time he needs to wise up or run out of cash, then get back to work. Same as last time.

Usman spent some time with Alison, as unsure about her as he was about Martin. She had started work in the bar across the street from her old place. Alison was chuffed about it, but Usman didn't like her working for Jones. He warned her to be careful there, but she was so sure that she was safe. Spent some time with his brother, doing some menial work he didn't need to do. That was track-covering. Let the people who knew him think that he still had to work, let them think that he didn't have much cash in his back pocket. Last thing he wanted was someone who knew him well enough to know where to look poking around to try and find out where he had gotten his money from.

That was the one downside to having a lot of money in a big, neat pile. Hadn't happened for him before, not two big scores within a few months of each other. Now he had more money than he could reasonably explain to anyone, more than he knew how to easily hide.

'You're not very busy,' Akram had said to him. There was a hint of suspicion in his voice, like he was 51 per cent sure that his brother was hiding something.

'Yeah I am, I got a bunch of stuff on the go,' Usman said with a shrug. 'Loads of wee things though, nothing worth shouting about. Why, you need a hand with something?' Asked as though he was eager to help, eager to get his hands on any extra cash that might be fluttering around his brother.

'Nah, nothing yet. I'll give you a shout if something comes up though,' Akram had told him, the suspicious tone fading as the percentage dipped to 49.

That left Usman to go back home and sit in his bedroom, looking at the wads of cash that he'd stuffed into a slit in the mattress. Not even a good hiding place in a flat this small. He took the money out and looked at it every few days, just to see it and touch it. Sixteen grand from the bookies that he'd only shifted half of when he got his hands on thirty-five grand from the Comrie job. Too much to move in big lumps without inviting suspicion. He was filtering some into his bank account, but only a couple of hundred a week. Some he was spending, wiping out any bills he had with loose cash, cheerfully running up other bills to annihilate with stolen money. But there was still thousands left, and every time he looked at it he thought about the dead dealer and the threat that he would spend the rest of his life living under.

It had been good, the last four months. Martin did no work, living off the money he'd made. Joanne liked the fact that he obviously wasn't working any more, despite the fear of money running out, and they were happy. A few months where they were able to create normality for themselves. The cash was basically gone, much of it on the deposit for a flat, and the rate at which Skye paid rent, it wasn't likely to make its way back to his pocket very quickly. He didn't care, and he didn't let Joanne pressure Skye much either. She wanted to, but in the back of Martin's mind was the fear that Skye might move back in with them, proclaim herself unable to live in the little flat they'd got her, out of spite.

There had been a couple of people in touch with him in the last few months, looking to set him up with work. Przemek had called, offering him a gig working with some importers. Martin turned it down. He hadn't heard of the people looking to employ him, didn't know if they might be connected to Chris Argyle. Wasn't worth the effort anyway.

'I know they're not paying great,' Przemek told him, 'but

you need to make connections if you want to make a living round here.'

'I'm doing fine,' Martin had told him.

'Living off the lover, eh?'

'No,' Martin told him, 'living off my own money.'

But that couldn't go on much longer, so he was going to have to pull in more cash from somewhere. Then Usman called.

Martin ignored him. Ignored the call and ignored the message that was left in its wake. Usman telling him that he had another job they could work, that there could be good money in it. Talking with the relaxed confidence of a man who couldn't see the dangers coming. Asked Martin to call him back for the details. Martin didn't. If he called Usman back and they worked another job, there would be an escalation. Bound to be, it was how these things worked. The job on the bookies had been fine, a little bit of violence but they got away with it. The job on the dealer had been dirty work, a killing that paid well. The next job wouldn't be any better. These things always spiralled down until you reached the kind of pit he'd almost been trapped in back home. More money, more risk, more violence.

Usman had thought there would be a period of fear, a couple of months maybe, after the killing. Then, when the police had stopped looking for Comrie very hard, and the people involved in the deal had moved on with their lives, the fear would fade. But it didn't, and Usman had come to realize that it never would. The police would keep an interest in Comrie's disappearance for evermore. They might not actively look for him, but it would only take Martin telling them about it for Usman to get a life sentence. The other people involved, the Allens and Chris Argyle, would never stop trying to find out what happened either. That was good money for them, not the sort of thing angry professionals would ever just shrug off, and a major business opportunity scuppered.

And it had been scuppered. Gully had confirmed it in a meeting not long afterwards. People were pissed off about money going missing and word had gotten to the Allens that Argyle wasn't convinced of their innocence in the matter. That may or may not have been true, it didn't really matter. The deal was dead in the water, Gully's employers happy with a sly piece of sabotage.

Usman's mind kept going back to Martin, the cold-blooded killer. What would happen if he got arrested? He wouldn't keep his mouth shut, not if he thought it would help him get a smaller sentence. He would drop everyone else in the shit and then flee Scotland for the old dangers of home when he eventually got out of jail. Hell, if they were able to deport him to face more charges over there they probably would. No, Martin wasn't a man who could be trusted. This wasn't like working with his brother, where flesh and blood tied them together.

He had wanted Martin to be a friend. He'd wanted him to be someone that he could trust and enjoy working with, form a bond that he could depend upon. If that had happened, if Martin had become the kind of friend Usman had wanted him to be, then the proposal Gully put to him would have been dismissed.

Usman was a loyal friend to those that earned it, that was what he told himself. He would never turn his back on his friends, on his brother, on anyone that returned his loyalty. He would do time for them, if it ever came to that. But Martin wasn't returning his calls, and seemed determined to put a vast amount of space between them. That wasn't a man you could rely on.

Gully came to the flat, earlier in the morning than Usman liked to be awake for. He wasn't expecting visitors and was still half-asleep when he heard the knock at the door. Slung on whatever combination of clothing was closest to the bed and went out into the corridor, just wanting the knocking to stop. He jerked back a little with surprise when he opened the door to Gully Fitzgerald. It had been a few months since they'd spoken; as far as Usman was concerned they had nothing left to say to each other.

'Morning, lad, now a good time to speak?' Gully seemed bright and cheerful, and, more importantly, alone and un-armed.

They sat in the living room, Gully doing a good job of looking sympathetic. Seemed sorry to have dropped in out of nowhere and alarmed the boy. Usman sat opposite and waited for Gully to take the lead on this. Wherever it was going, it was nowhere Usman wanted to rush.

'I've got a proposal for you,' Gully said, the friendly undertone always there to make the industry talk less intimidating. 'There's been some trouble within the organization, the aftermath of that job on the bookies. Your pal, Martin thingummy, he's a wanted man.'

'Shit,' Usman said, running a hand through his hair. If Martin was most wanted then Usman had to be next on the list.

'Now, he's the one people are talking about right now, not you. He's the one that really pissed people off and I think we can keep it that way. He cracked Donny Gregor on the skull, and that's what's gotten people worked up. See, Donny's been suffering from what happened that night, health problems and the like. Blackouts, headaches, all sorts of stuff, it's really affected the poor bastard. People have noticed, and they want to see us do something about it. They expect it from us. It's bad timing, more than anything,' Gully added.

'Oh?'

'If this had happened when Jamieson was free, and the organization was at its strongest, we probably wouldn't be having this conversation. Problem is, at a time like this, we can't afford to look weak, not in any way, so we have to be seen to do something about it. Punish anyone who hurts us. Reassures people. So that's why I'm here, we need to do something. We, us, you, me and Nate. We were all there that night, so we all need to clean that up. People won't put you under any pressure if they know that you helped us punish the guy who caused all the bother. Gets you off the hook, you see.'

Usman nodded along. Wasn't going to sit there and argue with Gully Fitzgerald anyway, but he was hearing some good things. He liked the idea of *we*, of being bundled in with Gully and Nate. Talk about protecting Usman from the people who wanted to hurt Martin.

'What, uh, what were you thinking of doing?' Usman asked him, leaning forward in the chair to listen.

'We want you to set up a job with him, make it seem like a right good score. You and him go and work a place over, let's say a warehouse or somewhere like that; somewhere there won't be anyone to get in the way. You get him in there, and, well, you can probably take a guess at the rest of it.'

Usman could guess, and guess with unerring accuracy. He nodded his head, picked at the seam of his trousers, tried to think of something he could say. Martin wasn't a friend, not really, but he wasn't a bad guy either, and only bad guys deserved that sort of ending. But he was dangerous, that was the fact he couldn't escape. He was a man who no longer seemed to want to work with Usman, who knew what Usman had done and could get him into a hellish amount of trouble.

'He doesn't want to work with me now,' Usman said. 'We got a good score last time out, I don't think he'll want to work again for a while. He ain't greedy.'

Gully nodded. 'That was, what, four months ago, something like that?'

'Something like that.'

'Well, there you go, we're starting to get into the time when it's safe for him to go to his work again. The man might not be desperate for work, but he'll be tempted if you dangle a pretty-looking carrot in front of him. Something lucrative and something safe as well, that'll be the clincher. You go to him and tell him there's good money in a job and that he won't even have to bring his wee gun with him, that'll get him interested. Low risk, high reward. He won't be able to turn it down.'

Usman didn't look convinced, but he knew what he was being told. Gully wasn't saying that Martin would jump at the chance; he was telling Usman that he had to find a way of pushing the gunman to accept it.

'What do I tell him?'

'Tell him there's a warehouse you know some drugs move through. Tell him it isn't well guarded because they're scared of drawing attention, it's a legit place most of the time, stuff like that. Tell him you know people you can shift the drugs on to as well, so there'll be no hassle in selling it.'

'He doesn't like drugs, anything to do with them.'

'Tell him you already have a buyer, and it was the buyer that brought the job to you. Money already agreed, you just got to go in and grab the gear, nice and easy. Talk about the dough, not the drugs.'

'He'll want details,' Usman said. 'He always wants details.'

'Sounds like a pro, this boy. All right then, tell him it's a warehouse out Clydebank way. I know we have a good place out there you can use for it, I'll get you the full address in the next few hours, before you talk to him. You tell him there are pills going through the place, party drugs coming in from the continent. Stored there, then distributed round the city. Tell him it belongs to James Kealing, someone like that.'

Usman nodded enthusiastically, this was something he could do. Telling lies, spinning a yarn with just enough detail to convince a man like Martin. Once you started dressing it up, it looked like one of his jobs. This could work, it really could.

'You're going to kill him?' Usman asked.

'I'm not,' Gully said with a sorry smile. 'You are.'

Usman just looked at him. Sat there and stared across the room. The only way to extricate himself from the wrath of the Jamieson organization was to kill the man they blamed for hurting the bookie.

'I'm not . . .'

'I know this ain't your sort of gig,' Gully said, 'but you got to be serious about the situation you got yourself into. People need to see that you've helped us, done something for us that nobody else could do. That happens, and they'll welcome you into the organization.'

Usman jerked his head up, having been staring at the floor. He looked across at Gully, eyes a little wider. 'Into the organization?'

'Into the organization, yeah. You've already proven that you're a useful fellow to have around. The job on the bookies was well done, even if it had this fallout. If you'd done that against someone else we'd all be very happy with you. The job on that dealer, shit, that was very well done as well. Textbook stuff, I would say. You pulled it off beautifully, even though it was a tricky wee thing to have to work. If you have other jobs like that, things you can work that weaken other organizations, then we'll look after you. You'll need to earn it, keep working jobs,' he added with a shrug, 'but I don't think there'll be any trouble in that, eh?'

'I've got loads of jobs I can work,' Usman said, 'if I get the help. Against other organizations as well. They'd be good for Jamieson. But, yeah, I got to kill Martin?'

'You do, yeah.' Silence for thirty seconds, Usman looking at the floor again and Gully letting him. Letting him see how dark the job was before he offered a little more light to guide him towards justification. 'Don't look at it as a negative thing though. Look at it as a chance to step up and join the organization. Look at it as the chance to make sure that the boy Martin whatshisname doesn't come back and bite you on the arse down the line, you know what I mean?'

Usman looked up and nodded. 'I can do it,' he said. 'I'll get in touch with him, set it up, let you know.'

'Good lad, good lad,' Gully told him, getting up. 'We'll help you as much as possible.'

It wasn't betrayal, that's what Usman started convincing himself of before Gully had closed the front door behind himself. Martin would have done the same if the roles were reversed, and there was a chance that he still would. If Usman was scared of Martin dropping him in it, then Martin had to have the same fears, didn't he? And he was a gunman. He might already be planning to wipe out Usman. This wasn't betrayal, it was self-defence.

A few weeks went past and there were no more calls from Usman. Seemed like he had moved on, maybe found himself another pair of bloody hands to work the job for him. A part of Martin was relaxing at the prospect of not having to work with the boy again. Another part was starting to get nervy at the thought of not having enough money. He needed a reliable income.

Then Usman called again. This time Martin answered.

'Martin, man, where the hell have you been?'

'Nowhere.'

'Nowhere, aye, right, good one. Listen, you fit for some work?'

'I don't think so,' Martin said, but it didn't quite sound like he believed himself.

'I got something to put to you, man, it's worth hearing. You want to listen?'

Martin held the phone in his hand, thought about it. Money was running down. Joanne had just started working an extra shift in the bookstore, extending the opening hours in the hope of a few extra quid. Less time for them to be together at home. Money was another thing they didn't talk about much, something that Joanne didn't like to make an issue of. She had always looked after herself and Skye, didn't need Martin or anyone else trying to help her out. Didn't change the fact that he wanted to help.

'Look, I ain't leaning on you here,' Usman said, leaning heavily, 'but this is a good one, man, real good. None of the shite we had with the last one, that's guaranteed. No, what's the word, complications. Come on, what do you say, eh? Come round to the flat, the one in Mosspark, I haven't used that in ages, we'll have a wee chat about it. Never hurts to have a chat, does it?'

Martin was silent, standing in the kitchen with the phone in his hand. This felt like home now, felt like a place he was sharing rather than occupying. It was hard to imagine being anywhere else, being *with* anyone else. This house, Joanne, that was life now. The life he hadn't realized he wanted and now couldn't live without.

'Jesus, you still there, man?' Usman asked, shouting a little because he thought Martin had put the phone down and wandered off in a moment of sudden senility.

'I'm here,' Martin said, his voice harsh. 'I'm thinking.' He paused again. 'I don't think so, Usman, I don't think I need the trouble of another one of your jobs.'

'Listen to me, Martin,' Usman said quickly before Martin could hang up on him. Too quickly, sounded a little desperate. 'This job isn't going to have trouble. I have something, not going to be as big as the last one for cash, but it's going to be damn good. I been saving it up, a nice easy one, you know? Something to break us back in gently after a long break. Good money, twenty-five, thirty grand maybe, to split between us. One night's work. In and out of a place, that's all it is. Not even anybody there to interrupt us. Get in, get a few boxes of gear and get out. I got a guy already to buy the lot, so we get the money on the night. It's that easy.'

'Thirty thousand pounds of gear has security.'

'Not good security, not this lot,' Usman said, his voice sounding insufferably smug down the phone line. 'Look, I'm not giving you all the details over the fucking phone or you could go and pull the job without me. Let's do this the proper way. Come to the flat, tomorrow afternoon. Two o'clock, right? Martin? Two o'clock.'

More silence before a reluctant answer. 'Maybe,' Martin said, and he hung up.

He went. Two o'clock the following afternoon he was walking through the little alley and knocking on the door. Usman answered, smiling broadly as he welcomed Martin in. They went up the unlit stairs and into the small flat, a place no more welcoming than it had been the last time Martin was there. They sat in the living room, Martin watching warily as Usman did all he could to make this seem like a meeting of old friends.

'It's good to see you, man, how have you been?'

'Fine,' Martin said, and shrugged.

'Good, yeah, chatty as ever, huh? I'm glad you came though, seriously. I have this job, right, and it's pretty basic stuff, but I need a second person there with me.'

'What is it then?'

'A warehouse job. Down Clydebank way. You heard of James Kealing?'

Martin half-shrugged and shook his head. He had heard the name, but it wasn't mentioned as frequently as the likes of Jamieson and MacArthur.

'Well Kealing's got a decent little operation, not as big as the real big beasts, but he's been around a good long time and he knows how to run an organization. His old man was, like, some mad bastard or something. Anyway, Kealing knows how to keep himself in expensive suits. Dangerous enough guy, is what I'm hearing. He moves some gear, and a lot of it is, like, that synthetic shit, party drugs, legal highs, highs that used to be legal and ain't any more. That sort of thing. Plenty of buyers, but it's a crowded fucking market, margins aren't great unless you got the latest flavour of the month. Gets it from Europe, Holland or somewhere, and stores it in his warehouse before he moves it on.'

'You want to steal these drugs.'

'Yes I do.'

'And you think that this man, this man who has a good operation, will not have any security at all at this warehouse? He is that good?'

'There's going to be some security, Jesus, I ain't saying the door will be wide open and we can just walk right in and there'll be a sign pointing to the gear. What I'm saying is there ain't going to be much, not as much as you might think. There'll be cameras, maybe alarms, shit like that, but we can handle that. We can handle it because we'll be moving fast, you see. No guards. Nobody armed. We won't even have to bring any weapons along with us. Just a van. We scout the place, see what's there, deal with it when we get there. In and out fast, like, in a proper fucking hurry, you know? That's going to be the challenge with this one, getting in and out fast enough.'

Martin started to nod his head. Working against the clock, rushing in and out. If there were no guards on site then it could be possible.

'Best thing is, right, I already got someone to buy all the gear off me. Haven't confirmed anything yet because I don't know for certain how much there'll be, but there should be plenty. It was that lad that pointed me in the direction of it and that was months ago, so this has been well scouted. We take it straight to him from the warehouse, get our cash, and we're done. And he'll pay nice. Not market value, but you don't get market value on stuff you've nicked out of Kealing's warehouse, do you?'

'This man is dangerous?' Martin asked.

'Kealing? Dangerous as usual, no more than that. Probably less dangerous than the people we've worked over so far, you know. He's got a smaller operation than any of them.'

They were both silent this time, Martin thinking and Usman watching him, wondering what there was to think about. He could sense that Martin was close to biting, that the hook was bouncing around right in front of him.

'I would like more details,' Martin said quietly. 'About the money, about the warehouse.'

Usman smiled. If he wanted detail then he was basically saying yes, because he had to know that he wasn't getting any good detail until he committed to the job.

'I think we'll clear twenty-something thousand on this one. I'm hoping over twenty-five, but that depends on how much of the stuff is in there and what it all is. I think I know, got a guy that used to work there that gave me a good idea of what was in there a couple of shipments ago. I'm guessing it's roughly the same this time around; they probably have a pretty consistent supply. What they had then would get us between twenty-five and thirty. Let's say roughly twelve and a half each, but don't go nuts if it's a wee bit under. We scout the place, we spend ten minutes max robbing the place, I handle the sale afterwards. Minimum ten grand each.'

'The warehouse?'

'I will tell you about that when you tell me that you're in on the job. Them's the rules.'

There was another pause, Martin seeming reluctant to acknowledge that this was the best job offer he was going to get any time soon. Twelve and a half probable for robbing a warehouse with basic security. Almost impossible to say no to.

'I'll help you,' Martin said. 'But we have to do this properly, make sure that we have all the knowledge we need before we go in.'

'Of course we will, of course we will,' Usman told him, grinning and leaning back in his chair. 'We'll scout it until we know every fucking brick.' And then, surprisingly quickly, the smile faded into a more serious expression.

Martin left a few minutes later, drove back home. The house was empty, Joanne at the bookshop again. It was peaceful in that house, but never lonely. Even when she wasn't there, there was a sense of her presence. The smell of the place, the feel of it. Everything was a reminder of her, of the life they had together.

There was nothing he wouldn't do to keep that life. It was a strange feeling, to realize that the things he was prepared to do weren't about money any more, weren't about power or position, they were all about maintaining the value of the good life he'd built. That was a change. Something he'd never considered before, when he worked with men who were married or had kids. Always assumed their motivations were the same as his, that it was all about the money and family concerns were something separate. But they weren't, and he was beginning to understand that. The need to protect the good things you have, the best thing you've ever had.

# 20

It was a small warehouse, sharing its yard with two other equally unimpressive buildings. The place had seen better days, all the buildings too small to house the major stock that could pay for upgrades. They were innocuous, which made them ideal. There was no gate at the front of the yard, nothing to stop Usman and Martin getting a van right up to the doors of the warehouse. The other buildings were in use, the area busy through the day. Martin and Usman were in a yard across the street, this one seemingly unused. Sitting in Usman's car, watching.

'I can see a camera at the door of the warehouse,' Martin said.

'Uh-huh, there'll be some on the other buildings as well, might cover all of the yard,' Usman said. 'Don't mean it's anything to get too worked up about though, does it? I mean, we knew there were gonna be cameras, just means we have to work extra fast.'

They watched a little longer, aware that in the daylight they couldn't linger long. There were people using the yard next door to the one they were in, although not many, and there was a danger they would stand out if they stayed.

'You're sure there's no guard on that building at night?'

'Sure.'

'What about the other two buildings?'

Usman paused, thought about it, realized he hadn't even asked Gully about the other two. Didn't know this warehouse shared a yard with them, something Gully should have warned him about.

'Well, I doubt it, right. I mean, if there was a guard he would be working the whole yard.' He paused. 'Okay, I don't actually know about the other two, right, but that's what scouting's for, eh? Come on, that's what this is all about. Good prep, and then we go do the fucking job. I'm right, you know I am.'

'So we will have to come back at night and watch this place, make sure that they don't have guards. And if they do have guards, then it becomes a very different job.'

Usman sighed, fed up already of the miserable bastard he was having to work with. One last time, he told himself, and then stopped sighing. One last time because he was going to kill him. One last time because he was going to give him a punishment he didn't deserve. Martin had only gone into that bookies because Usman offered him the job. He'd only become a threat to Usman because Usman hired him in the first place. That wasn't Martin's fault. And, yes, he was miserable, and he could be annoying, and he was as distant as the sun most of the time, but he had never let Usman down. Not once. He was nothing worse than a professional who wanted detail to make sure that they did the job well. But Usman was still going to kill him.

'We were going to have to come back and scout the place at night anyway,' Usman said calmly. 'We'll scout it tonight and if things look good, we'll do it tomorrow night. My contact that worked here said there were no guards, I thought he just meant for the building, maybe he meant for the whole place, the other two as well. I don't know. I'll call him, check what he has to say about it. We come back tonight and see it with our own four eyes.'

'And your man is sure that the gear is in there?' Martin said, keeping the solemn tone that Usman had uncharacteristically adopted. 'I don't want to go in there and find a warehouse full of toilet roll or something.'

'My guy says there's always stuff in there, a constant stream of it. Kealing brings it in in small amounts, always has about the same supplies running through it. Sounds like taking it in regular, small amounts is the safest way for him to get it in without being seen. Think it comes by boat or something like that. Fishing boats, is what I heard one time, but I don't know if that's what Kealing does. A fishing boat leaves, like, Holland or Portugal or one of those places, and it meets up with one from here out at sea, they transfer the stuff across. The second boat brings back a small amount of stuff pretty much every week. Someone picks it up from a wee harbour somewhere and they store it in the warehouse, then it gets

278

distributed out in smaller amounts. Always plenty of it though. If it reeks of fish we'll know I was right.'

'If it reeks of fish nobody will buy it,' Martin said, knowing that wasn't true at all. The detail was relaxing him.

They left; Usman dropped Martin at his house and went on back to his own flat. His proper flat, the one Gully came to, not the one he met Martin in. He wouldn't use that again. Not that they'd need a meeting place from now on anyway.

Gully was in the kitchen, making lunch for him and Lisa. She had been shopping that morning, bustling around the house the rest of the day. They were converting the spare bedroom into a study, something they could afford to do with Gully working again. They were busy, active, doing things together. Taking on projects. Converting the spare room felt like it might just be the start of it. They had a three-bedroom house, but Sally's room was off-limits, not spare while it still contained her memory. Still, these last couple of months had felt like the best in years.

His mobile rang on the kitchen table as Lisa entered the room. Gully picked it up.

'Hi, Gully, it's Usman.'

Gully smiled at Lisa and walked casually out of the room, phone to his ear, not saying anything. He wasn't going to rub her face in it by taking work calls in front of her.

'Sorry about that,' Gully said quickly. 'What's up?'

'Martin's in. All the way in. We're going to do it tomorrow night if nothing comes up, so, uh, I thought you might want to get ready. I'll text you as we're leaving. Um, so, yeah, I was thinking about a gun. Do I need to take one with me or what?'

'No, don't take a gun in with you in case he sees it ahead of time. If that dangerous wee bastard sees you with a gun then he's going to turn into trouble. He can't get suspicious until it's too late. Take something in with you, a crowbar or something like that. Use it to crack a door, there's a staff door next to the loading dock you can go in through. Get inside and give him a thump on the head with it. We'll leave the stuff there you'll need to tie him up. A chair, and there's a metal loop on the floor. Then you come for me and Nate, I'll give you an address. You come get us, we all go back together, you kill him, we get rid of the body, right? That way you're not leaving a dead guy behind at any point. Worst thing you can ever do is leave a body unwatched.'

'Yeah, that sounds . . . I don't know, sounds right, I suppose. I never done this before.'

'And you won't have to do it again either. People just need to see that you're one of us, that we can trust you. This is the key to the door, lad, it gets you into the organization. You do this, and it's much easier after. Trust me.'

'Yeah, okay.' Usman paused, ready to put down the phone, and then remembered another reason he had called. 'Listen, the other buildings at the site, what are they like? I mean, the security? Do they have guards?'

Gully chuckled. 'All three of them belong to us. You don't need to worry about guards or cameras or any of that crap, okay? You can cartwheel round the yard with a firework up your arse and nobody's going to see it. You just do the job and don't be worrying about that.'

It was in the hours afterwards that Usman thought about the job, processed the details. Knocking down Martin, a tough guy that would be hard to catch out. Tying him in place and going to get the other two. That seemed like a risk. A big risk. Why wouldn't they just be nearby? Wasn't that the professional way to do these things? Maybe it was, but he knew why they weren't doing it that way. They didn't want to be anywhere near an amateur like him when he tried to get a professional like Martin all tied up. There was a chance things could go wrong, and experienced professionals knew better than to stand close to the amateur juggling dynamite with a blindfold on. They had no faith in him.

It wasn't the thought of killing Martin that was getting under his skin now; it was the thought of trying to tie him up in that warehouse. Martin was tougher than him, more experienced than him. Smaller, sure, but experienced and a scrapper. The chances of something going wrong were huge. He could feel his heart thumping, could feel himself sweating just thinking about it. When he killed Martin, that would be different. It would be safe by then, he would have Nate and Gully with him, he would have a gun.

When it was time for the evening scout, he picked Martin up a few streets away from his house, which seemed stupid. That was the gunman's choice, didn't want Usman anywhere near his precious house and his even more precious girlfriend. Probably a good thing, Usman thought, that he didn't go anywhere near the place now. Better not to be seen hanging around with a man who was about to disappear.

'You called him?' Martin asked as they made their way west.

Usman turned quickly and looked at him. 'Who?'

'Your man, the one who worked at the warehouse. You said you were going to call him to find out about the guards and security at the other warehouses.'

A rush of relief. 'Oh, him, yeah, I called him. No guards. Cameras, but no guards is what he said. That's what he'd meant at the start, that there were no guards in the yard. Far as I can see, nothing's changed. Only challenge we've got is getting this done good and fast.'

They drove on in silence, Usman focused on the road ahead. They weren't able to park in the yard directly opposite their target at this late hour, that place was locked up. The clock in the car said eleven o'clock.

'Place looks silent,' Usman said, leaning forward. They

were parked on the gravelled forecourt of a car valet service, looking down the street at the warehouses. Not a perfect view, but good enough.

'This would be a good time, tomorrow night,' Martin said quietly, looking across at the entrance to the warehouse.

Usman nodded slowly. 'I guess. Wish we could get close enough to the warehouse to have a look at the entrances though.'

'Your man told you nothing about them?'

'Told me the door beside the big corrugated loading gate leads right into the storage place. We can get direct access through there. He says there are storage boxes, plastic things I think, against the back wall on the right-hand side. That's where it's always put. We get them out, into the van and we fuck off with them.'

'The van?'

'I'll get the van, don't worry about it. A small one, won't need anything big and heavy, won't be that much gear. Something nippy, you know. Only be about eight or ten boxes. Four or five trips each.'

'So we come here at about eleven. We go into the yard and we get the door open how?'

'Break it,' Usman said with a shrug. 'We're going to be on camera anyway, we're going to be racing the clock. No point trying to be clever about it, fannying about with locks and stuff. I'll take along a crowbar or something; make sure we get in fast.'

Martin didn't look enthusiastic. 'Fine. We get in, we get the boxes into the van.'

'Five minutes we'll be in that yard, tops. Maybe even less if we break the door quick and find the boxes straight away.'

'Should we not check the boxes before we leave?' Martin asked.

Usman puffed out his cheeks, then swirled saliva around in his mouth for the sake of making a noise. 'I don't know, that's a risk. I think I'd rather cut the time we spend in there, wouldn't you?'

Martin shook his head. 'If we're going in there, I'd rather we weren't wasting our time. I want to know that when we leave here, we have what we came for.'

Usman smiled a little. 'Your English ain't as shite as it used to be, you know that? But yeah, I get the point. Okay, fine, we check the boxes. But we set a time limit. Five minutes and we leave, even if we're leaving stuff behind.'

'Fine,' Martin said. His English might have been better, but he wasn't in the mood to share his new skills with Usman.

They stayed and watched for nearly an hour, searching for anything that might alarm them. Nothing suspicious, nothing that should make the following night's job any harder than predicted. They drove back into the city, Usman dropping Martin off. By the time he got home, his heart was racing again.

# 21

Joanne was up early the following morning, getting ready to go to work. She had showered and dressed by the time Martin rolled out of bed. She was in a hurry, planning to do one of her kiss-on-the-cheek-and-run-for-the-door exits. She heard him come downstairs to intercept her in the kitchen.

'What time will you be back tonight?' he asked her.

'Late,' she said. 'Seven, maybe, perhaps closer to eight.'

Martin nodded. 'I should still be here then.'

Joanne paused and looked at him, picking up the dismal tone. He was going out to work, and this was his stumbling attempt to talk to her about that fact. His way of letting her know that this was work he wanted to talk about. They had agreed on no details, but that agreement was ready to collapse. It was increasingly obvious that Martin wanted to tell her everything.

'You're going out?' she asked, letting the unwanted question in. Starting a conversation that was going to go down one of those dark roads they'd both worked so hard to avoid.

'I am,' he nodded, taking his time. He wanted to get the words and the tone right. She could see the effort Martin was making. He wanted to speak to her with clarity, but speaking in a second language clouded that attempt. 'I have a job tonight. It is nothing special, simple job, but I could be late back. I don't know how long it will take, some of it. It will not be dangerous; it is something I've done many times before so there is no need to worry.'

Joanne frowned, folded her arms. She pursed her lips, looking at the tough little man she'd welcomed into her life. 'When people tell me not to worry about something that's usually a reason to worry about it.'

'There may be some dangerous things; there are dangerous things in every job. I think it's safe, a good job, so . . . But I wanted you to know that I would be out, that you might not see me when you come back tonight. Maybe I will be out already.' Repeating himself, trying to make sure she understood what he was really saying. The truth had retreated behind his struggling English.

'Is there—?' she said, and stopped before she finished the question. She knew she wore the hard look she got when she was confronting something bigger than she was ready for, something big enough to do her real harm. 'Is there a chance that you won't come back?'

Martin wanted to be reassuring. Smile and tell her she couldn't get rid of him that easily. Laugh and ask her if she was fearing or hoping. He couldn't though, because he was going to be honest with her. This time he was going to be as honest as he could be.

'There is always a chance,' he said with a shrug. 'Less with this job than most. If the police catch me or a security guard or some other dangerous person. I am good at my job though. I am. I have done so many things more dangerous than what I will do tonight and I've always been okay. I will be okay. I just wanted you to know that I am working, that's all.'

They stood a couple of feet apart for several more seconds, both silent, Joanne watching Martin and Martin watching the floor. He didn't have the courage to look her in the eye, to see what was there. The fear that he would see revulsion, a woman realizing that she was sharing her life with a thug. The fear that he would see the end of their relationship silently declared on her face. Then Joanne stepped towards him and hugged him.

He watched her leave and began to wander round the house. Walked and walked, room to room, taking it all in. When was the last time he had felt so at home in one place? Not since he was a child, he figured. This was it. This was the reason he had done all those jobs, all the work he hated. You do the work and you take the money and then what? There has to be something after that, or all the work is pointless. Used to be that he would spend it. Parties, women, drugs. Then he'd buy himself gifts, like motorcycles or expensive watches. None of those things had any real value though. Had to leave most of them behind when he ran. They weren't worth the effort it took to pay for them, no matter how hard he tried to persuade himself. Then he met a woman. A smart woman, so much in control of herself. So far removed from the kind of women he'd spent money on before. Eight years older than him and with a grown-up kid. Now he had a reason for everything, which instantly made even a small risk seem colossal.

He sat in their bedroom. Their bedroom. Not hers that he happened to spend a lot of time in, theirs. They had been talking about converting Skye's room into an office, a chance to draw a line under the scary prospect of her returning. They were planning a long way ahead, holidays and other things. They were planning for a life together.

It was different before Joanne, when life meant being as close to death as possible. A third-rate cliché, but true. It was the most fun he ever had, putting his life on the line for the hell of it. He walked into those jobs, not overly concerned if he came out the other end of them or not. There was nothing to lose. Life was the job and if the job killed you then so be it, that was the risk you enjoyed taking. Perhaps too strong to say he had nothing to live for but his work. He had life to live for. But he never had anything outside of the job that mattered more than the job itself.

Should have had something to eat before he left, but he didn't. Should have done all sorts of things to prepare, but he didn't. Not this time. This time he sat and let time tick away, watching the clock through the afternoon and wondering what was taking so long, watching it in the evening and trying to work out why it was going so fast.

Which left him with another struggle. It was after eight o'clock and Joanne hadn't come back home yet. She was staying away, probably to avoid him, make sure that they didn't have to go through the torture of another awful goodbye. He wanted to see her again; he was desperate to spend more time with her, but not now, not in these circumstances. Later, when he got back. He would wake her up and they would talk the night away. But he didn't want to see her right now. He was too close to the job, in need of separation. If he saw her he would get more nervous, put his ability to do the job at risk. He called Usman.

'Come and get me, we will scout a little before we go in. You have everything?'

'Yeah,' Usman said, 'I have everything. Haven't picked up the van yet though, didn't think we'd be going this early. I'll need time.'

'Get the van now; pick me up from the same street as last night. We'll kill some time.'

Usman sounded nervous, didn't like the idea of getting the vehicle this early. He was right not to like it. If he had any sense he would have refused, told Martin to sit tight and wait another hour and a half so that they'd have the van for as little time as possible, but he didn't. He went along with Martin's lack of professionalism because he didn't have the strength to argue.

Cut the cord and cut it fast. The only way you can do it. Don't stand around in the house, moping about the future you might have had and the person you love. Don't risk her coming back and finding you still there, all nervous and miserable. He went and grabbed a coat and pulled the back door closed behind him. Walking quickly for a few streets until he reached the one he'd been collected from the night before. He had to sit on a wall and wait for Usman to turn up, waiting twenty minutes on a street where he didn't belong.

# 22

Nate sat at the table, watched Kelly loading up the dishwasher. It had been hard, at the start, to form a proper relationship with her. Would have been hard with anyone for a man like Nate, it wasn't Kelly's fault. But they'd met because Kelly's boyfriend had been killed, and Nate had always been convinced that this would cast a long shadow. For many months he resisted any attempt on her part to get close to him, too many reasons to keep her away.

Bad experiences in the past, bad experiences inevitable in the future. Nate's life was a succession of brutal moments strung together by periods of waiting for the next dark event to arrive. Plenty of reasons not to let a woman you liked anywhere near you. But he did like her, and she liked him, and Kelly Newbury knew the business well enough to know what Nate was. There wasn't a hint of naivety in that woman, no danger that she didn't know the threats. It had been tentative at first, two people who'd sustained a lot of damage, who had a lot to hide from each other. But it was working. Slowly and surely, it was working, mostly because she understood his work and his life, and he understood hers. She was in the industry, organizing the storage of a lot of Kevin Currie's illicit goods.

'I'll be out late tonight,' he said from the table. 'Got a little job on.'

Kelly nodded, turning round to face him. They had gone out for dinner to celebrate her thirty-second birthday a few weeks previously, but if she was a better liar she could convince you she was ten years younger. She ran a hand through her long dark hair, a giveaway that she was a little nervous. Kelly was tough enough now to rarely get a lot nervous.

'Risk?'

'Not for me,' Nate said.

There was a time she had asked the same question of the previous man in her life, and he had given the same answer and then ended up dead. He had told her that only the person he was meeting faced any risk, and she hadn't believed him. She believed Nate Colgan though, because if risk saw Nate coming it was likely to turn on its heel and sprint away.

'Good,' she said, 'be careful.'

He smiled. If he was a careful man, he wouldn't be working in this business in the first place, but it was nice to have someone who cared. So many nights he had wandered off into the darkness, knowing that the only person who would be concerned about his survival was his daughter, Rebecca.

That was the next challenge, introducing Kelly to Becky. That worried Nate more than anything he did in his work. He wanted them, needed them, to get along or he would never have peace of mind. If Becky reacted badly then he would have to reconsider his relationship with Kelly. He thought they would like each other though, saw no reason why not. Kelly stayed over a lot through the week, Becky stayed with him every weekend. That was when Kelly went back to her own flat, out of the way. In the next few weeks, they were going to have to think about changing that. Spending a Sunday afternoon together, something like that, just to make the introductions. Becky lived with her mother's parents, but hadn't seen her mother for a long time. Surely she would want to like Kelly.

'Probably won't be back until after one,' he told her with a smile. Letting her know that he'd be waking her up, and if she wanted to sleep at her own place tonight, he would understand.

'That's okay,' she said.

He kissed her before he left. Nate had never been tactile, had never known how to be romantic or to show his true feelings to another person, but he was trying. The effort was clumsy and sometimes made him uncomfortable, but the fact that he was trying so hard was enough.

By the time he reached his car, Nate's mood had changed. No more happiness, no more optimism that life was going to be good and everyone was going to get along famously. He was thinking only about the next few hours, and the next few hours were work. Bad things were going to happen, necessary things. He had been pulling strings to set these puppets up for months and he needed to deliver. He still didn't like his own place within the Jamieson organization, still didn't trust many of the people he was working with, but he could solve a part of that problem in the next few hours.

The first thing he needed was a van. Would need to move a body in it, and all the gear required for burying its recently deceased passenger. Nate used Ross French for things like this. French had a car dealership, moved all sorts of vehicles and let Nate use one or two, now and again, for the right price. Nate had called him in the afternoon.

'No problem, big man, you can park round the back of the building, I'll have a van left there for you. Everything out of sight. You need anything in it?' Ross was getting friendlier than ever now that rumours had started flying about someone in the Jamieson organization setting up a car ring. There was a gap in the market, created when the orchestrators of the previous ring got locked up, and French wanted a slice of whatever filled the vacuum. The rumour was, Nate suspected, just a rumour, but it was a helpful one.

'Nothing else,' Nate told him.

There were other things he needed, but he wasn't going to get them from French, not this time. He had been planning this long enough that he didn't need to take risks with it. Get the van and nothing else from French. Maybe French could take a guess at what it had been used for, maybe, but he couldn't be certain. Ask him to load a body bag, a couple of shovels and two pairs of gloves into the back of the van and it wouldn't half kill the mystery. He parked alongside the silver van behind the showroom and switched vehicles. The van was spotlessly clean and empty inside, the keys under the visor as usual.

The second point of collection. If Grant Connelly had ever been anything in the business, Nate wasn't aware of it. He was nothing more than a man with a grubby-looking garden shed and a willingness to destroy absolutely anything he found in it. The organization paid him, probably not very well, and in return if you needed something destroyed and didn't know how to do it, you dropped it in his shed. Whatever new arrivals he found, he got rid of. He also kept things of his own in there, things that didn't look out of place in a suburban garden shed but came in very handy for men like Nate. Shovels and large plastic sheeting. The sort of things anyone would have in their shed. The sort of things a man like Nate couldn't keep buying on a regular basis, so borrowed from Connelly.

Connelly, a man Nate had never even seen, lived alone, in a house with a driveway right up the side. His shed was beside the end of the driveway, almost hidden under the tall trees that ringed the garden. The only person who could see you going in and out of the shed was Connelly, and he was always careful to make sure he didn't look.

The shed was, as always, unlocked and Nate took out two

pairs of thin gloves and a square of plastic sheeting. He filled a plastic bag with cleaning materials and left.

Now he drove out to the warehouse. He was driving a van whose owner would say he had permission and the only things in it could be explained away as gardening tools. Out to Clydebank and into the warehouse yard. There were a few vehicles still there, a few people still working. Only one in the warehouse they would use. Nate went in through the door beside the loading bay and nodded to the thin young man inside.

'Ryan Deek,' the thin young man said to him.

Must have been in his early twenties, a scrawny-looking kid hoping to make his way up the ladder. Nate had seen him working at Kevin Currie's main warehouse, the same one Kelly worked at. This was another of Kevin's, less used and its ownership more carefully hidden. If you told a person it belonged to James Kealing, they'd have a hard time proving otherwise.

'Everything ready?' Nate asked, scanning around. It looked right.

'Yeah, everything where you asked,' he nodded, eager to please.

The warehouse looked ready for the job, the metal shelving pushed back against the far wall to create space in the middle of the floor. Large plastic boxes were stacked against the near and side walls, giving the place a look of being busy, and some boxes were left separate in a corner on the right-hand side. Temptingly placed, and ready for a collection that would never happen.

'Good,' Nate said, 'give it twenty minutes and then leave. Lock up like you normally would, nothing out of place.'

The last meeting. Nate went to the pub in the city centre where they were going to meet Usman later. Parked a street away, walked down the hill and went in through the back door and up the stairs. Hated this place, hated it. Couldn't go in there without seeing the shadow of Kelly's ex, the bloody splatter his brain had become on the carpet and skirting board. First time he ever met Kelly was in here, standing over the bloodstain, going to collect the body.

Nate went upstairs and into an ugly little room. Glanced at his watch; his last meeting would be in eight minutes' time. This one would be bang on time.

Dale Duggan knocked on the door and stepped slowly inside. A fat little man, looked like he belonged behind the wheel of a delivery vehicle, which was ironic as that was his cover story. He looked nervous about meeting Nate Colgan. A lot of people did, and it was always reassuring to see. Duggan walked over to the small table where Nate was sitting and took a bag from inside his coat pocket. He was fat and unshapely enough that he could carry the bag under his coat without the package being noticeable.

Nate pulled an envelope from his pocket and passed it to Duggan, not a word spoken between them. The fat man stuffed it into his pocket, crumpling it as he did. Wasn't like him to be nervous, he was an experienced man who worked for a good, longstanding supplier, a family business. There had been some serious changes in that family business lately, but it all seemed to have calmed down and Nate was sufficiently reassured to keep using them. Make the Bowens their regular suppliers.

Duggan nodded, turned and walked out of the room, probably glad to be away from the beast of a man he had just dealt with. A beast with a reputation that made even Duggan, a man who sold guns to killers, nervous.

Neither man had looked at what they'd been given when they were in each other's sight. Duggan would be pulling the envelope from his pocket now and checking the money as he went down the stairs, knowing the right amount would be in there. A man like Nate Colgan, working for an organization like Jamieson's, doesn't screw you on cash when they have so much of it. They pay well to protect their reputation. Colgan carefully unwrapped the bag, knowing that it would have to be destroyed now that he'd touched it with gloveless hands. He didn't touch the gun, but it was there and it looked as deadly as a gun should look.

Nate leaned back in the creaking chair and waited. When you work a job like his, you quickly learn to sit in empty rooms and stare at nothing. Patience is a much underrated skill in the world of organized crime. The things that do happen tend to be dramatic enough to distract people from the fact that much of the time nothing is happening at all. Took another twenty-five minutes before Gully walked into the room, not feeling the need to knock. He went across to the round table and sat.

'We just playing the waiting game now then?' he asked with a smile.

'Afraid so.'

They sat and talked about the job, where they would take the body, how they would work it. When they had exhausted that, they talked about the holiday Gully and Lisa had gone on. It had turned out better than Gully expected, the mood relaxed and happy. He was warily beginning to think it might be a turning point for him and Lisa. She had gotten through a holiday without guilt and come back home to familiarity without settling into the usual patterns. Had her mind set on renovating the spare room, on doing ordinary things together. They talked about Becky too, because Gully liked to hear Nate talk about his daughter. He didn't ask much, didn't say much in response to Nate's stories about the girl, but he loved to listen. Gully found a deck of cards in the room across the hall and they played badly for a while. They kept glancing at their watches, wondering what the hell was taking so long. And they waited.

# 23

Usman pulled up in a VW Caddy, stopping at the side of the road for the few seconds it took Martin to drop in. They drove in silence for the first few minutes, neither man comfortable with the other.

'It's too early to head out there,' Usman said eventually. 'I mean, I've got everything we need, but I don't want to turn up there and find the lights on and some bastard working overtime to put more pennies in his pocket. We linger while he works and he's going to spot us.'

'Fine,' Martin said. His tone always seemed flat to Usman, so this was no different.

They both accepted that they couldn't go to the warehouse this early, and Usman didn't want to stop anywhere else they might be spotted together. He had to find somewhere secluded and peaceful, somewhere they could watch the clock.

They parked on a side road, little more than a track, that had a gate at the end of it. Seemed to lead to some footpaths and had signs for cyclists and dog walkers. At this time of night there was nobody around.

'We'll give it another forty-five minutes, then head back to the warehouse,' Usman said, glancing across at Martin.

Martin said nothing, looking out the window in silence. He didn't seem to be looking at anything in particular, didn't seem to want to talk. Some people were like that, clamming up in advance of something scary. It was nerves; it was a pro getting into the mood for the job. It was nothing Usman needed to worry about, even if he was the opposite. His nerves loosened his already flappy tongue.

'I got what we need,' Usman said. 'Balaclavas, gloves. Got a crowbar as well, big heavy thing. We crack the door to the warehouse fast, get in, grab the boxes and we get out. I'm going to time it, right, five minutes. No longer than that, even if we don't have time to check every box. Five minutes dead.'

'Mm-hm.'

Martin didn't seem to care. It was starting to get to Usman, the way he was behaving. A man miraculously cured of his obsession with correct detail. He was more fun when he was asking questions and doubting Usman's answers. Annoying, yes, but more fun than the silent lump sitting in the passenger seat, radiating a sense of impending doom.

'Is there something wrong?' Usman asked. If Martin suspected anything then there was no way Usman would go ahead with this. Going into that building with a gunman when the gunman knew you intended to harm him? No fucking way. That was a death sentence for the wrong man. He'd just drive him home and they'd forget about the whole fucking thing.

Martin turned and looked at Usman, looking up at the

taller man. There was sadness in Martin's expression. He held Usman's eyes for just a little bit longer than seemed right.

'Home things,' he said, and turned away again, thinking those two words ended the conversation.

'Home as in where you came from, or home as in where you are now?'

Martin sighed through his nose, the question unwelcome. 'Where I am now.'

Usman nodded. Strife with the woman, that was reassuring. If that relationship was falling apart then it would explain his mood. Might even cause him to take his eye off the ball tonight, something that might make this a little easier. Would also mean one fewer person to get worried about him disappearing, which might drive the number of people concerned down to a healthy round zero. Hell, if his love life was taking a dive down the toilet then maybe he'd leave Glasgow, leave Scotland and none of this would be necessary. Go somewhere else where he wouldn't be a threat any more. No, that would actually be worse, Usman figured. If he left Glasgow he would still be just as dangerous but much harder to find.

'Well, if there's anything I can do,' Usman said quietly.

'There isn't.'


They sat in silence for another half-hour, both miserable and both wondering what was going through the mind of the other. Should have been around this time that Usman picked

Martin up, but Martin had made it earlier, forced them into this tense, unpleasant time-killing exercise. Wanted out of the house, it seemed. Wanted away from the woman he was with.

'We'll head in then, yeah?' Usman asked.

'Yeah,' Martin said, and nodded his head.

Usman drove and Martin reached into the glovebox for the balaclavas and gloves that were stashed there. He slipped on his gloves, put his balaclava on the top of his head, like a badly chosen hat. About half a mile from the warehouse, Usman pulled the van over to the side of the road and put his own gloves on, his balaclava on the top of his head.

'Should probably put these on a few hundred yards from the warehouse, eh, better to be covered up in advance so they don't pick us up on any cameras they have on the street.'

Martin hadn't noticed any cameras out on the street, but it was a reasonable precaution. He pulled his balaclava down before they reached the last corner, covered his face, Usman doing the same. They drove the final few hundred yards in yet more silence, Usman pushing up against the speed limit the whole time. Nervous driving, something Martin didn't like but wasn't willing to criticize. Didn't want Usman getting any more jittery, getting things wrong.

They turned into the open yard and Usman swung the van round, reversing up to the front door. He pulled on the handbrake, cut the lights but left the engine running. The two men jumped out quickly, going round to the back of the van, pulling open the doors. There was a crowbar sitting in the back, which Usman quickly grabbed, nearly dropping it. They left the doors open, ready to receive the boxes.

They would say nothing from this point forward, no noise that didn't absolutely have to be made. That was professional, and a relief for two men who had nothing to say to each other. Martin stepped back away from the warehouse door and let Usman get close to it, the crowbar in hand. There was a brief second of eye contact, both faces hidden under balaclavas. Impossible to know what the other one was thinking.

Usman was trusting Gully and Nate at this point. Trusting that there would be no alarm screaming at them when he cracked the door, that there would be no phalanx of police officers standing behind the door sniggering at him. That would be a hell of a set-up. Get them both punished for the robbery at the bookies by having them caught red-handed at the warehouse. Or there could be a dozen guys inside with far more than crowbars, waiting to batter them both senseless. But no, there wouldn't be, Usman knew that. Men like Nate Colgan and Gully Fitzgerald didn't go to this much trouble unless there was something big at the end of it. Killing Martin, that was big enough for them.

He was trusting them to have made sure the warehouse was ready as well. Door locked but not so heavily bolted that even the crowbar couldn't get them in. He wedged the end in against the doorframe, beside the lock, and started to twist, putting all of his weight into it. He was grunting, getting louder as he struggled.

'Fuck's sake,' he wheezed quietly, just in time for the lock to crack and break out of the doorframe. The door was open, they were in. There was no screeching alarm, no shout or other surprise.

Usman paused and looked at Martin. He felt stupid, standing there with the crowbar, waiting for his victim to go in ahead of him. Martin returned his gaze, a hard look in his eye; it looked like frustration.

'Hurry,' Martin said, and gestured for Usman to go in first.

Made sense, Usman supposed, he was the one with the crowbar in his hand. If there was someone in there, hiding in the shadows, he was the only one in any position to do something about it.

A couple of careful steps, looking around for anyone or anything that might be a hidden danger. Nothing; just the darkness and silence of a warehouse after hours. If there were any dangers here then they were too well hidden to spot. There were metal shelves pushed back against the walls, most of them filled with large boxes, mostly plastic but some looked like cardboard that had seen better days. There was a surprising amount of space in the middle of the floor. A door on the wall off to the right-hand side that obviously led into an office.

Usman turned back and nodded for Martin to come in with him. But Martin moved slow, stepping over the threshold and stopping again, looking at Usman. The inference was clear; this is your job so you lead the way. Usman turned, walked quickly across the floor, over to the far right corner where he had been told the boxes would be.

Wasn't supposed to have gotten this far, he was supposed to have had Martin in front of him by now. Get him inside the door, out of view of the street, and get it done fast. Don't waste a second; but now seconds were ticking away and the crowbar was feeling heavier than ever in his hand.

He stood in front of the boxes and tried to work out what to do next. Couldn't pick one of them up without putting the crowbar down, the boxes were too big, too heavy. Usman slowly put the crowbar down on the floor with a clink and slid a box off the shelf.

'Hold this,' he whispered to Martin, turning quickly. Martin was right behind him, looking down at the crowbar. 'You hold it, I'll check it.'

Martin took the box; Usman unclipped the top from the sides and lifted it open. Underneath a couple of layers of dog-grooming products, he found small plastic boxes of pills, all labelled. He lifted one out, showed it to Martin, waving it cheerfully in his face, and put it back into the box. He sealed the lid, relieved that it had been in there, that he had something to convince Martin with.

'Take it to the van; I'll get the next one.' Speaking in a low whisper, looking Martin in the eye. They were supposed to have been silent throughout, but Martin was being awkward.

Usman watched Martin turn, watched him take the first few steps away towards the door. In that split second he decided he couldn't do it, that this was too tough, too much of a betrayal of a man who'd done him no wrong. Killing a person was too big a step for Usman Kassar. It wasn't who he was and it certainly wasn't who he wanted to be. He was a crook, yeah, but there was a limit to that. He took money, but he always left people breathing. Then he thought of Nate Colgan and Gully Fitzgerald. The sort of punishments they gave to people who let them down. Then he changed his mind.

He leaned down slowly, picked up the crowbar without it scraping on the concrete floor. Martin was moving slowly and with an awkward gait, Usman was taller and faster. He took two steps in silence, realized he wasn't closing the gap fast enough and ran the last three. Martin turned his head, just slightly, hearing the movement behind him, but he didn't even have time to drop the box.

Usman hit him hard, harder than he had intended, the momentum from his run-up carrying into the swing. He watched Martin slump forward, dropping the box in front of him and then landing on it, rolling heavily onto the floor. He lay still, the sealed box beside him. Usman stood there, crowbar in hand, for what felt like a long time. Looking and seeing what he had done, taking it all in, wondering if he'd killed

Martin with that hit, and wondering too how the hell he was going to manage to get through the rest of this night.

Martin moved. Not much, but he tilted his head sideways on the concrete floor and groaned a little. He was still alive, and suddenly Usman wished he wasn't. If he was dead from the blow to the head, this would be over already. Done; and he would be a big step closer to the worst night of his life coming to an end. But Martin was stubbornly alive, and that meant going through all the things Gully had told him to do. Think them all through, step by step.

Before that though he wanted to check, wanted to know what damage he had done. He pulled Martin's balaclava off and stuffed it into his pocket, lifted up his own so he could have a look at the head wound. There was a small cut, but it didn't seem like much to get excited about. No dent to the skull, nothing that could turn fatal without outside assistance.

Looking around for the chair. It was over near the door through to the office at the back, so Usman trotted across. Tried to walk faster than usual, the effort making him realize that his fear and nerves were doing funny things to his legs. He was wobbly, drunk without the good stuff. He reached the small chair and paused, taking a couple of deep breaths. No, don't stop, don't recharge your batteries and don't congratulate yourself on a job well done when the job hasn't been done at all. You don't pause for a second until the gunman on the floor is tied to the chair and the danger he poses has passed.

He started to move the chair across, holding it with one weary hand, dragging it so that the legs scraped noisily along the concrete floor. Pausing halfway back to Martin and realizing he didn't need to be carrying the crowbar any more. He dropped it to the floor, grimaced at the unexpected clatter, and carried on over to his target. Usman placed the chair beside Martin and looked around, remembering his instructions. Detail, detail, detail, the obsession that every good professional shared. A metal hoop in the floor, the plastic cords in a box beside the front door. Remember the details, get it right. When you're nervous, Gully had told him, the little things you need to remember most can be the first ones to go.

He put the chair down beside the metal hoop and walked quickly across to the boxes at the door, finding the thin plastic straps in the first one he opened. He walked back across slowly, looking down at the straps in his hands and across at Martin, still flat on the floor. He needed to work out the best way of doing this, and he didn't have time to think. Put the straps on now, or after getting Martin into the chair? Now, right now, he decided. Martin moved again, regaining another lost shard of consciousness. The straps had to be on before he woke up.

Usman knelt beside Martin, pulled the gunman's arms round behind his back. Looping the strap round the wrists and pulling it tight. Maybe too tight, he realized, as he saw them dig into skin, but it didn't matter. Martin would be dead in an hour or two, it didn't matter much if he got his wrist cut in the process. Discomfort was the least of his problems. Another strap around the ankles. This one not as tight, just enough to make sure it couldn't slip off.

He stood again and looked down at what he'd done. Martin lying on the floor, hands tied behind him, ankles bound, blood running from the cut on the top of his head where the crowbar had landed. He breathed heavily, building up courage to grab Martin, to lift him into the chair. Martin mumbled something, it wasn't obvious what. Might have been in Czech, or it might have been an attempt at English from a brain still three steps away from functional language. He was waking though, and his next words could be hard to deal with rather than just to understand. Usman needed to get this done.

He kneeled again, grabbing Martin under the arms and dragging him a few feet towards the chair. Martin didn't struggle, didn't seem to understand what was happening to him now. Another pause to gather strength into weary limbs, and Usman lifted Martin up. Nearly knocked the chair over, struggling to hold the weight of the smaller man. Martin slumped forward as soon as Usman let go, not making this easy. Usman shoved him back, angry, willing to hurt him now, hardly thinking of him as a person. He was nothing more than a lumpy burden. He was a dead man making the life of a living person much harder than it needed to be. There was no guilt in hurting a man who was already dead.

He shoved Martin backward. The impact seemed to bring a little more life back to the gunman. At least enough to hold his weight in place, anyway. Usman dropped back down to his knees, taking another strap from his pocket and looping it through the metal hoop on the floor and the strap around Martin's ankles. This one he pulled as tight as possible, a burst of energy rushing through him as he realized that he was finished. He had Martin in place, he had done it.

Not finished. There was one thing left to do. The worst thing, the thing that would change his life forever. He stood in front of the chair with his hands on the top of his head, looking down at Martin. The gunman wasn't aware of him, or didn't seem to be. Sitting there, leaning back, head dropping forward, lips occasionally moving without saying anything. Now he had to go, leave Martin here and lose more time. The bit he still didn't quite understand, resented. Nate and Gully staying away in case he botched this.

He took backward steps towards the door, looking at Martin as he went. Thought about saying something, but he didn't. There was nothing he could say that would mean anything now. Not after what he'd just done and not when he knew what he was going to do next. Martin was moving more, his head shifting slowly sideways, like a man waking. He owed him a quick ending. Martin deserved to be spared the torture of waiting for a death he knew was coming for him.

As he pulled the door shut behind him, Usman thought he heard something, a quiet voice. It spurred him to move faster, not wanting to hear his betrayal mentioned. Usman stepped outside, felt the cold air hit him and gasped. The fast intake of breath caught in his throat, the tiredness and the misery of the night, the churning in his stomach. He had to fight down the bile, take another gasp of air that didn't help much. Usman got into the van and started driving.

Usman knew where he was supposed to go. He remembered the details that Gully had given him, spelled out carefully. They were right at the front of his mind, and he was ignoring them. Driving the van back into the city, not aware of his speed, not aware of anything other than the need to throw up. He knew he was supposed to go straight to the pub and meet them. He knew he was going to piss them off by being late, but he knew too none of that mattered. Home wasn't far out of the way, and he needed it. The chance to stop and breathe, to compose himself before the next step. He had to make a good impression, and he couldn't in this state. And what were they going to do anyway? They wanted him to pull the trigger, and that meant waiting for him. They would just have to work to his schedule, this one time. He'd only be a few minutes late.

Usman went into his flat, closed the door, and felt an urge

rush through him to never leave the place again. You go out there and you have to kill a man. You go out there and you won't be the same person, won't live the same life. It all changes. Every single thing you think about yourself gets swept away, and you become a killer. He fought it down, felt his stomach turn another sloppy cartwheel and ran into the bathroom.

He threw up, at least once, maybe twice. He couldn't remember, for a few minutes, where he was or what was happening. He knew that his heart was thumping its way out of his chest, knew that he had never felt so suddenly exhausted in all his life. Those two things seemed so huge that no other thought could compete for space.

There was nothing left to vomit now, so he dropped onto his backside and slid across to the bath, leaning against it. Dropped his head back and stared at the ceiling. Forgetting the rest of the world, focusing on breathing and not having a heart attack. Never felt his pulse move that fast before, all the high-pressure situations he'd been in. He closed his eyes. Opened them suddenly a few seconds later, terrified that he'd fallen asleep.

He hadn't, his watch told him little time had passed and he'd only been in the flat for a few minutes. But he should have been at the pub half an hour ago. They'd be sitting there, the two of them, waiting for him with a gun. Waiting for him to do all the dirty work, them just along for the profits. He hated the pair of them in that moment, but he knew that would pass. His hatred would slowly morph into something else, something more professional. A tolerance of the men who made him kill, because they'll become the men who make him money.

Usman leaned his head back against the bath again, hating himself more than he'd ever hated anyone else, and he'd hated a few. He closed his eyes again, hoping that some of the lethargy would leave if he just gave it a few minutes. This time he did sleep, although he didn't realize it. Was only for a few minutes, and it helped. He was mentally drained, physically weak, but he knew what he had to do. The fog was clearing and those careful details were elbowing their way back to the front. He knew that sitting back against the bath wasn't going to get the job done.

Up and through to the kitchen, taking a drink of water from the fridge to try and wash out the taste of puke. Over to the sink to splash a little tap water on his face. He was pouring with sweat and he knew it was going to show in his matted hair and stained clothes. He thought about changing, but decided against it. All this, finding little things to do that killed more time, was a pathetic delaying tactic. His brain finding reasons to dodge the effort his body had to make.

Out to the van and driving through the street. His arms were so tired it was hard to even turn the wheel. He needed more time to get his head together. The van weaved across the road, Usman's concentration weaving with it, pulling him back to reality just before he hit anything. There was anger in there now as well, bubbling up and telling him that this wasn't his fault. This was Nate Colgan's fault, and Gully's fault. They were the professionals, why the fuck weren't they doing this? They should have been there, should have been sitting outside the warehouse waiting for him to clobber Martin. They should have had a proper gunman there with them, or one of them should have done it. Fuck's sake, this was their job, the thing they wanted more than he did. They should be the ones carrying the can for it. But no, not them. All the powerful ever had to do was clean up afterwards.

The details. He remembered them all, everything Gully had told him. He remembered the instructions and little else, because little else mattered. In through the alleyway, through a metal gate, across a small yard and in through the back door of the pub. Up the stairs on your left, and they'll be in the room opposite waiting for him.

They were sitting there, ready for him. Probably annoyed with how late he was, but relieved that he hadn't botched it. They took him down to their own van, and they all made their way back to Martin.

# 1.44 a.m.

Now they're in that silver van, Nate driving and Usman squashed between them. The boy looks twitchy, moving around in his seat. Gully can see him watching the clock on the dashboard, like he can't quite believe how much time has passed. Wouldn't have realized how long his drive had taken under pressure. Now he's too aware of the seconds ticking past, too aware of how long it's taking to get back to the gunman.

'Take your time,' Gully's saying again, sensing the growing nerves from the kid beside him.

Usman's nodding. 'And then afterwards?'

'Afterwards me and Nate take care of the body; you don't have to worry about that. We do all that work. We'll drop you off back home, or wherever you want to go. You just have to do the deed, leave the donkey work to us old nags.' Gully's doing his best to keep that understanding tone in his voice, trying to sound like the only friend Usman has in the world right now. Hard to do, when the kid's so nervous and keeps going back to the same questions, hugging the same fears.

'And then I'll be in,' Usman's saying, quietly enough to have spoken only to himself.

Gully's glancing at him, nodding but not saying anything back. The boy's looking out to that happy future, convincing himself that what he's doing is worth it because there will be a reward he's long dreamed of. He'll be in the Jamieson organization, working his own jobs and everything he's about to do will be the reason why. Gully knows different. Gully knows that you don't just kill a man and move on from it because you're making money out of the deal. That isn't how it works, not for normal people. He's seen enough gunmen in his time, knows they're not normal people. For men like him, like Nate, and like Usman, killing a man is a step out of the life you know, and there's no turning back.

Nate's slowing the van down, knowing they're near the warehouse now. Time to be wary, to watch out for parked police cars or people peeking out of doorways. The nature of the job, leaving the target alone, anything could have happened. Some nosey bastard drives past as Usman is leaving, realizes that Usman shouldn't have been there. He goes in to check for trouble and finds the gunman tied to the chair. Maybe someone who works there turns up for no good reason, left something behind during the day. Things go wrong, frequently. People get involved who shouldn't, or someone makes a stupid mistake. Keeping distant from the initial event was as much of a precaution as they could take.

'Not seeing anyone,' Nate's saying quietly, talking to Gully. He's treating Usman like he's not there.

'Take a run past and circle back,' Gully's saying, stating the obvious. No way a man of Nate's experience is going to turn the van into the warehouse yard without scouting the area first.

Usman is pinching his eyes with his thumb and forefinger, trying to fight down his frustration. If they had been nearby, they could be finished by now. The gunman would be in the ground and he would be back home. Wouldn't need to worry about people finding Martin. Wouldn't need to make all these time-consuming defensive manoeuvres. They had to do it differently though, keep themselves as far away as possible from the warehouse when the job was going down. Only turning up now, when they felt they could control the risk. This is their fault, and if anyone's found Martin then they will have to take the blame. No way Usman's accepting it. No fucking way.

Nate's driving past the warehouse, all three of them looking into the yard as they go. No sign of anyone there. No vehicles that weren't there already, no lights on in any buildings. They're carrying on down the road and round the corner, along the next street. Looking for police cars, someone sitting in a car in the dark, that sort of thing. Anyone that might be trying to park out of view of the warehouse, waiting to jump on them when they return.

'If there's anyone around,' Gully's saying, 'they're doing a damn impressive job of hiding it.'

Nate's nodding his head. Finding a place he can turn the van so that they can go back. It looks safe. Might look it, but they'll still be keeping their eyes open; it could be that someone is better at hiding than they are at looking. It happens, and they need to be prepared for it happening to them.

Back round the corner and along the road, keeping eyes open for anything that might have changed since they were last on the street a minute ago. Looking for people who have come out of their hiding places when you went past the first time, thinking you wouldn't be back so soon. Nobody. Seems like there's nothing to be concerned about.

Turning left into the yard, swinging the van round and reversing up to the loading-bay doors. Lights off as quickly as possible. That's one thing that's going to stand out if anyone drives past. They'll see a van in a yard and think nothing of it; this is a natural home for it. They see a van with its lights on and they'll think it's odd that someone's working this late at night. So lights off, engine off.

Gully's the first to get out, slipping down off the seat. Usman's quickly out after him, obviously grateful for the fresh air, for the room to move his arms and legs. He's breathing deep, not caring if the other two see that he's terrified of this. What does he care anyway? Let them see it, let them understand how difficult this is for him. Should be difficult for anyone. Okay for them, they're not the ones that have to do the shooting, that have to kill a man they know. Neither of them ever has, in all likelihood. Both muscle, both guys who get to avoid the worst of it. Not true in Nate's case, but Usman doesn't know that. He just knows that men like them always have the option of pressuring people like him into doing the killing for them.

Gully's reaching out, putting a hand on the young man's shoulder. 'You ready for this?' he's asking him quietly.

Usman's nodding, trying to get a hard look on his face. The sort of look that Nate Colgan has on his face all the time. It fits this occasion.

'Remember what I said,' Gully's telling him, 'take your time. Get things right in your own head before you do it. Don't let the size of the job push you around, you know what I mean?' Looking Usman in the eye, concern on his face.

Usman nodding again, his lips shut tight, breathing in heavily through his nose. Nate's out of the van, walking round to join them, fiddling with something in his coat.

'We ready?' he's saying.

'Aye,' Gully's nodding. 'I'll wait in the van. Second it's done, you open the bay door, I reverse in and we get the body into the van. Get out of here as quickly as possible.' Talking low, just in case.

Usman's looking to Gully, then at Nate. Doesn't like that it'll be Nate going in with him and Gully staying outside. He has something like a connection with Gully, a trust, because Gully's a likeable person who's at least tried to make this as painless as possible. Nate, he's just been distant and unpleasant throughout. Making it clear that he doesn't care how Usman feels, how hard this is for him. Colgan's a man who doesn't care about the struggles of others and doesn't understand why he should.

'I don't have a gun,' Usman's saying.

Nate's frowning a little, like he shouldn't have to explain this. 'I've got it. I'll give it to you inside, not out here.'

Gully's nodding to Usman, making eye contact, one last look to make sure that he's as ready as he'll ever be. He's turning and walking round to the driver's side of the van, leaving Nate to take control of this.

'Come on,' Nate's saying, gesturing towards the door of the warehouse. Not asking if he's ready, not asking if there's anything he wants to say or do first. Walking up to the door and opening it, standing in the doorway to make Usman go in first.

He's doing as he's instructed, walking inside. It's darker in here now, or maybe it just seems that way. There's only the light of the moon coming in through the windows, but even before his eyes adjust to the difference, he can see that everything's as he left it. The box on the floor where Martin fell. The chair in the middle, Martin in it. Looks like he's moved slightly, his legs more stretched out than they were. Usman can see the crowbar on the floor behind the chair. Shouldn't have left it there, Martin might have been able to get to it.

He's conscious. That's the thing that Usman's noticing,

looking across the room and making eye contact with him. Martin looking back at him, obviously alert and aware of what's going to happen next, but not saying anything. Just staring, silent and angry. There's blood down the side of his face, but the thump on the head doesn't seem to have done anything more than cosmetic damage. This would be easier if it had, if he was still unconscious. Fuck's sake, they should have let him do the shooting right away, get it done quick and not have to look Martin in the eye now. This is punishment, not promotion.

Nate's closing the door behind them, letting the other two stare each other out. Usman's looking down at the floor, not wanting to say anything, hoping that Martin won't open his mouth either. He just can't look at him any more, not when he knows he's about to put a bullet through that head. He's walking slowly towards Martin, eyes cast down, walking past him. Martin watching him the whole way, keeping his gaze firmly on Usman until he's past him and out of sight.

Now he's behind Martin, no danger of eye contact. This is where he'll do it. He'll shoot him in the back of the head, because, fuck it, all that stuff about looking a man in the eye is bullshit. Why should he torture himself with that? Doesn't make you tough, just drives you nuts trying to look good in front of a bastard like Nate Colgan. He'll do this on his terms, he's earned that. Like Gully said, you do it in a way that lets you get your mind right first.

Usman's looking at the back of Martin's head. Martin seems to be looking over towards the door, where Nate is still standing, watching the more easily visible threat. Just glad he's not looking round, trying to get a view of Usman, glad that he's staying silent throughout this. That was always his nature, Usman's thinking. Always the quiet guy, always the guy who didn't want to give away a single thought or feeling. Thank fuck he's sticking to that, all the way to the bitter end. Others would be screaming and shouting, throwing abuse or pleading for mercy, but not Martin. He'll never utter another word.

Nate's starting to move, walking slowly towards them. Martin's tensed, Usman spotted it. Worried that Nate's going to be the one to kill him, Usman just there as a witness. He'll be thinking it was Usman's job to get him there for a proper killer to finish the job. Convinced, probably, that the big guy with the big reputation is the one he should be afraid of. Yeah, most people would jump to that conclusion. Assume that if Nate Colgan's in the room, he's the one that's going to hurt you. Maybe that'll make it easier, Usman's thinking. Nate will step behind Martin and hand Usman the gun, Usman will shoot Martin and Martin will think it was Nate. Die thinking that.

One more intake of breath, trying to do it quietly. Turning away from Martin and Nate, looking across at the office door. One squeeze of the trigger. How hard can that be? Forget that it's Martin, forget that you're killing a familiar face or even a living person. Squeeze the trigger and go home. After that, a good life. A better life. Working with a big organization to take home some serious money. All those dream jobs that have been rattling round in the back of your head, now made possible by the resources of the organization. This is the price you pay, and it's worth it. He heard Nate walking towards him, heard him stop. A deep breath, shutting his eyes tight and opening them, then starting to turn around.

# 1.51 a.m.

His hands have started to go numb, and wiggling his fingers and clenching his fists isn't helping much. Wish they would hurry up. No reason why they're taking this long, no reason at all. When he holds his breath, Martin can just hear passing vehicles on the road outside the warehouse. Not many of them at this hour, and none that have stopped.

Fighting the lethargy, the urge to fall asleep, to rest his body and mind. He knows if he falls asleep, he might not wake up, even if they come clattering in here. It wouldn't be sleep, it would just be unconsciousness. It would be passing out and staying out forever more. Shaking his head hard, but that's just giving him a headache so he's stopping. His throat is bone dry, his eyes are getting sore. Martin's failing the physical challenge of being tied to a chair and that's making him angry. He's flagging, and he knows that's going to make what comes next a hundred times more difficult.

Now he's hearing a vehicle outside, and everything's changing. His mind is clearing; he's able to ignore the pain and numbness. This is it. A heavy vehicle, at least a large van, turning out in the yard, its engine straining as it reverses back to the door and then stops. Two doors closing, and then nothing for a couple of minutes. They must be out there, whispering among themselves, planning how they're going to work this. Martin's making the effort to make his face hard, expressionless. Clear the pain and discomfort from it, don't let them see anything when they look at him.

The door's opening, there's a pause of a few seconds before anyone steps in. It's Usman first. Walking in and seeming like he's struggling with the darkness. Looking around and then looking at Martin. There's eye contact, Martin staring at him. Trying to make him feel uncomfortable, make this as difficult for him as possible. Coming here to kill a man who's only ever been a worthwhile colleague and never once a threat. Make him suffer every little pain and humiliation you can. This isn't supposed to be easy, and Usman's going to understand that.

Usman's looking away, down at the floor. He looks like a guilty man, a coward who can't spend a few seconds looking at the thing he's about to destroy. Nate Colgan has walked in behind him and he's pushing the door shut. Just the three of them in the large room. Two of them in control, knowing what's going to happen, and the third man the victim. Martin's glancing past Usman, looking at Nate Colgan, making eye contact with a man who feels no need to look away. Usman's still looking at the floor as he walks towards Martin. Martin's watching him, looking right at him as he walks on past and stands behind him.

Nate's walking across towards Martin. He looks calm,

expressionless as always, a man in command of the situation. Martin can see Nate glance behind him at Usman. Something's prompted him to move more quickly. This is the moment. Nate silent, crouching, a flash of metal suddenly in his hand. A small, sharp knife slicing the metal strip tying Martin's ankles. Leaning in close to him without a sound and slicing the strap holding his wrists together, too. Martin's pulling his hands round in front of him, flexing them silently.

Nate's straightened up and he's reaching quietly into his coat, taking out a small handgun. He's passing it down to Martin. The gunman has pins and needles in his hands, but the feeling is coming back to them, and the touch of the heavy gun is the reassurance he's been praying for. This could have gone the other way, the set-up could have been flipped round to work against him, but it seems Nate Colgan will be as good as his word.

The same day Gully had gone to Usman with the plan for this job, Nate had paid a visit to Martin. Turned up at the house, knowing Martin's girlfriend was fussing around in the bookshop she owned with her sister.

'You and me need to talk,' Nate had said to him when Martin opened the door.

It was a risk for Nate, turning up on the doorstep of a gunman like that. A man who had good reason to fear him, and when a gunman has reason to fear you he has reason to kill you. Martin let him in, they sat down in the living room and he waited for Nate to talk.

'Well?' Martin said. He didn't know this man, but he knew his sort. Tough and sure of himself. Confident that there was nobody in this world who could break his complacent superiority. Martin knew he had been at the bookies, knew he had reason to punish him if that's what he was here for.

'You know who I am?'

'I remember you.'

Nate nodded. 'You know that your friend, Usman Kassar, has been talking to us for months now?'

Martin said nothing, didn't move. Just looked at Nate, waiting for him to give more information than this.

'That job you did on the dealer, the guy working for Chris Argyle. We knew all about that, helped to make it happen. You think it was luck that kept Argyle's men away from you that day? You think they didn't go chasing after you because they were too lazy, or because they didn't care about all that money? Nothing they care about more. They didn't chase you because we made sure they thought it was us behind it. We stood between you and them, gave you cover.'

Martin looked at Nate for a few seconds, expressionless, then said, 'Thank you.'

Nate chuckled, a rare show of genuine mirth. 'Aye, you're welcome. You did us a favour that day, made up for what you did to Donny Gregor. It was that job you did on Comrie though, that's what I want to talk to you about.'

Martin frowned. 'I have nothing to say.' You don't talk about the people you've killed to a man you don't know. You sure as hell don't talk to a man who has reason to use it against you.

Nate shook his head. 'You don't understand, I don't want you to tell me about it, that's your business. Only thing I need to know about that job is the consequences for Argyle and Park and I don't need you to tell me those. I want to talk to you about it, not have you talk to me. You're a gunman, a good one if that job is anything to go by. You have experience, I reckon. No way that was your first time pulling a trigger. You're a gunman working shitty robberies and glorified muggings with some loudmouth kid. I can offer you something better, if you're willing to listen.'

This was unexpected, and Martin didn't like or trust the unexpected. But he didn't like the work he was doing either, and Nate Colgan knew it. Gunmen always thought themselves a cut above, and he knew Martin wouldn't enjoy slumming it with Usman. A proper job, working for a major organization, was what he had wanted when he first arrived in the city. Nothing had changed.

'Go on,' Martin said.

'We need a gunman, and I think you could do the job. If you're interested. Permanent work, doing jobs for us and nobody else. Good money, regular income, we'll make sure you make decent cash and we'll make sure that you're as well protected as you can be in this city.'

It was the job he wanted, and he couldn't say no. He needed money, something regular, something that protected him, and here was Nate Colgan offering him just that. That tough-looking guy, smart enough to know that Martin was going to say yes before Martin did.

'I will be interested, yes.'

'Good,' Nate said. 'There's something else though. Your mate, Usman, knows a lot more about you and your work than we're happy with him knowing. Don't trust him to keep his trap shut either. Only way to keep him quiet is by shutting him up or paying him off, and we don't want to employ him as well. Some kid running rip-off jobs, thieving money and killing people that don't need killing. It's not suitable work for an organization. You we need, him we don't.'

Martin already knew just where this was going. Nate was going to shine a light on the thought that had run through Martin's mind so many times in the last few weeks. Usman knew too much about him, and with a mouth his size he was going to cause trouble sooner or later. Time was going to come when Martin would have to deal with him, maybe silence him permanently. Reduced the risk if that time was now.

'We have a plan,' Nate said to him, looking at him with a solid stare.

Martin agreed to it all, and by the time Nate left the house they had the details worked out. He knew everything that was going to happen, right down to the phone call Usman made him, asking them to meet up again. Every detail of the job on the warehouse was exactly what Nate had said it would be, and Martin knew what Usman was planning to do to him.

He told himself he was doing it for Joanne. The only way they could have a settled life together was if he worked for an organization, someone who could both pay and protect him. No more high-risk two-man jobs with a kid he hardly knew. But it wasn't really about her or anyone else, Martin was doing it to protect himself. Wouldn't have to worry about Usman ever getting him into trouble, giving his name away as a bargaining chip.

So when Nate handed him the gun just now, Martin was ready for it. He'd tried to keep his legs from cramping, tried to make sure his hands didn't go so numb as to become useless. He hadn't tried to escape either; he's here to do a job. Accept the bump on the head and keep yourself ready for the key moment. Nate's put the gun in his hand and Martin's getting silently to his feet. A little unsteady, but he's standing.

Usman, still behind him, looking the other way, trying to build up the courage to overcome a challenge he'll never face. Martin's looking at him, emotionless, and raising the gun. Usman's starting to turn around. Martin isn't going to let him, isn't going to give him the chance to look him in the eye. He's pulling the trigger, the shot loud, filling the room as the bullet smashes into the back of Usman's skull, and he's falling forward on the concrete floor.

# 1.54 a.m.

Martin's standing with the gun in his hand, looking at the mess oozing out of the back of Usman's head and onto the dusty concrete floor. He's lowering the gun to his side, because there's nothing left for it to do. He knows there's only one bullet in it. This gun was provided by Nate Colgan, and Colgan would only give him the bare minimum required to finish the job. Enough to kill Usman, not enough to do anything else with it. A single bullet made sure Martin stuck to the plan. They sent Martin and Usman into the warehouse and waited to see who came out. Who followed the plan with enough intelligence to understand how to survive it. Gave Martin a better chance, but Usman could have avoided this. Martin passed the initiation, Usman failed.

Nate's already walking back to the loading door, reaching down and pulling it up. It's making a noise, clattering upward to allow the van to reverse in. Gully, sitting in the driver's seat, waiting for the door to open, has noticed it and he's starting up the van. Reversing it slowly in, watching Nate as much as he's watching where he's going. Nate looks the same as ever, which means everything went the way it was supposed to go. Which is a shame, in Gully's opinion, because they just killed a likeable kid who they could have found some use for. It was Gully who had wanted to give Usman a fighting chance, the one he didn't take. Enough time with the gunman to kill him with the crowbar if he was smart enough to see the need. Sure, the things the boy wanted to do weren't useful to an organization like this, and he was too bloody naive to last long in the business anyway, but it still seemed a waste. Fancy thinking they needed a thief more than a gunman. Just a shame to lose a good lad who could have learned.

As soon as the van's inside, Gully's getting out and closing the door, taking them all out of view. Nate's opening the back door of the van, pulling out the plastic sheet they'll wrap the body in. He and Gully are walking across to Usman, looking down at the bloody mess.

'I'll get the cleaning stuff,' Gully's saying, glad of the chance to go back to the van. Being familiar with blood doesn't make it any more attractive.

'Here,' Nate's saying to Martin, 'give me the gun.'

Martin, still standing by the chair, is passing the gun to Nate, watching him slip it back into his coat pocket. Martin hasn't moved since he shot Usman, letting the other two do the work because that's their job and because he wants to be sure he can move without falling over before he risks trying. If Nate thinks it's because he's getting his emotions in check then let him think that. Martin's not concerned by whatever conclusion Nate jumps to, because he knows it won't make a good impression if he tries to take a step, cramps up and falls flat on his face.

Nate's laying out the plastic sheet beside Usman's body, waiting for Gully to walk back across with the towels. Gully's past Martin, kneeling beside Usman and quickly putting a towel over the back of his head so that he won't have to look at the wound.

'Jesus,' he's muttering, tightening the towel and getting ready to lift the body.

'One, two, three,' Nate's saying, and the two of them are lifting Usman and dropping him onto the plastic sheet. Rolling the sheet around him until you can't see Usman any more, and that's helping Martin relax a little.

'Better get this cleaned as well,' Gully's saying, grimacing as he's looking down at the pool of blood on the concrete.

He has a bottle of bleach with him, wiping up as much blood as he can onto one towel before putting the bleach on the floor and scrubbing it. It isn't perfect.

'Get a splash of oil, something like that,' Nate's saying, looking at the pinkish smudge. 'Something dark that'll cover it up.'

'Aye,' Gully's nodding.

They're picking up Usman, wrapped in the plastic sheet, and walking him across to the van. Now Martin has to move, because those two are almost finished and about to leave. He has to go with them, has to start doing something to make it clear that he hasn't drifted off mentally in the wake of the job. He's their gunman now, and that means showing you're useful beyond just pulling a trigger. Display your professionalism in the early days often enough that others take it for granted.

There's more power in his legs than he expected. He's moving, walking a circle round the chair and then picking it up, carrying it across the room and putting it down against the wall where it won't stand out. Back to the middle of the floor, kneeling and picking up the cut strips that had held him in place. There's a brown patch on one where his blood has dried on it. He's pulling up his sleeves, there's a cut on his left wrist. Walking across to the van, passing the strips to Gully who's putting them inside a towel and putting the towels on top of Usman.

'There's a cloth and a bottle of water in the front of the van, lad,' Gully's saying to him. 'You can wash some of the blood off the side of your face before we hit the road. Don't want people seeing you like that.'

Martin's nodding, but he'd forgotten all about it. The cut on his head, the blood that had run down his neck and tickled its way under his clothes. He'll need to clean any of it that's visible before they leave the garage. He's walking to the van's passenger side, finding the cloth and bottle of water in the glovebox. Cloth doesn't look as clean and unused as he'd hoped it would. By the time he's finished it's a dirty red colour.

He can hear Nate and Gully muttering behind him, discussing the best route to where they want to go. Sounds like the grave is dug and ready to be filled, a third man there waiting for them. Sounds to Martin like they picked this warehouse because the burial site isn't far from here, an easy route on which they shouldn't be seen and definitely won't be stopped.

'You can come out to the grave with us,' Gully's saying. 'We got a guy there; he'll give you a run back into the city. Be safer going with him than in the van.'

'Okay,' Martin's saying, and not committing himself to saying anything else.

Gully's smiling a little, another gunman who never bothered to learn the art of conversation. Nate's closing the back doors, coming round and getting into the driver's seat. Gully's sitting in the middle this time, Martin beside the passenger door. No need to keep him squashed in the middle when his work is already done.

They were only on the road for eleven minutes, and now they're pulling off into the trees and stopping beside an old but sporty-looking car. In the moonlight Martin can see a tall and broad-looking young man, light brown hair with small eyes and a small mouth, standing beside a shovel that's planted in the ground. They're out of the van, Nate nodding a hello to the youngster.

'BB, come over and help us with this.'

The young man's moving casually across to the van, helping Nate pull out the body. The two of them will do the carrying, Gully and Martin standing by the van and watching. They don't need help; a third person would just get in the way of a two-man job. Nate and BB are carrying the body across to the grave that BB dug while the rest of them were at the warehouse. He'll have been waiting a while, given how far behind schedule they are. A patient, unquestioning boy, he'd have waited much longer if he had to. The body, the towels and the straps are all going into the hole. Thrown in casually, two men dumping the body of a stranger they care nothing for. Martin doesn't wince.

'It's a good organization,' Gully's saying quietly. Talking in a whisper as a precaution. 'Lot of good people doing a lot of good work. Don't matter about the boss being in jail when the rest of the thing is so well run.'

Martin's nodding slightly, and that's it. Gully seems to feel the need to talk, to try and create a connection between them. The sort of man who wants to connect with everyone, get to know people and be friends with them even when he might never see them again. Still a smart enough man to know that there isn't much point in trying too hard with this new gunman. Just good manners to make the effort.

Nate and BB are quickly filling in the grave, trying to return the ground to a presentable state. There's muttering between them, Nate giving some sort of instruction to the younger man. Martin can't hear what it is, but the glance BB gave him is enough to know that Nate was instructing the boy to drive the gunman home. Nate's taking both their shovels back across to the van, while BB walks over to Martin.

'I'm BB,' he's saying, sticking out a big hand for Martin to shake. 'I'll give you a lift home, if you're done here.'

'I'm done here,' Martin's saying.

Nate's putting the shovels in the back of the van, closing the doors and watching Martin walk across to BB's car. Martin's opening the passenger door, glad to be going home, when Nate calls across.

'We'll be in touch again soon,' he's saying.

Martin's turning and looking at the large man, standing beside the van. Martin's nodding, doing his best to seem like he's one of the team now, but there's nothing to say. Of course Nate's going to be in touch, there are details to be thrashed out about Martin's new employment. Of course Martin's going to accept whatever details Nate offers, he's hardly in a position to say no.

BB's driving back into the city a little too fast, but he's driving with confidence and he seems relaxed. That, in turn, is relaxing Martin, knowing that the job is behind him, that he has secure employment and the protection of a big organization. No more risky, two-bit jobs, smashing bookies on the back of the head and gunning down befuddled dealers. It's a step back to the life he had before he came to Scotland, the life he knows well and can live. He's found what he was looking for when he stepped off the plane that first day, despite it being so well hidden. You don't plan for someone like Usman, but he served his purpose. Helped Martin make some serious money, helped him get back into the business in the job he wanted.

'Whereabouts exactly mate?' BB's asking him.

Martin's giving him the name of the next street along from the house. Doesn't want this guy knowing his address, not yet. Might turn out that this boy can be trusted, they might end up working together again, but until he's sure of a person Martin will keep them at arm's length. That's the only way a gunman can live.

BB's pulling over to the side of the road on the street Martin named. He's turning and looking at Martin, smiling a little in a manner that seems to beg for a compliment. He's in his late twenties, but he looks younger, small features on a wide, youthful face.

'Thank you,' is as much as Martin can manage, getting quickly out of the car.

BB doesn't hang around, pulling away and driving quickly out of view, Martin standing on the pavement watching him go. The last nagging doubt has gone with him. There was a thought, the kind the industry specializes in creating, that maybe BB was part of a wider set-up, here to get access to Martin's house and hurt him somehow. If they were going to do it, it would have been at the grave, but the worry doesn't pass until the last of them is gone.

Martin's walking back to the house, glad of the chance to

get some exercise into his limbs, to breathe some fresh air and to think about what he's going to say to Joanne. Key in the front door and stepping quietly inside. Along the hallway he can see a light coming from the kitchen and it makes him feel good. She stayed up to wait for him, no matter how late he was. She cares enough to wait. He's walking along the corridor and pushing open the kitchen door, seeing her sitting alone at the kitchen table. There had been fear on her face, but it's collapsed into relief and she's getting up quickly. Martin's laughing just a little, hugging her tightly and kissing the side of her neck.

'You're okay,' she's saying, a statement rather than a question.

'I'm okay.'

'Are you going to be okay from now on?'

'Yes,' Martin's saying. 'I have a new job.'